THORNS & ROSES

USA TODAY & WALL STREET JOURNAL BESTSELLING AUTHOR

CHARITY FERRELL

Thorns & Roses

Copyright © **2022** by Charity Ferrell

All rights reserved.

www.charityferrell.com

Cover Designer: Mayhem Cover Creations

Editor: Jovana Shirley, Unforeseen Editing, www.unforeseenediting.com

No part of this book may be reproduced or transmitted in any form or by any means, electronic or mechanical, including photocopying, recording, or by any information storage and retrieval system without the permission of the author, except for the use of brief quotations in a book review.

This book is a work of fiction. Names, characters, brands, places, and incidents either are products of the author's imagination or are used fictitiously. Any resemblance to actual persons, living or dead, events, or locales is entirely coincidental.

Prologue

Rose

My life as I knew it came crashing down on me two weeks ago.

I'm no longer Rose Graves, the daughter of wealthy rock legend and lead singer of The Gravediggers, Ritchie Graves.

I'm now Rose Graves, the *broke off her ass* woman who's lost her condo and is close to being kicked out of college, only a year shy of receiving her degree, if she doesn't come up with tuition.

Three days ago, my dad's former manager stepped in and offered me a job.

One I'd never take if I wasn't so desperate.

But the pay is too good to pass up.

The problem?

I'll be working for the kind of person I despise more than anything.

A celebrity.

And not just any celebrity.

He's the worst of the batch.

My new employer is young, attractive, out of control, all over TMZ and is under the impression that he's God's gift to the female population.

Fuck my life.

1

Rose

I've never been someone who regrets the decisions they made. I look at them as life lessons.

Losing my virginity at sixteen to a lying asshole taught me that guys will say anything to get into your panties, even throw out that cherished four-letter word.

Stealing my father's Corvette to go on a weekend road trip with my bestie taught me that showing a little cleavage can get you out of spending the night in a jail cell.

My father turning himself into a federal correctional facility last week taught me there are only two certainties in life—death and taxes—and it's stupid to depend on someone else's money because when they go broke, your ass also goes broke.

As soon as I step out of the Uber, regret hits me. The California sun throws her heat down on me while I walk into the high-rise building.

Desperate times call for desperate measures.

"Thomas is running late, Rose," the secretary greets when I step out of the elevator and into the lobby. "You can wait in his office."

I sigh. "Thank you."

Damn you, Thomas.

I pull out my phone to text Thomas to hurry the hell up as I open his office door.

"It's about damn time you showed up."

His edgy, deep voice catches me off guard, and my phone drops from my hand onto the floor. I look forward to face the jerk, and my mouth falls open when I spot him standing across the room. He's casually leaning against the wall, his muscular arms folded over his chest, and he smirks.

He isn't Thomas, but I'm aware of who he is.

Like millions of other people in the world.

I've seen him on TV and on magazine covers, but never in person. People don't exaggerate when they talk about how attractive he is. He's solidly built, and his nipples show through his thin white tee. Days-old stubble is scattered along his lower cheeks and strong chin. A black baseball cap covers his head—most likely an attempt to appear inconspicuous—and strands of his toffee-brown hair peek out along its edges.

Everything about him screams masculinity and arrogance.

This man, ladies and gentlemen, is Knox Rivers.

My new boss and America's favorite bad boy.

"Fuck," he hisses with a hint of apology on his face. "I thought you were Thomas. Dude is always on my ass about punctuality." He throws out his arms to gesture to the Thomas-less room. "Yet I'm the only one here."

I nervously bend down to pick up my phone and slip it in my bag. He's not the only one who wishes Thomas weren't running late.

Knox's green eyes narrow at me with suspicion as he gives me a once-over. "Who are you?"

"Rose," I answer, like he should know exactly who I am.

He throws his head back and groans. "Shit, is that why I'm here? Are you another woman claiming to be carrying my baby?" He looks back at me. "You're wasting both of our time, sweetheart. I always wear a condom and do early paternity tests."

What the …

He can't seriously think I'm here to baby blackmail him.

I shake my head. "That'd be a huge negative."

He quietly glares at me.

"I'm the new hire," I quickly add.

He keeps staring.

What the fuck?

"Your new assistant," I clarify.

He scowls. "I'm sorry, you're my new what?"

"Assistant."

The hell?

That's why we're meeting here today.

"You have the wrong guy, sunshine. I didn't hire a new assistant, so whatever your little plan here is, it won't work."

I'm tripping Thomas when he gets here.

I jump at the sound of a loud clap and turn around to find Thomas standing in the doorway with a bright smile on his face.

Fucking finally.

Of course, he had to show up post–*awkward baby-mama* conversation.

"Great, I see you two have met," he says, shutting the door behind him and walking to his desk across the room. He plops down on the massive leather chair and tilts his head toward the two chairs in front of him. "Have a seat."

I do as I was told. You know, rule follower and all.

Knox obviously isn't because he stays exactly where he is with the same scowl on his face, like Thomas told him he couldn't have any more cookies.

Knox points to me. "This chick said she's my new assistant, which is news to me, considering I don't recall hiring her."

I gulp and look back and forth between the two men.

This meeting is definitely not going as planned.

I expected Knox to give me a hard time. Men like him think if they have money and a Grammy on display in their living room, they can do whatever they please, but I figured Thomas had given him a heads-up that he was receiving a new assistant.

"You didn't hire her," Thomas states. "I did."

"I like the assistant I have just fine," Knox fires back.

"You like her because all she does is stay on her phone and allow you to do whatever you want. You were missing important events and not taking your job seriously, so I fired her." Thomas signals to me. "And I hired Rose. I had to put a stop to your shenanigans before you lose the career you've worked your ass off for. Rose's job is to help you get back on track and behave."

"I don't need a goddamn babysitter," Knox snarls. "I'm perfectly capable of taking care of myself. Sure, I enjoy having a drink and a good time, and I might fuck a few women now and then. Last time I checked, those aren't crimes."

"You also punched a paparazzo in the face and are acting like you have no repercussions for your actions. Not only did your album release this week, but you're also about to depart on a world tour. You need to work on your image. Rose has been given a pay advance, and I expect you to respect her."

I tense when Knox glares at me.

"*Rose*, I'll respect you by kindly asking you to leave," he says. "Keep the money. Merry fucking early Christmas. Again, I don't need a goddamn babysitter."

"And I'm not a babysitter," I argue, now fully ready for the challenge.

He needs to know he can't walk all over me.

"Did you not listen to a word Thomas said?" I continue, forcing a smile. "I'm assisting in managing your career and making sure you don't do anything stupid. Don't worry. I won't be fixing you peanut butter sandwiches or tucking you in for naptime."

He points at me. "You do know I'm the one cutting your paychecks, sunshine? I'd reel in the attitude if you want another one."

Thomas grins at his response, like we're two kids who just hugged out our problems on the playground. "Rose starts tomorrow. She'll be at your place at noon."

"Yeah, whatever. I have shit to do," Knox grumbles before storming toward the doorway. He doesn't pay us another glance on his way out the door.

"Are you sure this is a good idea?" I ask Thomas, blowing out a breath. "Isn't there someone else I can work for?" I appreciate him giving me a job, but I have a feeling Knox and I won't get along.

"You'll be good for him." He opens a drawer, stands from his chair, and hands me a binder. "This is everything you need to know. You got this, Rose."

I wish I had as much confidence in myself as he has in me.

This will be an interesting three months.

2

Rose

I walk into a mansion packed with people.

It's noon on a Tuesday, for fuck's sake. Although I'm sure the loud music, endless amounts of alcohol, and half-naked women aren't out of the ordinary for Knox.

I guess when you're twenty-six and you have a net worth of hundreds of millions dollars, you can party whenever you please.

My anger heightens with every step as I work my way through the crowd of sweaty bodies and search the sea of people, scanning the face of every shirtless man.

"You've got to be kidding me," I mutter when my eyes finally land on Knox.

He's stretched out on a massive leather couch in the middle of the living room with not a care in the world. His feet are kicked up on the glass coffee table while he watches the madness around him like he's the king of the party.

I inhale a deep breath and stomp toward him, knowing the exact moment Mr. Pop Star notices me coming his way.

My body stiffens at his dominant stare, and a brief silence passes when I make it to him, like we're waiting for the other to speak first.

Why is this so damn awkward?

Because he wants it to be.

He enjoys making me squirm.

He leans back, watching me in amusement, fully telling me he's in charge of this game … or whatever the hell it is.

He's shirtless, and swim trunks hang loose on his hips, showing off the hard ridges in his chest. There's no ball cap covering his disheveled hair today. He has a six-pack, of course, because a bad boy can't exist without having an amazing body, apparently.

"Did you forget you have an interview in an hour?" I yell over the music.

I don't know what you're talking about, he mouths back to me with the grin still on his face.

The chick sitting next to him gives me a nasty sneer, like she's afraid I'll ruin the chance of her life-changing screw. I turn around and race to the corner of the room. Faces, including Knox's, morph from ecstatic to pissed when I yank the cord from the stereo system, and the room goes quiet.

"This party is over," I scream. "Everyone, out."

They scowl at me, but no one moves.

"You have five minutes before I call the police and have you escorted out," I warn.

There's no missing the dirty looks and rude remarks from the people passing me on their way out the door. It takes a good fifteen minutes for everyone to clear out with the exception of the woman next to him, and it looks like she has no intention of leaving.

"You too, girlfriend," I say, tossing my thumb over my shoulder toward the door.

She crosses her arms and pouts. "I'm not leaving." She peeks over at Knox with a silent look that he'd better defend her and put my ass in place.

"He'll call you later if he's still interested," I answer for him.

Knox pats her thigh and brings himself up. "I'll call you later, babe."

I'd bet my last ten dollars that's a lie.

She nods and gives him a much friendlier look than she gave me even though I told her the same thing. A smile is on her lips as she kisses him and leaves.

It's only the two of us now.

Yay.

Knox stalks over to the minibar in the corner of the room, and there's no way he misses my hesitation when I sit down on the arm of the couch and open up the binder Thomas gave me. He refills his glass and leans back against the bar with his eyes on me—the same stance he had when we met. He's waiting to see how I break this tension.

I can't blame him for not taking me seriously. I don't have the look of a reputable and professional assistant. I'm only twenty-three. My blonde hair with pink streaks doesn't help my cause, and I have yet to grow out of my baby face. My cheeks are still on the chubby side, and dimples stick out from each one of them like a Cabbage Patch Kid.

"You have an interview in forty-five minutes now," I say, looking at my watch. "We wasted a good fifteen, clearing out the house. The station is *at least* a thirty-minute drive, and that's if traffic isn't backed up. Why aren't you dressed and ready to go instead of throwing a party?"

He gulps down his drink before answering, "I'm not going."

"You canceled?"

He shakes his head.

"You're going. Set the booze down, go brush your teeth, and put on some clothes."

"I'm not going. I hate interviews. They all ask me the same shit. *Who am I sticking my dick into? Did I really get arrested?*" He waves his empty glass in the air. "The bullshit list goes on. No fucking thank you."

He isn't wrong about what will happen, but that doesn't give him an excuse to bail on a commitment.

"You're going. End of discussion," I tell him.

He holds up his glass. "I've been drinking, sunshine, and trust me, I'm not the most professional person under the influence of alcohol. I'm sure you've heard the stories."

"I don't think you're the most professional person, period," I mutter underneath my breath.

At least my dad made sure he attended all promotional events that furthered his career.

"What? I didn't catch that."

He heard me.

I shake my head. "We don't have time for arguing. You're not drunk. Canceling interviews last minute is terrible publicity, especially one with the most popular station in the country. If you stand them up, they'll tear you apart and never play your songs again."

He surprisingly sets the glass down and grunts while making his way to the couch. He grabs a shirt draped over the back of it and pulls it on. "This is all you're getting from me. Take it or leave it."

I'll take anything right now. He can show up in a chicken suit or a rhinestone-embellished thong for all I care.

I stand, grab a stick of gum from my purse, and toss it to him. "Where are your keys? I'm driving."

He looks at me like I said I'm about to castrate him. "No way in hell am I letting you get behind the wheel of my car. We'll take yours."

"I don't have one."

He points to my purse. "You have a two-thousand-dollar handbag, but no car?" He stares at me in that intense, studious, weird way again. "Are you a hooker?" A smile cracks on his lips. "No wonder you know Thomas. That fucker loves to pay for pussy and then tries to do the whole *ho into a housewife* shit."

"I'm not, nor have I ever been, a hooker," I snap, my hand itching to slap him. "Thomas is a friend of my father's, not my fucking sugar daddy. Now, I'd love to stay here and chat about how I don't open my legs for a handbag, but we have somewhere to be." I hold out my hand. "Keys."

"Do you know how to drive a stick?"

"Sure do."

I follow him to an office, where he opens a cabinet, punches in a few numbers into what I assume is a safe, and pulls out a set of keys.

He holds them out before pulling away suddenly. "Are you lying?"

"No. Now, give me the damn keys," I push.

He holds them up in the air. "If anything happens to my baby, it's your ass."

I snatch the keys from his fingers before he gets the chance to stop me.

What's up with men referring to cars as their babies?

He leads me out of the office and into a garage filled with expensive cars.

I point to the neon-green Lamborghini. "Can we take that one?" It's a newer model than the one my dad taught me to drive in. I even took my driving test in it.

"Hell no. We're taking the Porsche."

I shrug, perfectly okay with that. He opens the door of the black Porsche Cayman and plops down in the passenger seat. The scent of leather and cinnamon hits me when I slide into the driver's side and start the engine. I plug in the radio station's address into the GPS and see the surprise on his face when I shift the car and reverse out of the garage, but he doesn't comment.

I don't know why I'm expecting a pat on the back or something.

The only emotion this guy knows how to show is arrogance.

The ride is silent, and I keep my eyes on the road while he pays attention to his phone. I follow the directions the GPS gives me and merge onto the freeway.

"Jesus Christ," he yells out, causing my grip to tighten

around the steering wheel. "We're not going to make it to the station unless it's in a body bag." He stretches the seat belt across his body and buckles it. "Do you even have your driver's license? Is that why you don't have a car—they revoked it from your crazy ass because you drive like a damn lunatic?"

"I don't drive like a lunatic," I argue, swerving into another lane.

The car behind us honks, and I'm positive the driver is waving his middle finger through the air.

He snorts. "And I don't have a penis."

"Oh, we all know you come equipped with one of those."

"How so?"

"You've sent your fair share of dick pics."

He gives me a sly look. "So, you've seen them?"

"Negative. I'd actually like to keep my eyes and not acid-burn them from their sockets."

"Your loss, and by the way, there're no dick pics of mine out in cyberspace. They're all impersonations."

"That's good to know," I mutter. Selfies of his cock are the last thing I want to talk about. "How about we go over this interview?"

"What about it? I've done thousands of them. Same shit, different person asking the questions."

"Anything off-limits?"

Another horn blares in the background when I merge into a different lane.

"Stella. My latest arrest. I don't like discussing my personal business with strangers, which is why I don't want to go. The assholes only want to talk about my so-called scandals, my fuck-ups, my problems because that's what gives them listeners."

"You have to talk about your arrest and sound apologetic. Tell them it was a stupid mistake that you regret and it will never happen again. That you hate that you disappointed your fans."

"That's what every celebrity who gets into shit says. I'm not about to be as pathetic as them. I punched a pap who had his camera shoved in my face, wouldn't move, and was saying some bad shit to me after I asked him to step away *three* times. I don't regret doing it."

"Definitely don't tell them that. For future reference, if you don't want to talk about getting arrested, don't get arrested. Your new album recently released, and your tour is paramount. You need fans to support your music and buy tickets."

"My fans won't let me down."

We both go flying forward when I slam on the brakes.

"*Fuck*, woman, no more talking," he yells. "Keep your eyes on the road."

3

Knox

Today is a goddamn nightmare.

Showing up for this interview is at the end of my *shit I want to do* list.

Kayla, my old assistant, let me ditch anything I wanted. She did her job when it was needed but knew to keep her mouth shut and not challenge me. I have a feeling this new girl won't do the same.

I'm surprised we make it here alive when she pulls into the parking lot to the radio station and parks the car. I want to jump out and kiss the ground, but there are probably video cameras out here.

"Please go in there, act professionally, and try to refrain from using profane language," my lovely new assistant says, like she's lecturing her child.

I don't know where Thomas found her, but Punk Malibu Barbie doesn't look like she's qualified enough to work for one of the top celebrity agents in the country. Whoever she is, I'm positive she's going to be a pain in my ass.

"I can't make any promises," I say in all honesty and open up the car door. "My politeness will depend on their questions."

"Have you ever heard of killing people with kindness?" she

asks, trailing behind me while I make my way through the entrance doors.

"Can't say I have."

"If they ask something you don't want to talk about, change the subject or give them some vague, bullshit answer. I'll tell them what's off-limits, but I can't promise they'll listen."

It's a live interview, and I can tell Rose is nervous when I leave her and walk into the recording room. She'll look incompetent if she can't even control me on her first day.

The hosts, on the other hand, look like children on their way to the candy store. I shake their hands and sit down. They're both in their late thirties, and they have been in the business for over a decade. I've interviewed with them several times, but that was when I was known as the golden boy and there were no juicy scandals to talk about. They asked about Stella, but I didn't mind that then because shit was good and we were happy.

I take a seat and put the headphones on. They crack a few jokes to break the ice, talk about my latest single that's flying up the Billboard charts, and congratulate me on the album's success.

My jaw goes tight when they ask the first question Rose told them was off-limits.

"Are the rumors true?" the woman asks. "Did you and Stella break up for good this time?"

I swallow down the lump in the base of my throat before leaning forward to answer through the microphone. "We mutually decided to go our separate ways," I say, trying to control my shitty tone but doing a bad job at it.

"So sad," she whines. "Is it true there's a sex tape you're threatening to release if she doesn't take you back?"

Is this chick fucking kidding me right now?

Is she deaf?

I told her two minutes ago that we *mutually* decided to end things.

I snort and dig my fingernails into my swimming trunks.

"There's no sex tape, and even if there were, I wouldn't make it public. I'm not a goddamn snake."

Their phony smiles collapse.

"Is that the answer you were looking for?" I ask.

Neither one can muffle up a response.

"Yeah, didn't think so."

They flinch at my reply.

Then, glee spreads across their faces.

Shit.

I didn't entertain the whole sex tape story, but they managed to get a rise out of me, causing me to look like an asshole.

" 'Ecstasy' is a great song," I say, trying to control my breathing and stay calm. "The entire album is kick-ass. My tour starts in two weeks. Tickets are on sale now. Get them before they sell out."

I rip off the headphones, chuck them onto the table, and storm out of the room. Rose grabs her purse and jumps up from her chair while I rush to the exit. She scurries behind me when I push the door open and hustle back to the car. I slide into the passenger seat and slam the door.

What a fucking day.

My party got crashed for this shit?

"Do you understand now why I didn't want to come?" I ask when she dips into the driver's side. "They didn't give two shits about my album or tour." I slam my hand against the dashboard. "You know what they care about?" I wait for a response, but she stays quiet. "They act like I'm the only person who's fucked anyone." I scrub my hands over my face.

That interview will be all over the internet. *Fucking fantastic.*

Rose looks over at me. "That's a part of the life. You know what you signed up for."

"What I signed up for? I signed up for this shit when I was thirteen years old with no damn clue what fame even was. I love music. It's my passion, what I live for. I thought that's what I would be doing."

"There's never a good without a bad." She gears the car into drive and pulls out of the parking lot.

Her response lights a fire inside me.

"Why don't you do your job and keep your comments to yourself?. You don't know what it's like to have people expose every personal detail about your life and then be scrutinized for it. I get a ticket and people tweet that I should kill myself. I don't want to take a selfie while pissing in a urinal, I'm a dick whose music should be boycotted."

"You're right," she says, her tone somewhat cold. "I have absolutely no idea."

"If I have any more interviews, you let them know I'm not talking about who I'm screwing, my arrest, or Stella. They ask, I walk and will never do anything for them again."

"Got it."

And with that, our conversation ends.

I probably sound like a dipshit for complaining about my situation. Don't get me wrong; I'm appreciative of how far I've come and how successful my fans have made me. The fame and money are nice. I'm thankful for everything I have, but it can also be a burden. If I make one wrong move, it's all over the news. I get more publicity than the damn Pope. I can't go to a club or hang out with a woman without the world hearing about it.

I grew up poor—dirt fucking poor—to a single mother, living off food stamps and the welfare system. She, Mason—my younger brother—and I lived in a small two-bedroom apartment that could fit in the living room I have now. I was teased in school for the hand-me-downs I wore and for receiving free school lunches.

All I wanted to do was escape my miserable life.

And that was what music did for me.

It helped me evade the hurt and insults.

When I was twelve, I tagged along with my grandma to a garage sale. That was when I found the guitar that changed my life. I begged her to buy it for me, promising to mow her yard every week, and she agreed. It felt like Christmas when I brought it home. I finally had something that was all mine. I spent all my time learning different songs and then went out on the streets to play for people's spare change. Someone recorded me and posted the video online, and Thomas showed up on my doorstep two days later.

I was discovered at thirteen, and now, thirteen years later, everyone knows my name, and I can buy anything I want. I became the poster child for the successful young musician and allowed the people over me to make my decisions and tell me how to act and feel. I was afraid to rattle people's tails, but that changed three years ago. That was when I decided to live the life I wanted and let loose, and everyone lost their shit.

I make business calls during the ride home until Rose parks in my driveway. I get out and head to the front door but stop to look at her when she doesn't do the same.

"You coming in or staying out in the heat all day?" I yell.

She doesn't reply but gets out of the car and follows me inside. I stroll through the large foyer and head straight into the kitchen. I bought this place on my eighteenth birthday when I decided it was time to go out on my own. Plus, it meant I could move my then girlfriend, Stella, in. I gave my mom the house I'd bought two years prior.

My new home was nice, but not my style, so I had everything renovated. It's now sleek and modern. The kitchen is equipped with stainless steel appliances, the cabinets are black and flat-paneled, and the countertops are white marble. The outside has everything needed for entertainment—hot tub, pool, fireplace, and pizza oven.

I hold out my hand. "Keys."

She tosses them to me, and I walk around the island, open a drawer, pull out another set of keys, and hand them to her.

She eyes me in confusion. "Where are we going now? There isn't anything else on your schedule for today."

"Nowhere. Keys are to my Jeep in the garage. It's yours while you work for me since you have no transportation. Try to do the speed limit and not kill anyone."

My cousin, Nate, has been using the Jeep while he's staying with me, but I texted him in the car and told him to leave the keys in the kitchen.

I jerk my head toward the hallway that leads to the garage. "You're off for the rest of the day."

All I want to do is sit by the pool, write new music, and rid my thoughts of that bullshit interview.

She tries to hand the keys back to me. "I can't take these."

"How did you get here today?"

"I took an Uber."

"Exactly. Uber isn't dependable. I won't be happy, waiting around for an Uber driver to drop you off when I need you here. Use the Jeep. Consider it a company car."

She blows out a long breath. "Okay, thank you."

Typically, I'm not the nicest guy, especially lately, and handing out cars to strangers isn't something I do on the regular, but this chick surprises me. She hasn't pried for information about my private life, isn't afraid to challenge me, and hasn't asked for my autograph, like most employees do. Thomas once hired a chick who attempted to Snapchat our entire conversation and even followed me into the bathroom.

This Rose chick is straight business.

"Do me a favor," I say, causing her to raise a brow. "Give Thomas a satisfactory progress report. He'll be pissed about the interview, and I won't be answering my phone. That means, he'll blow yours up. Try to talk him down for me." I smile and wink.

She rolls her eyes and holds up a finger. "First off, never wink at me again. Winking is never a turn-on. It's actually creepy." She lifts her hand up and wiggles the keys in the air. "Thanks again for the wheels. I really appreciate it, so I'll give you a B-minus for today. But before you get rid of me, we have to go over this week's schedule. What I walked into today had better not happen again."

So much for being in peace.

I collapse onto a stool, and she takes the one across from me. We spend the next twenty minutes going over my schedule —*twice*. She grabs my phone and punches everything in my calendar, just in case I get amnesia or some shit.

"I'll see you tomorrow," she says, bringing herself up from the stool.

"See you tomorrow," I reply.

I watch her leave the kitchen. My new assistant is sexy but in an innocent type of way. She's wearing a loose black dress that hits her ankles but hugs her in all the right places and accentuates her plump ass.

Nate comes strolling in a few seconds later and whistles. "Damn, bro, who was that?"

I recently agreed to let him temporarily move in with me to help him get his shit together. I didn't want to, but my mom had begged me. A year ago, I'd agreed to pay for his college, but he failed his classes and got kicked out. He's now working at a club to save up enough money for his own place.

"A new assistant Thomas hired because my old one wasn't exactly doing her job. Rose is supposed to keep me in line," I answer.

"I wish I could get someone like that to keep me in line." He shrugs at the hard look I give him. "And assistant? I don't understand why you won't give me the job. No one works harder for you than family."

"You couldn't survive freshman year of community college. There's no way in hell I'm putting you in charge of my career."

He chuckles while opening the fridge and grabbing a beer. "So, instead of hiring me, Thomas gave you a babysitter." He pops off the cap and takes a big gulp. "At least she's hot. Am I allowed to screw the help?"

"Shut the fuck up." I narrow my eyes at him. "Leave her alone, or your ass will be kicked out, do you hear me?"

The last thing I need is her filing sexual harassment against his dumbass.

He holds up his hands in surrender. "Sorry, man, I was only kidding."

I turn around at the sound of a throat clearing to find Rose standing there with her hands folded in front of her. There's no doubt she overheard our conversation.

She bites into the edge of her lip. "I, uh … forgot my purse in your car."

I shake my head at Nate and jerk my head toward the front door. "Let me get it for you."

Rose follows me outside, and I unlock the car.

"Sorry about that," I say, handing it to her. "Nate is my cousin. He can be a raunchy asshole but is harmless. I promise."

"Sounds like it runs in the family." She grins, clearly proud of her comeback.

I return the smile and point at her. "You'd better shut that pretty mouth and go before I make you scrub my toilets and give me a foot massage."

She laughs. "Okay, I'm out of here."

"Drive safe and obey all traffic laws."

I wait until she pulls away before going back inside to find Nate heating up day-old pizza.

"That's why you took my Jeep?" he questions. "To give it to some chick?"

"It's not *your* Jeep. Rose works for me, and that's more important than you riding around, trying to pick up women."

His face pinches together. He doesn't like my answer but won't challenge me on it. "Emeralds is going to be crazy tonight. It's going to be killer. You in?"

"You know clubs aren't my thing anymore."

"Come on. Emeralds is known for its privacy for celebrities."

"Fine, whatever, but if it gets too crowded, I'm out." I used to enjoy clubbing, sitting in the VIP section, and getting shit-faced while underage, but that shit gets old and usually leads to trouble and crazy tabloid pictures.

I grab my phone from the counter when it beeps and frown when I read the text on the screen.

Stella: What are you up to?

"Who is it?" Nate asks, like he's my mother or some possessive girlfriend.

"None of your damn business, you nosy ass," I answer, closing out of the text.

"Stella?"

I don't answer.

"Dude, let it go. She's always playing games, leading you on and then dumping you."

"I have let it go. I broke things off with her, but she's not the only one to blame. I've done plenty of stupid shit myself."

"Not as much as her, and the fucked up thing is, she always ends up looking like an angel while you're left behind, being the bad guy."

4

Rose

I pull in front of my best friend's condo in my new loaner Jeep. It's the most expensive model they make—equipped with black leather seats and an off-market GPS and stereo system. I can't believe Knox gave this to me after only working for him a day.

The past few days have been a whirlwind. I thought I'd prepared myself for meeting the infamous Knox Rivers, but it was nothing like I'd imagined. I'd geared myself up for dealing with a jackass who would order me around and act like I was beneath him.

Instead, I got someone different.

Thomas stuck me with him because he knows I'll do a good job and not put up with Knox's shit. I'm used to dealing with high-maintenance rock stars. A pretty-boy pop star shouldn't be too much harder.

Maybe that's why I despise the entertainment industry so much—because I've dealt with it for so long. I hate it but know a lot about it. I know people and have the right connections. I can get last-minute reservations at the nicest restaurants with yearlong waitlists and book secret luxury suites people don't know exist. I know PR and have experience twisting bad images into shiny ones. My dad nearly appointed me his personal assistant by the time I was fifteen.

I inhale a deep breath and release it slowly before getting out and going inside. Claire moved here about a year ago when she decided she didn't want to live in a building with hundreds of people any longer. Her parents found her this kick-ass two-story condo in a gated community, complete with a private entrance and front porch.

"Hey, bestie," Claire calls out when I walk in. "How did the new job with celebrity boy go?"

I stroll into the kitchen to find her ass planted on the counter, a box of cheese pizza open next to her and a glass of wine in her hand. Her pitch-black hair is pulled back into tight French braids, and she's only wearing a sports bra and yoga pants.

Claire has been my best friend since third grade. We were both crushing on the same playground heartthrob and hated each other at first, but after he kissed another ponytailed girl, we ditched him, banned together, and swore off boys for the rest of elementary school. She's been my rock through this entire IRS mess and is letting me stay in her guest room, free of charge.

I sit on the counter on the other side of the pizza box and snag a slice. "Pretty much how I imagined it would go."

She kicks her bare feet back and forth. "Is he as big of an asshole as the media makes him out to be?"

"I'm not sure. I haven't exactly figured him out yet."

Yes, there were times when Knox acted like a complete jackass, but I can tell there are more dimensions to him. He hides parts of himself, and the hidden parts are always the best ones. He didn't have to loan me a car. He could've been an asshole and refused to work with me, leaving me unemployed. But he didn't.

"Did he hit on you?"

I scoff. "He's my boss. I highly doubt he'll be trying to sweet-talk me out of my panties."

"I don't know, girl. I've heard the stories. I don't think he minds banging his employees."

"Even if he does try to sleep with me, it's not happening. The only things on my mind are making money and getting my degree. That's it."

"Does he know who you are?"

"I don't think so. Even though my father was in *that* world, he wasn't in the same circle. His fans and my dad's don't exactly run in the same crowd. Knox's are girls who make posters, asking him to marry them. My dad's are mosh pit–loving lunatics and women who want him to sign their tits."

"You're probably right, and I doubt the dude reads the tabloids." She hops off the counter and brushes crumbs off her stomach. "I'm getting in the shower." An innocent smile presses against her lips before she turns around and yells something over her shoulder. "Oh, and by the way, we're going to Emeralds tonight."

I slide off the counter and follow her upstairs into her bedroom. "Hell no. You know I hate that place."

"So do I. I'd much rather sit on my couch and watch Netflix documentaries. But it's Dixon's birthday, and his brother is throwing him a party there. It will look pretty shitty if his girl-friend doesn't show up. So, tonight, we both suffer."

I groan and dramatically fall face-first on her bed. "I'm sure Dixon will be okay with ditching the party and hanging out here if you ask him."

She and Dixon have been dating since high school, and I'm positive he's going to pop the question soon.

"True, but I can't miss it." She lowers her bottom lip and pouts. "It's one night. If anything goes down, we'll leave. I promise."

I roll my eyes, sighing. "Fine."

Like me, Claire is an only child—a spoiled only child.

"But we're not staying late. I have to work in the morning," I add.

"Girl, Knox probably won't be up until noon."

5

Knox

I regret coming to Emeralds as soon as I sit down in our VIP section and make myself comfortable on the leather sofa. The music is bumping loud from the speakers. Dancers are hanging from the ceiling or swaying their hips to the beat on the dance floor, and I've already had three servers come over to give me complimentary bottles of alcohol.

Nightclubs aren't much of my scene anymore. I prefer parties at my house, where George, my bodyguard, can confiscate phones and make people sign nondisclosures.

"Oh shit," Nate hisses next to me.

I jerk my head in the direction he's pointing and force down a sick feeling while I watch the bouncer move the rope aside to allow three women entry. They head directly in our direction. This is what I've wanted to avoid for months, and it has to happen here out of all places.

"Fuck me," I mutter.

Why is she here?

We agreed to end things for good this time, to cut off all communication, and not keep playing the *let's be friends* bullshit game that ends up being more than that.

"Do you think she'll be chill tonight?" Nate questions.

I bend forward to snag a vodka shot and drain it before grabbing another. "I never know when she's going to be chill." I take the next shot at the same time Stella and her friends make it to us.

Stella's glossy red lips tip into a bright smile when she plops down next to me, like we're good ol' pals again.

I glance over at her. Her long midnight-black hair is down, flowing against her back in loose curls. I used to spend hours in bed with her, running my hands through the thick strands. Her sleeveless blue dress hits right above her knee, and her golden skin shows off her Spanish heritage.

We met when we were sixteen years old—both of us starting to get our feet wet in the entertainment industry and experiencing what fame truly was. I was into my music, and she was the star of an Emmy-winning prime-time show. Our situations were what made our connection so strong. We were both going through life-changing events together.

But we grew up and grew apart. I was busy with my music and touring. Her show ate up her schedule. We would break up, get back together, and then break up again. She hooked up with other people. I hooked up with other people. It was a toxic and endless cycle.

First loves aren't always meant to be a constant in your life.

She leans into me and drapes her hand around my arm. "I texted you earlier."

Her voice is loud and clear. A warning to the women around us. Stella can be jealous and possessive.

Her smile grows when I stare down at her.

"I know," I answer.

"You ignored me?"

"I told you, I'm done playing the games. We both agreed to move on."

"We can't be friends?"

"No, we can't. I won't be dragged by the tabloids and labeled the asshole again because we decided to hang out as friends and people think we've reconciled. If I'm around another chick after that, the media rips me apart, assuming I'm fucking around on you. And you stay silent."

I flinch when she moves in closer, her tits brushing against my arm. "Screw what the media thinks."

She's in a mood. If I ask her to come home with me tonight, she will.

"Our relationship was toxic. We don't trust each other. It's time we stop heading somewhere that won't end up in a happy ending."

Her nails dig into my skin. "One more night," she pleads. She doesn't want to see me touch another girl here. She doesn't want to see me leave with another girl tonight.

I drag her hand away from me. "You have to quit texting and calling. Why do you keep fucking with my head? You can't find dick as good as mine?"

She rolls her eyes. "Why do you always have to be so complicated?"

"I'm not in the mood for this discussion. Let me know when you're done playing games." I refuse to look down at her while I bring myself up. I eye the exit and gear to head that way but stop to look back at her before I do. "Actually, don't. We need to quit living in the past."

I fight myself from comforting her when heartache passes over her face.

I can't be that man for her anymore.

My head is throbbing as I bolt past everyone in our section.

I need a fucking breather.

"Rose fucking Graves!"

I freeze at the sound of her name.

It can't be my new assistant.

It's only her first name and probably not even her.

There are most likely millions of Roses in this city, but that doesn't stop my curiosity. I wander over to the section I heard the name screamed from and look into it like some creep.

My mouth drops open.

It's her.

I fold my arms over my chest and lean back against the wall —an attempt to stay in the shadows. My sexy new assistant is parked at the end of a couch in a short black number. A martini glass is in her hand, and she looks miserable as hell.

That makes two of us.

I glance away from her and look at the drunken dude moving her way. He's dressed in a polo shirt and khakis *in a fucking club.*

Jesus, get this guy some loafers, and I'll mistake him for my accountant.

He reminds me of one of those douchebags who tells you his attorney father will sue you if you kick his ass.

"You finally decided to make an appearance," Douchebag yells out. It's the same voice that called her name. He lets out an annoying laugh. "Do you still think you're too good for me now that you're broke as a joke?"

Every muscle in my body tenses when he bends down to get face-to-face with her. He stumbles back when she pushes him away.

"It doesn't matter if I'm broke or not," she replies. "I'll never be with you."

He throws his arms out and lets out a condescending laugh. "Why are you here then? No one likes a freeloader hanging around, and we all know you can't afford cover to get in here."

The dark-haired girl next to Rose leans forward, like she's acting as her bodyguard, and draws her hand at the guy. "Josh, cut the shit," she yells. "You're drunk, and you look like an idiot."

"I look like an idiot?" he asks. "I'm only stating the truth, and all of you know it. She'd be fucking dumb not to get back with me. I'm her meal ticket."

Why am I standing here, watching this?

Why can't I tear myself away?

I look down and notice my fists are balled up.

The guy sitting next to the girl who defended Rose gets up and stands in front of them. "This is my birthday," he tells the dude. "Keep your mouth shut, or I'll kick your ass. Leave her alone. You hear me?"

Asshole backs away. "It's cool, Dixon. I'm not trippin' over some chick."

The dark-haired girl snorts. "Obviously, you are, *psycho.*"

Rose looks over at her. "Claire, drop it, or he'll keep acting out."

"Fine," Claire groans, tossing her hair over her shoulder before looking around.

A gasp leaves her, and I freeze when her eyes hit me.

She points my way. "Oh my God. There's your new boss."

Oh fuck.

Do I make a run for it or act normal?

I give them a polite wave and feel like a complete dumbass when everyone looks at me. Rose's mouth drops open like she's not sure if she's seeing clearly. I turn around and stalk back to my table to find Nate surrounded by a crowd of women. I grab his arm and pull him away.

Curiosity is eating at me.

I nod toward Rose's section. "Do you know those people?"

Nate works here and knows everyone.

He lets out a mocking laugh. "Oh, them? They're the I Live Off Daddy's Money Club. Those assholes came into the world with silver spoons in their mouths and attended private schools that cost as much as your Lambo." He arches a brow while looking at me in curiosity. "Why? One of them catch your eye?"

He must not have noticed Rose.

I shrug. "Just wondering."

I pull out my phone and Google *Rose Graves.* I start reading about her father being some rock legend and look back her way. She whispers something to her friend and gets up. My eyes follow her as she starts walking toward the exit. I'm reading about when and where she was born on Wikipedia when I notice Polo Boy heading in the same direction.

I shove my phone into my pocket. "I'm out of here."

"You serious?" Nate asks.

"I have my video shoot in the morning and can't be hungover."

He nods in response and heads back to his fan club. I text my driver to let him know I'm ready and to have the car waiting. I never drink and drive even if I've only had a few drinks. I can't risk getting a DUI.

I walk along the edge of the crowd, trying to go unnoticed in the dark, and make my way toward the back entrance, where the people who don't want to be seen pay to walk through. I hear her voice when I hit the bottom stair.

"Josh, get the hell away and don't touch me again," Rose says.

"You can't be serious," Josh groans. "What do you have going for you now? Nothing, Rose. No one else is going to want a chick whose dad is a criminal and who has to live off her best friend."

I turn the corner and spot them arguing. Rose is backed into a wall, and he's stopping her from moving around him.

I slide my hands into my pockets and walk into their space. "Hey, Rose. Whatcha doing?"

Josh looks ready to pummel my face in, and I focus on him, daring him to try. I don't bullshit or take shit, and I think I've hit enough paparazzi to prove that.

"Nothing," Rose sighs, glancing back and forth between Douchebag and me.

"I've been looking for you." I hold up my phone. "I got your text. You ready to go, babe?"

Josh looks at me in shock, and I point my phone at him.

"Keep your hands off her, or I'll break every bony-ass finger on them," I say.

Josh chuckles, but I can see the annoyance of my interruption on his face. "You have nothing to do with this, *pop star boy.* Go back to singing on the streets and begging for money."

I smirk, and he flinches when I take a step closer. "I dare you to say something else. I fucking dare you, *rich boy.*"

He slowly backs away. "Whatever, dude. She's not worth it. I don't like broke strays. You two are perfect for each other." He gives Rose a dirty look, turns around, and disappears up the stairs.

Rose runs a hand through her hair, and I notice a flush creep across her cheeks when she looks at me.

"I was about to leave," I tell her. "You need a ride home?"

I want to ask her about the guy, how she knows him and how the fuck she got involved with a jackass like him.

She gives me a questioning look. "You were about to leave, or were you being nosy?"

"Both."

She doesn't say anything.

"My driver is about to pull up. You can come or not. It's your choice."

6

Rose

"So, *Rose Graves*, how is it that everyone knows who you are but me?" Knox asks as soon as he slides across the backseat of the SUV after me.

The aroma of vodka and peppermint drifts through the air. He makes himself comfortable, resting his back against the door, and we leave as soon as his driver gets back in the vehicle.

It's dark, and the windows are tinted, so the only time I can make him out is when we pass a bright streetlight, but I can feel his eyes on me. I sense him studying me, waiting patiently for my answer.

"Not everyone knows who I am," I reply, shifting in my seat.

I didn't plan on working for him to play out like this. I expected him to be a rich asshole who would let me work without asking personal questions or playing the *get to know each other* game.

"That's what it looked like to me. Tonight isn't the first time you've been to Emeralds. Even though it looked like you were having a bad time, you sure seemed comfortable with everyone in your little VIP area."

"Were you spying on me?"

"No, I saw you on my way to the restroom and decided I was interested in you. Consider it employee screening."

"You can easily screen me through Google, if you're so interested."

That's what everyone does these days anyway—search for what they want to know and instantly believe that whatever comes up is true. If it's on the internet, it's apparently a fact.

"Trust me, sunshine, I'm the last person who uses the internet as a credible source."

"It's complicated."

"I know complicated very well."

What does he want from me?

To sit here and confess my life story?

"I was there because tonight is my roommate's boyfriend's birthday party. She'd begged me to go with her," I say.

I should have said no. Josh's dad co-owns the club, so he thinks he controls the place. He's been constantly texting me, asking to go out and offering to be a shoulder to cry on since the news about my dad went public. I've ignored every single one.

"Huh."

I tense up, waiting for the next question of his interrogation.

"My driver needs your address."

I relax and give it to him before pulling out my phone to text Claire, letting her know I'll meet her back at the condo.

"Was he your ex?" he asks.

"No," I answer. My breathing catches when he reaches up and turns on the overhead light.

His deep-set eyes meet mine, urging me to keep going.

Why do I feel like I owe him answers?

"I wouldn't consider him an ex. We had a thing—a temporary one—in high school. He was a rebound after a bad breakup. Josh thought it was more serious than I did," I say.

"I never did see you as a tease."

"I'm not a tease. The only reason Josh keeps pursuing me is because I don't fall at his feet for his money."

"You mean, his daddy's money?"

I nod, and his words feel like a sucker punch to the gut. *Is that how people looked at me? Like I was some spoiled brat who lived off daddy's money and didn't work for anything on her own?* Yes, my dad paid all my expenses, but we made a deal that I had to keep my grades up and was on my own after graduation.

"It's this neighborhood right here," I tell the driver, pointing to the gate.

I give him the entrance code, and a sense of relief hits me when we pull in front of Claire's condo.

"This is a nice place," Knox says, looking out the window.

"It's my best friend's. She's letting me stay with her until I save up enough money for my own."

"Good friend."

"I'll see you in the morning. Eight o'clock sharp."

"Eight o'clock sharp," he repeats, a smile tilting his lips. "Damn, I hate early mornings. Good night, mystery Rose."

"Good night," I softly reply.

I stop the driver from getting out and opening my door. I don't look back on my way to the front porch—even though it's killing me—and I rest against the door after slamming it shut.

I never thought I'd run into Knox outside of work.

Why was he being so nice to me?

And why did I like it?

7

Knox

I toss my phone back onto the nightstand after reading her text. She sent it at three in the morning, which means she was probably wasted off her ass, feeling jealous or wanting to fuck.

Or all of the above.

She has plenty of guys to do the job for her, so why is she suddenly all over my dick?

Before last night, I hadn't seen her in months. She did text me a few times after my arrest to check on me, but we weren't necessarily on speaking terms. Nor do I want to be. She did a long-ass interview with a magazine and told them she was done talking about me and wanted to move on with her life and be happy.

That's what I'm letting her do.

I grab my phone again at the sound of another text.

There's a link to a web page attached to his text. When I click on it, a photo of me leaving the club with a blonde woman pops up. I squint, looking at it closely.

It's Rose.

Fuck.

This isn't good.

The person who's supposed to cover up shit like this is the one involved. I wonder if she's seen the picture and, if so, if she has a statement ready.

I hop out of bed, shower, and pull on a pair of workout shorts and a T-shirt before heading downstairs. I look at the clock when I make it into the kitchen. Seven fifty in the morning. I don't remember the last time I was up this early, but I wouldn't be surprised if Rose came and dumped water on me if I wasn't up when she got here. I make myself a drink, snag a banana, and start to peel it when my phone rings.

"Hello, sunshine," I answer.

"Hey," Rose says on the other line. Her voice is sweet, almost angelic-like this morning—definitely better than her snippy-ass attitude yesterday. "I'm outside. Can you let me in?"

"On my way."

I jump off my stool and meet her at the front door. She's in another one of her maxi dresses—this one tighter than yesterday's, but not as revealing as what she was wearing at the club last night. Her honey-blonde hair with hints of pink hangs down in loose curls, pink gloss covers her lips, and nearly a dozen bracelets dangle from her wrist. In one hand is a planner. In the other is a clear cup, filled with a green drink.

"Remind me to get you a key made," I say, moving aside to let her in.

She walks toward the kitchen. "I'll make a note of it."

"Just don't start sniffing my boxers or go hiding in my closet to get a peek at my goods."

"Trust me, that won't be happening. Your *goods* are safe around me."

I plop back down on my stool and take a long swig of my drink as I watch her stand in front of me, looking awkward. Her arms are folded across her breasts, the cup and planner dangling from each hand, and she looks uncomfortable as hell.

I gesture to her cup. "Whatcha drinking?" I ask in an attempt to break the silence.

She looks down at it. "A spinach and kale smoothie."

I curl my upper lip before holding up my stainless steel bottle. "My trainer makes me drink that shit sometimes, but I can guarantee you, it's not as delicious as what I have."

"And what *exactly* do you have?"

I give her a careless shrug. "Just some whiskey and Coke."

"You're kidding, right?"

I shake my head in response.

"Throw it away," she demands, her voice turning harsh. "You have a shoot today, and I'm not dealing with any drunken bullshit."

"No can do, sunshine. I'm not wasting good whiskey."

She scoffs, "I'm sure you can afford to replace it."

"I'm not dumping it out."

She throws her planner down on the counter and sets her drink next to it before stomping my way. She stops in front of me, a snarl on her upper lip. "Oh, yes, you are." She holds her hand out like I'm a child who has something he shouldn't.

"How about this? You drink the rest of it for me."

"I'm not drinking whiskey for breakfast. I don't drink whiskey … ever."

I hold back my laughter and press the lid of the cup to my lips, testing her. It's working. *Perfect.* "Either you drink it or I chug this thing right now and show up drunk to my shoot."

"Seriously?"

"Seriously."

She snatches the drink out of my hand. "I haven't had this much peer pressure since high school."

She plugs her nose before taking a gulp. I wait for it, watching her face as it dawns on her.

"You're an asshole," she snaps.

She shoves the bottle into my chest, and I catch it before it falls in my lap.

I give her my best innocent look. "What?"

"It's chocolate milk."

I can't hold back my grin any longer. "Nesquik, to be exact."

"What are you, twelve?"

"Chocolate milk is the drink of real men." I take another drink while she gives me a dirty look. "What's on the agenda today, boss?"

She takes a few steps back and rests her elbows on the island. "You have to stop by the office and okay a few tour ads, and then we're going straight to the shoot, so make sure you have everything you need now because we're not going to have time to come back."

Damn, this chick sounds like my mother, only she does a better job than her.

8

Rose

"Where in the fuck is the model?" Thomas yells, barging into the room, his eyes focused on his watch. "Has anyone seen the goddamn model? We're scheduled to start in thirty minutes."

His attention goes from his wrist to me, like I have the answer to his missing model problem.

I shrug and point to the open door leading to another room. "Don't ask me. I'm already in charge of one drama queen, and he's in that room, getting spray-tanned … oiled up … glittered … something along those lines."

"Screw you, Rose," Knox yells from the room. "I'm getting dressed, not fucking glittered. If you don't believe me, you're more than welcome to come see for yourself."

I'm seriously working for one of the biggest man-whores in the industry.

Thomas starts nervously pacing in front of me. He's a control freak who expects everything to always go according to plan. He's the best in the business, and he is business all the time —Monday through Sunday, twenty-four/seven. It's like hitting gold, getting him to crack a smile. He's not married, and he has no children even though he's drifting into his late fifties. His receding hairline and stray grays tell me his job takes a toll on him. He's the one who discovered The Gravediggers and worked his ass off to get them signed to a label. Then, he went on to give other people, like Knox, the ticket to fame.

I open my mouth, ready to volunteer to hunt down this CLAIRE model, but the sound of Thomas's phone ringing stops me.

"Tell me you found her," he barks into the speaker. Sweat forms at the base of his forehead. "You've got to be kidding me. Yeah. Fine. I'll figure it out, as usual." He ends the call and tosses the phone on the table in front of me, curse words flying from his lips.

I click my tongue against the roof of my mouth—my nervous habit—and wait for him to tell me what's next. "So ... no model?" I finally ask.

"No model. Apparently, she can't make it in today. She canceled because she has some audition for a movie role that's *a better opportunity*."

"Should we reschedule for tomorrow?"

He scrubs his hands over his face. "Everything is already a go for today. The director is the best of the best and is doing this as a favor to me. He's leaving the country tomorrow, and he won't be back for weeks."

He stops his pacing and looks straight at me.

Shit. Stare-downs are never a good thing.

I bring myself up from the couch, fully ready to scurry off and find some bullshit errand to run. He stops me before I get the chance.

"Rose will be filling in for the model today," he calls out.

I freeze.

What the ...

Knox dips his head out the doorway and looks at me, a grin on his face. "Sorry, Thomas, but I don't think Rose is going to want to do that, considering what happens in this video."

He's absolutely right.

"We'll cut down the sex a bit and make it work," Thomas argues. "That way, today won't be a total waste, and we won't have to wait to get the video done. We need everything released on schedule."

I shake my head violently. "Uh, no, Rose isn't going to fill in. I'm an assistant, not some video vixen."

I read what the video consists of.

It's sex. All sex.

Correction: it's supposed to *look* like sex.

And there's no way in hell I'm fake fucking my boss.

"Exactly, you're an assistant," Thomas says, grabbing his phone from the table. His mood has changed from pissed off to chipper now that he's decided to ruin my life. "And your assistance is needed today." He gives me a reassuring look. "Don't worry. I can see the look on your face. You think we're shooting porn, but that's way off. Everything will be PG and tastefully done."

"Don't you have a backup?" I ask, my voice almost pleading. I'm reaching for anything to prevent me from doing this. Hell, I'll even go pick up some random girl off the street. "Surely, there wasn't only one woman who auditioned for this part."

There was probably a line out the door for women who wanted to be his love interest.

"It'll take hours to call in a replacement. You're here now." He shoves his hands into his pockets. "You'll be getting paid for this. Five grand." He grins, like that should immediately change my mind. "Not too shabby, huh? Hair and makeup will be in to get you in a few minutes."

He walks out of the room without waiting for a response from me.

Thomas isn't dumb. He knew to throw in the fact that I'll be getting paid a decent chunk of change.

Knox walks into the room, not glittered up or looking much different from when we left this morning. The only difference is, he's now wearing a white T-shirt and dark jeans. It seems to be his signature look. It's basic yet sexy. I also know all those articles of clothing don't stay on throughout the entire video.

"Oh, come on," he says, giving me a mischievous smile. "It won't kill you to act like you're attracted to me for five minutes."

"Sorry to burst your ego, homeboy, but, yes, it will. Not every girl wants to have sex with you," I argue.

He rests against the wall and crosses his arms. "So, are you one of those girls?"

I nervously nod while he pushes himself forward to come my way, getting so close that I can feel his breath against me.

Is he trying to get me worked up so I say yes?

"You're telling me if I asked you right now to fuck—no strings attached—you'd turn around and walk away?" he asks.

My chest tightens as he stares down at me and grins. He's fully aware of the reaction he's pulling out of me.

I stumble back, hitting the arm of the couch. *Shit.*

He crowds in closer.

"Damn straight," I say, trying to keep my voice level. "I'd actually kick you in the balls *and then* turn around and walk away."

He puts his hands up and retreats backward. "Let the games begin."

"What the hell is that supposed to mean?" I shout.

He shrugs and disappears from the room.

Jackass.

9

Knox

I walk away from Rose with a satisfied smile on my face.

Excitement ran up my spine at her reaction when I asked what she'd do if I tried to fuck her. I didn't miss the way her breathing changed or how her eyes suddenly refused to meet mine.

Rose is fighting her attraction to me. She might not like me personally, but that doesn't mean she is repulsed by my sex appeal or looks.

I'm not saying she's ready to straddle my dick and ride it into the sunset, but there's some internal conflict within herself, and I want to make her question it even more.

Which is a bad fucking idea on my part.

Thomas has told me since day one not to fuck the people who work for me. Venturing into that territory never ends well.

Period.

And I've done a good job of sticking with it.

Rose is a good assistant so far, and I'd hate to lose her.

The crew is almost finished, setting up the scenes for the shoot. I'm coproducing the video, and I've spent over a month planning out every single detail with my team. Thomas and the director, Mike, are immersed in conversation, most likely trying to figure out how to shift shit around so Rose feels more comfortable yet not change the entire concept of the video at the same time.

Thomas looks at me worriedly when I reach them. "Please tell me you didn't say something to piss her off."

"Really?" I question, giving him a dirty look.

"She's a good girl, Knox." His face goes soft. It's the first time I've ever seen him show an ounce of emotion.

"Let me remind you that her being in the video was *your* idea. If she's not cool with it, we'll reschedule. It'll be a son of a bitch, but not the end of the world. I can handle it."

"It would be too complicated." He juts his finger toward me. "Be on your best behavior, so everything goes smoothly."

"You know I always am."

He snorts at my response and then snaps his fingers when my stylist comes into view to get her attention. "Mallory," he yells.

She whips around to look at him.

"Change of plans," he tells her. "Rose, Knox's new assistant, is doing the video with him now. Find her something to wear and then send her straight into hair and makeup. Do it quickly, but don't half-ass it either."

"Got it," Mallory answers, brushing her blonde hair over her shoulder. "Are we going for a more modest look now?"

Mallory has worked for me for two years and is damn good at her job. She'll have this under control.

"Let her pick whatever she wants to wear," I say.

Mallory raises a brow.

"I'm not saying give her a clown costume, but options."

She nods in response and scurries away.

"You sure this is a good idea?" I ask Thomas. "There are already pictures of us leaving a club together last night."

"What?" he questions. "Why the hell were you at a club with her?"

"I wasn't there *with her*. I ran into her, was about to leave, and she needed a ride home."

He nods, but I'm not sure he buys my story.

"Now that we're doing this video together, people are going to speculate we're fucking. I can guarantee that."

Thomas shrugs. "Maybe that will be good for your image—make it look like you're settling down and making better choices."

This had better not be some kind of setup by my team.

"No, it won't be good for my image. It will fuck it up more. If they think I'm dating Rose and I hang out with another woman who's not her, they'll say I'm cheating. Make sure that doesn't happen."

"Let's not worry about that right now. Today's goal is shooting this video. We'll figure out all of the necessary PR later."

I salute him. "Got it."

He walks away to talk to someone else, and I sit down and pull my phone out before searching my name on the internet—something I haven't done in years. It makes me sick to my stomach when I read the bullshit lies they wrote up.

That's what sells.

Sex and lies.

I scroll through the results.

Knox Rivers Has a Wild Night Out at Emeralds: Booze, Partying, Drugs, and Women!

Knox Ditches Stella for Mystery Blonde! Stella Leaves in Tears!

New Girl for Knox Rivers?

Jesus Christ, it's worse than I thought.

At least they don't have her name yet.

I look away from my phone when Rose comes stomping out of the room, her makeup halfway done, with a copy of the script in her hand.

"There will be no tongue. You need to do a rewrite," she tells me.

"I'm not rewriting it," I reply. "If you're not comfortable making out with me, say it right now, and we'll leave. I'm not changing this entire video."

"What if we change it to light kissing?" Thomas suggests, making his way over to us. He looks over at Rose. "It won't be as bad as you think."

"It'll be *much better*," I add, resulting in a dirty glare from the both of them. "You'll probably be proposing to me when it's over."

She rolls her eyes at me.

"It's one minute of kissing," Thomas goes on. "You need the money."

"Why does that make me sound like a hooker?" she snaps.

"She's right," I say, nodding. "It does." I bring myself up from the chair and stand in front of her. "But there's a lot less needed in this job than that of a hooker, considering you don't have to blow me. So, are you in or out?"

She looks at Thomas, who gives her a slight head nod. "In," she answers. "I'll be fine."

I don't believe her. This video is sexy, and the storyline is that of a forbidden romance. I'll be playing Rose's boyfriend's best friend, who she sneaks around with and has an affair with. The set is going to look like we're in a cheap motel room in the middle of nowhere. The actual *building* is a cardboard cutout that will look like the real thing once the video is finished and editing gets their hands on it.

It takes Rose another twenty minutes before she comes back out.

My jaw drops.

Goddamn, she looks fucking stunning.

My hands are already itching to peel her black tank top off her chest.

She slowly comes my way, giving me time to appreciate the

cutoff jean shorts that barely cover her thighs, and I can already feel my dick starting to throb.

Fuck, don't let me pop a boner while we film this.

"So … how do I look?" she asks, throwing her hands down her body.

"Damn good. I can't wait to take those clothes off," I say, causing her to blush and look down at the ground. "You ready to do this?"

"I think so. I popped a Xanax about ten minutes ago, so I'll probably feel better when it kicks in."

"What?"

She slaps my chest, a smile cracking on her lips. "I'm kidding! Let's make this fun, okay? Otherwise, it's going to feel *and look* like we're uncomfortable, which won't be good for your image and will take away from the entire video."

"I completely agree."

I grab her hand and lead her to where we're shooting the first scene—on a bed.

"And we're starting with the big one," she mutters. "Don't you believe in saving the best for last?"

"Nope. The first take is always the best." My tone turns serious. "I know you read the script, but do you want to rehearse a few times before we shoot?"

"No, it seems pretty basic, so I think we'll be okay. If we mess up, we'll reshoot it."

"Pretty basic, huh? You make out with random dudes on camera regularly?"

She nods. "All the time. Make-out porn is all the rage, the most hard-core stuff out there."

I've never shot a video without rehearsing first. I'm a perfectionist in the sense that everything has to be planned and done right before we start shooting, but I guess there's a first time for everything. I don't think she understands that by not rehearsing, we're most likely going to have to kiss and touch more.

I twist around on my heels and tell everyone we're going

straight into shooting. They all look at me like I've lost my damn mind but start to move into their places.

Mike, the director, shrugs. "I guess we'll get started then."

I shake my arms out and start to bounce on my toes before they turn the music on.

"Action!" Mike yells.

My heart pounds at the start of my song, and I have no idea why. I've shot dozens of these videos. I've kissed and done more with plenty of models, so why does it feel like my heart is about to come barreling out of my chest?

I shrug off the feeling and push myself forward to start walking through what'll look like a deserted parking lot. Rose is in one of the rooms, pacing back and forth nervously, waiting for me.

A rush of adrenaline punches through me when I knock on the door. She peeks through the peephole before letting me in and lets out a gasp when my arm immediately spans around her waist as soon as I make it through the doorway.

She's apprehensive.

Hell, we both are.

She pulls in a breath when I push her against the wall, my body moving into hers, and I tilt my head down to look at her, waiting for the right time to advance. I edge in closer to draw her lower lip into my mouth, sucking on it gently, and press my lips against hers.

They're as soft as feathered pillows, and she expels a deep breath before kissing me back. She tastes delicious, like fresh citrus and peaches.

The attraction between us sparks to life.

I don't want this scene to end.

Hell, I'll do this entire video with my mouth and hands on her.

I tighten my hold on her hips, and my body is begging for more when I sense her excitement.

I have to stop myself.

I have to keep this professional.

But it's taking all of my strength not to wrap her legs around me and give it to her against this wall … and we haven't even made it to the bed yet.

10

Rose

Knox kisses me like he owns me.

I stupidly believed I was safe—that I wouldn't be able to focus on anything, except the camera—but I was so wrong.

Right now, all I can think about is how I want more of him.

This attraction, this pull, is blindsiding me.

The song's sexual lyrics playing in the background isn't helping either. They're only driving my desire harder.

I'm dizzy—so damn dizzy—as Knox keeps me pinned against the wall with his lips on mine. My knees start to wobble, and I'm grateful when he picks me up in his arms and carries me across the room to the bed.

My pulse is pounding so hard that I can almost hear it over the music. I gulp as he levels me down on the bed and starts to crawl over me. Goose bumps take over my skin when he draws out a long breath against my exposed neck before his lips find mine again.

My tongue darts into his warm mouth, demanding more and surprising the shit out of him.

I mean, I'm only doing my job, right?

I have to make our attraction look as real as possible.

My thighs tingle when I lose his mouth, and he starts to drag my shirt over my head, messing up my hair. That's my cue to do the same to him.

Everything is so fast-paced.

I need him to slow down.

I want this to last longer.

"Goddamn," he hisses between his teeth while drinking me in underneath him.

I tried convincing Mallory to find me a sports bra instead of this red lace bra, but she wasn't having it.

I brace myself, aware of what's coming next, and gasp at the feel of his soft lips hitting the skin right above the button of my shorts. Heat pools through me as he circles his arm around my back to bring me closer to his mouth.

He trails kisses up my stomach, and everyone around us fades away.

It's only him and me.

The pressure builds up, and reality starts to hit me.

He's going to make me come.

Why the hell is my body letting this happen?

If I have an orgasm right now, I'm quitting.

I'll work a drive-through, asking people if they want to supersize their fries, before I'll face him after that.

"All right, cut!"

The music stops, startling me, and my throat closes up as I try to calm myself down.

Knox looks down at me, grinning. "Are you sure you'd turn me down?"

"Holy hotness," the director shouts. "I think it's a blessing the other chick didn't show. You two just fucking killed it."

The air in the room feels tight. I push at Knox's chest, unable to look at him, and probably look batshit crazy as I roll off the bed and hit the floor with a thud.

"Is that a wrap?" I ask, catching my breath. I grab my shirt off the floor and pull it over my head. "I … I think that should be a wrap."

Knox stands up. "Actually, I'm positive I made some mistakes." He looks over at me. "We need to reshoot. Better safe than sorry."

"It was fine, Knox," Thomas says sternly. "We need to move on."

Thank God.

I keep my eyes on the ground when I head back to hair and makeup for my second look, and we spend the next six hours shooting scene after scene, which—thankfully—aren't as sexual as the first one. We sneak around in different rooms and share a few *light* kisses, and I scream like a madwoman when Knox gets into a fight with my on-screen boyfriend.

What a fucking day.

I take one last look at myself in the mirror and try to process what happened today.

Everyone who watches the video is going to witness me bare myself to him. They'll see the spark I felt when his lips touched mine. There's no missing the connection, how my nerves tingled underneath my skin while I wanted more of him. I was in a euphoric haze at the feel of his soft fingertips running along my skin.

Which is why something like this can't happen again.

Panic starts to ride through me while I change my clothes. Too many people are going to see this. His videos get hundreds of millions of views. I need to give my dad a heads-up before he hears about it. He's tried to keep me out of the spotlight and even resorted to throwing me in private school and banning me from traveling with him after what happened, but now, I've slapped myself right back into it.

What was I thinking?

I should've said no.

But there's nothing I can do now.

I made my decision.

I only hope Knox doesn't like the video and decides to reshoot it with someone else.

Anxiety, shut up.

I'm slipping on my sandals when I hear a knock at the door.

"Come in," I yell.

It swings open, and Knox appears in the doorway.

He points down the hall. "They're about to show some clips of the video. You want to see them?"

I hesitate for a moment, biting into my lower lip.

He steps into the room and shuts the door behind him, concern now on his face. "Rose, if you don't feel comfortable with this going public, I'll reshoot it."

"It's not that. I'm comfortable with it. I'm only trying to figure out the best way to tell my friends and dad about it."

"Claim it's not you and there must be some secret twin of yours running around somewhere."

"You're terrible at coming up with lies."

He laughs. "I stupidly tried using that excuse once."

"You can't be serious."

"I threw a party in my hotel room when I was underage. The media found out about it and went nuts. When I was questioned, I told them it must have been my secret twin."

"You were a dumb kid."

I feel paralyzed when he moves in closer. The high from his touch is still driving through me. I'm unsure how I will react if he does it again.

I might rip his clothes off and screw him against that door.

"Can you do me a favor?" he asks. His eyes are focused on me, giving me that intense stare I'm beginning to grow familiar with.

"What?" I stutter out.

"Admit that you enjoyed kissing me and it didn't gross you out like you'd said it would."

I gulp, hearing the challenge in his voice, and force out a laugh. "You've lost your mind."

"I know when a woman is attracted to me. I know when a woman is turned on, and you, sunshine, were most definitely attracted to me and turned on."

"I was *acting*."

He lets out a sarcastic snort. "If that helps you sleep better at night." He starts walking backward, away from me, and grabs the door handle but doesn't move. "I'll meet you out there, but before I go, I just want to make it clear that I wasn't acting."

My mouth falls open, and I just stare at him, unable to form words and taken aback by his truthfulness.

"I'm only being honest." He shrugs and finally opens the door to leave.

Why does he keep doing that?

He says something to test me and then walks away, like it's no big deal. He's getting in my head, and he knows it.

I release a steady breath, grab my bag, and exit the room. I walk down the hallway to find everyone hunched around a computer. Knox smiles and waves me over.

"We look pretty damn hot, eh?" he asks, elbowing me in the side when I reach him.

I slowly nod and stare at the screen.

He's right. The pull between us is transpicuous. There's no faking that strong of an attraction even if you're the best actor in the world. I watch him take my breath away and light me up.

I'm so screwed.

The director drags me out of my daze when he claps his hands. "This is going to be a hit."

That's what I'm afraid of.

I glance down at my watch and fake a gasp. "Wow ... it's getting late. I have to get going." I look at Knox, and it hits me that I'm his ride. "Unless you need me to stay or take you home?" I rush out.

Spending thirty minutes in the car with him isn't what I want to do right now, but he's my boss, and he owns the car I'm driving. It would be rude.

"Nah, I think I'll stay here and work on some editing. You go ahead. I'll have Thomas drop me off at home," he answers, giving me a reassuring smile that shows off his perfect white teeth.

I nod at his response and say my good-byes. The sun is starting to set as I walk through the parking lot to the Jeep. I toss my purse in the passenger seat and am about to get in when I hear Knox yelling my name.

I turn around, and he's running toward me with a shopping bag dangling from his fingers.

"Hey," he says, catching his breath when he reaches me. "Thanks again for doing the video. You have no idea how much I appreciate it."

I stare at the bag in his hand.

He holds the bag out to me. "I had my stylist bring this over. You helped me big time, so it's the least I can do."

I keep staring until he shoves it into my hand.

"Take it."

I don't look away from it because I'm too nervous to face him.

He bought me a present?

Do I open it now?

Wait until I get home?

"Open it," he urges.

I do as I was told and gasp when I open the box inside. "I ... I can't accept this." I run my hand over the soft leather, appreciating the beautiful piece. I was eyeing this purse and planned on asking my dad to buy it for my birthday before we lost everything. "This is a three-thousand-dollar bag. I'm already getting paid to do the video."

"Don't worry about the price. I can afford it."

"But—"

His words cut me off. "Keep it. Sell it if you need the money. I wanted to show you my appreciation; plus, I know you love your handbags. I'll take it as an insult if you don't accept it."

He gives me a smirk and turns around without waiting for my response. I stand there with the purse in my hand and watch him disappear back into the building. I gently place the new bag into its box and set it in the backseat.

What the hell is going on with my life?

"Hey, girl, hey," Claire shouts when I walk through the front door.

I move into the living room to find her and Dixon snuggled on the couch, watching *The Bachelor*.

Dixon looks miserable as hell, and I don't blame him. The whole idea of trying to snag a guy who's making out with dozens of other women doesn't appeal to me, but whatever. To each their own. I'd prefer not to share spit with a plethora of strangers.

"Hi," I answer, setting my bags down on the love seat before falling down next to them in exhaustion.

"Rough day?" Dixon asks. His shoulder-length hair is pulled into a man bun, one that looks better than anything I can do on my best day.

Dixon is a professional surfer and spends all his time at the beach, catching waves. His dad has one of the biggest surfing clothing companies in the world, so he doesn't have to rely on a job while he trains.

"You have no idea," I grumble. All I want to do right now is take a hot shower and collapse in my bed.

"What's in the bag?" Claire asks.

"A gift from Knox."

"A gift from Knox?" she repeats slowly. "Your boss?"

I nod, and she grabs the remote to pause her show. You know she means business when she hits that button.

"You've worked for him for, what? Two days? And he's already gifting you shit from Neiman Marcus? I hate to tell you this, but you're so wrong about him not wanting to sleep with you." She jumps up from the couch and grabs the bag before I have a chance to stop her, and she lets out a whistle, admiring my new Gucci purse. "And, he's trying hard. This thing is beautiful."

I hope to God she doesn't make this day any longer by pressing me for details. I debate on telling her the real reason, but I don't want her to think I'm dodging a boss who wants to stick his penis in me.

"He didn't give it to me because he wants to bang me. He gave it to me because I shot a music video with him today."

I wait for the incoming dramatic reaction I know I'm about to receive.

She drops the bag, her mouth falling open. "I'm sorry … you did what with him today?"

"He had a video shoot today for his newest single. The model didn't show, and there was no backup, so Thomas asked me to do it. I said no at first, but they were desperate; plus, I couldn't pass up the pay." I shrug. "So, I agreed."

"Like one that's going to be on TV … YouTube … everywhere on the internet?" she asks, falling back down on the couch.

I click my tongue against the roof of my mouth before answering, "That's correct."

"Holy fucking shit."

"By model, do you mean, love interest?" Dixon asks.

I nod.

Claire claps her hands. "Oh my God. I seriously cannot wait to see this. I bet you're going to be trending when it releases.

Everyone will be dying with curiosity about who the mysterious, hot blonde is in his video."

"I hope not," I grumble.

My phone beeps, and I see a text message when I grab it from my purse.

> Thomas: Look up Knox on the internet right now. You might have your first problem to fix.

I type Knox's name in the search box of the internet browser. My breathing falters, and my fingertips go numb when I start to scroll through the headlines.

Oh shit.

"I have a feeling I'm going to be trending before the video releases," I tell them.

I click on the first link and hold my phone out so they can read the story.

"He's who you left the club with? I thought you took an Uber home?" Claire asks.

"I was about to book a ride when Josh followed me into the back room and pretty much started to harass me. That's when Knox suddenly appeared. His driver was already on his way to pick him up, so he offered to give me a ride. It saved me money and the awkwardness of riding in the car with a stranger." Okay, it might've been more awkward in the car with him.

"How convenient. Your knight in shining armor."

I give her a dirty look. "Coincidence, not convenience."

She shrugs and grabs her wineglass from the coffee table, taking a big gulp. "I still think he wants to get in your panties. The guy gave you a car."

"He didn't give me a car," I interrupt. "He *loaned* me a car. It's no different than providing a company vehicle."

"So, he *loaned* you a car, practically followed you in a club to give you a ride home, convinced you to costar in his video, and gave you a handbag that costs more than some people make in a month."

I look down at my fingernails. It does sound a bit extreme for only working for him for a few days, but celebrities are extreme, especially young ones.

"He was watching you at the club," she goes on, taking her two fingers and pressing them against her eyes. "I saw it with my own two eyes."

I knew she'd make a big deal out of this. "He was surprised to see me there. He didn't know I'd be in the wealthy ... or whatever they call us group of friends. Our relationship is one hundred percent professional."

She snorts. "Good luck convincing people of that. You're hanging out with one of the most famous people in the world." She raises her legs and rests them on the coffee table. "What are you going to do?"

"I haven't figured that out yet. I'll talk to Thomas and ask what's the best way to handle it."

They watch me as I reply to Thomas's text.

> Me: Release a statement with the true story.
> We ran into each other. I needed a ride home.
> The end. Completely innocent.

> Thomas: It's your job to fix it, Rose. Write up a
> statement, and I'll release it.

His response isn't what I was hoping for.

"What did he say, you video vixen, you?" she asks.

"That it's my job to fix it." I get up from the couch. "And you're annoying." I head toward the stairs to go to my bedroom, hearing her laughter in the background, and close the door before sinking down on my bed.

I hit Knox's name and text him next.

> Me: Not sure if you've seen the viral picture of us leaving the club yet, but how do you want me to handle it?

> Knox: Tell them whatever you want. You're in charge.

Shit!

I wanted one of them to fix this problem for me.

I grab my laptop and start writing out a response to let the world know we're not screwing.

Fuck the paparazzi.

11

Knox

I completely spaced mentioning to her the pictures of us leaving the club together. So much shit was going on that it slipped my mind.

When Thomas came in, bitching about the model being MIA, I was close to losing it. My hands were shaking, my mind going nuts over the thought of having to cancel the entire shoot after spending so much money on booking everyone. I'm glad I was in the other room because I almost fell over in shock when Thomas said Rose would step in.

I could tell she wasn't completely sold on the idea, and there was no way she would've done it if she wasn't working for me, so I texted my stylist and told her to find Rose the perfect bag. I don't know why I bought her the purse, but it was the best way I could think of to thank her for stepping out of her comfort zone and saving my ass.

I hit Reply ... but I'm not sure what to say back.
Should I even respond?

I'm stretched out on the sheets of my California king bed, the ceiling fan on above me, listening to the TV in the background. It's on some reality show about finding the love of your life or some shit. I laugh to myself. No one ever finds the love of their life on a damn TV show.

> Me: Do you know ...

I delete that.

> Me: Any plans tonight?

I backspace that.

> Me: So, what are you up to?

I hesitate. Will she think it's weird if I ask that?
I delete it when I come up with a better idea.

> Me: What's on the agenda for tomorrow?

I toss my phone down next to me and rest my head on the pillow until she responds.

> Rose: We put everything in your phone, remember?

> Me: Yes, but I'm too lazy to look it up right now.

And I want to talk to her.

> Rose: Tour meeting tomorrow at 9 a.m.

Me: Cancel it. I'm not going.

Rose: You've got to be kidding me.

Me: Nope.

Rose: You're going. I don't care if I have to break into your house and drag you out of bed. And don't forget about getting me a key made, BTW.

Me: You threatened to come and drag me out of bed. You can't expect me to give you a key now.

I wait a few seconds and no reply. I reread my last text, wondering if I said something wrong. I even held back my urge to fuck with her and say I'd rather she climb into my bed than drag me out of it.

I text her again, blaming it on my boredom.

Me: Calm down, killer. I'm only fucking with you. I'm not canceling.

This meeting is too big of a deal to cancel. Tours are where I make the most money.

My phone beeps.

Rose: Fucking with me seems to be your favorite pastime. I'll see you in the morning. Be ready to go. Traffic is most likely going to be a bitch.

Fucking *her* would actually be my favorite pastime … if I had the chance.

Me: Yes, ma'am. See you in the morning.

I click off her message and hit Thomas's name.

> **Me:** Is Rose coming with me on tour?

> **Thomas:** Undecided. I thought we'd talk about it tomorrow.

> **Me:** I think it's a good idea. She seems to know what she's doing, and she keeps me on track.

> **Thomas:** Don't try to be slick with her. She has people who will destroy you if you touch her. I'm not joking.

Whoa. Not the response I expected. *She has people who will destroy me?* I need to question my little assistant more and find out what I'm dealing with. Maybe sunshine has a bit more of a cloudy edge to her.

I'm elated for this tour and counting down the days until I leave. It'll be a breath of fresh air and nice to get out of the city for a while. It clears my mind, and I do my best writing on my tour bus. Performing for my fans is what moves me, drives me, and makes me the happiest. I have a purpose for a few hours.

I email the producer and tell him to send me the unedited video so I can work on it.

I can't wait to see it.

12

Rose

I have my bedroom light off, *Friends* is streaming on my TV as background noise, and I reach over and snag my phone from the nightstand to double-check the time again. I've probably looked at it at least twenty-four times since I climbed into bed after showering.

I groan when I see it's three in the morning. Sleep is not my friend tonight. Even the Ambien I popped earlier isn't giving me any love. I guess my anxiety beats out pharmaceuticals.

Why the hell can't I fall asleep?

I'm not a hundred percent sure of the *exact* reason, but it most likely has something to do with the fact that I'll be facing Knox in about six hours and it's going to be awkward city. I'm positive of it. And if there's anything I can't stand, it's awkwardness.

I grab a pillow, press it over my face, and scream into it a few times. I toss it next to me when I'm finished having my meltdown, grab my phone again, and hit his name.

He probably won't get my text until the morning, but I need to make sure he knows, so I can attempt to get some shut-eye.

Me: I'll just see you at the meeting tomorrow.

Knox has his own car … or his own *cars*, to be more accurate. There's no reason why he'd want to ride with me.

My phone beeps with a response a few seconds later, surprising me.

What is he doing up at this time?

Oh yeah, party boy.

He's probably sitting on his couch, feet kicked up, and getting wasted while not even thinking about the video being that big of a deal. Later, he'll go to his bedroom and screw some other chick without me on his mind.

That's the attitude I need to have—well, minus the *screw a chick* part. I can't let this get to me. I have a job to do.

> Knox: I'd prefer you meet me at my place and I ride with you, sunshine. I need you to pick me up some breakfast.

Well, my brilliant little plan just flew out the window.

> Me: I thought you hated my driving?

> Knox: True, but I love your company.

> Me: I'll be there at nine. What do you want for breakfast?

> Knox: Whatever sounds good to you. Treat yourself. You have a credit card.

I was given a business credit card to charge any expenses to get what Knox needs.

> Me: You're my boss. Tell me what you want.

> Knox: Oh, sunshine. You know what I want.

He's drunk. He has to be drunk.

> Me: I could sue you for sexual harassment, you know.

I grin at my response. That will teach him to keep his sexual remarks to himself.

> Knox: Sexual harassment? I was referring to wanting an Egg McMuffin. There's nothing sexual about that, and if you think there is, you must be into some kinky shit.

> Me: You're seriously the most frustrating man I know.

> Knox: And you're seriously the most sexually frustrated woman I know.

I stab each letter of my response forcefully.

> Me: SEXUAL HARASSMENT!!!

> Knox: Damn autocorrect, putting sexually in there. Don't file a complaint against me. File one against Apple. They're the ones who are always changing my fuck to duck. It's quite frustrating.

We need to move on to a new subject.

> Me: Why are you even up?

> Knox: Why are you even up?

> Me: Good point.

> Knox: Insomnia can be a bitch. Now, answer my question. Are you out, drinking champagne on the golf course with your cashmere polo-wearing boyfriend?

> Me: Judgmental much? And I told you, he's not my boyfriend.

Knox: Sunshine, you're the last person who should be calling someone out for being judgmental.

> Me: What's that supposed to mean?

Knox: You judged me the second you walked into Thomas's office. Shit, probably before you even stepped inside.

> Me: You asked me if I slept with you and was lying about carrying your love child!

Knox: So, you judge someone because they ask if they've fucked you?

> Me: No, I judge someone who shares a bed with everyone who has a vagina.

Knox: You have a vagina, and I haven't shared a bed with you.

> Me: OMG, this conversation is so over. Go to sleep. I'll have your Egg McMuffin in the morning.

The man is seriously a pain in my ass.

Knox: Yummy.

I keep my phone in my hand, waiting to see if he's going to say anything else, but he doesn't.

Yummy?

Did he really just end our conversation with the word yummy?

"Asshole," I mutter to myself, turning my attention back to Ross and Rachel drama.

My alarm goes off, and I have it set to "Happy" by Pharrell Williams in hopes it'll make me happy when I wake up. It's unfortunately doing the opposite of that.

I want to hurl my phone across the room, but I'm broke now, so there's no throwing shit I can't afford to replace.

I don't know when I actually fell asleep, but I think I was another four *Friends* episodes in before my eyes slowly shut.

It takes me a few minutes to convince my brain that it's time to get up, and I finally drag myself to the bathroom to shower. I throw my hair into a messy bun and then take it down. We're meeting with Thomas and Knox's tour manager today. I need to look a little more professional. I run to my bedroom for my straightener, and thirty minutes later, I'm walking out the door with my hair and makeup done.

I make it to Knox's only a few minutes early because the line at McDonald's was a fucking nightmare.

"Good morning, sunshine," he sings out when he spots me walking into the kitchen after realizing the front door was unlocked.

I hand him the bag of food, and he starts to pull everything out.

"Did you not get yourself something?"

I shake my head, and he looks at me in disappointment.

"Why not?"

"I'm not a big McDonald's fan."

He unwraps his sandwich, takes a giant bite, and swallows it down before replying, "How can you not like McDonald's?" He takes another bite and groans. "When I was little, going to McDonald's was like Christmas for us even if it was something small, like a cheeseburger. My brother and I thought it was the best meal in the world."

His words hurt my heart. McDonald's was never a big deal

to me, growing up. I didn't care about Happy Meals. I actually hated them and would bitch at my dad if he tried to go there because none of my friends' health-nut parents would let them eat it.

It's funny how much the environment you grow up in affects your life and what you're grateful for, and it's sad there's no way to change it either. You don't get to decide who your parents are. Some of us get lucky while others … not so much. Fast food, like a damn McDonald's cheeseburger, was something I took for granted, but it was something another kid was wishing for.

I give him a small smile. "Anytime you want something from there, you just let me know."

"Got it, and you're going to get something too."

"Maybe. As soon as you finish up, we have to get going. I'll meet you in the Jeep."

"Change of plans. The tour manager and Thomas are meeting us here." He taps on the stool next to him. "So, make yourself comfortable, and if you didn't get a chance to eat something, my fridge is full."

"I'm okay."

"There's healthy shit in there. My chef went to the grocery store last night, and I'm pretty sure he bought the ingredients to make one of your drinks."

I want to ask him if he purposely had his chef get the stuff for me or if it's a regular thing, but I don't.

Only a few seconds pass before the doorbell rings.

"Can you get that for me? It's probably Thomas and Max," Knox says.

He takes the last bite of his sandwich, crumples the wrapper in his fist, and throws it back into the bag. He's on his way to the trash can as I go to answer the door.

We all gather around the dining room table. I grab my notebook from my bag and take the seat next to Knox. I listen to the three men and hastily scribble down everything I can, as if I were going to be tested on it later. I know how important tours are—they're the butter to your bread, and you need them organized properly to make sure everything goes smoothly.

They go through every stadium he'll be performing at in every city and decide whether he'll be staying on his bus or in a hotel after each one. It's my responsibility to book the suites and make sure he has everything he needs upon his arrival.

"Don't forget to book a room for yourself," Knox says, looking over at me. "I'd prefer yours is on the same floor as mine."

A room for myself?

I drop the pen in my hand. "I'm sorry … a what for who?"

"You are going to need a place to sleep. You're more than welcome to crash on the bus or a hotel room. It's your choice. I pay for it, so don't worry about the price."

All eyes are on me. I'm not looking around to make sure of it, but I can feel them.

I shift around in my chair. "I'm going on tour with you?"

Knox nods, and I whip around to glare at Thomas. This was never part of the arrangement.

"I'm going on tour with him?"

Thomas nods this time.

"You never said anything about me going on tour and traveling across the country."

Thomas gives me a hopeful look. "We were undecided until last night. Knox seems to like you working for him, so I think you're suitable to take over for a while."

"I have school," I fire back. What's the best excuse to try to get out of this, but not lose my job at the same time?

"You can come back in three months when school starts. We'll look for a replacement then," Thomas says.

"I'm confused." Too many questions are flying through my mind, and my brain is incapable of spitting out one in particular at the moment.

"Don't worry; we'll provide you with everything you'll need,"

Knox says, giving me a bright smile. "You'll be doing the same stuff you're doing now, only on the road."

"I'll need to go over my schedule and make sure it's okay," I lie.

"You're getting paid good money to do this, Rose," Thomas adds, starting the same lecture he gave me before. "There's nothing you'll find that will give you anywhere near the salary you're getting with Knox."

"I'll give you a raise, if need be," Knox throws out. "You traveling with me obviously puts a damper on your party or whatever."

All eyes are on me, and I feel like the biggest pain in the ass that's ever lived.

"You don't have to do that," I reply, blowing out a breath. "It's fine. It just took me by surprise—that's all."

The room grows quiet as we all pretend to be engrossed in studying the paperwork.

Knox finally breaks the silence. "I told you I need more days in Houston."

"I thought one was enough?" Max asks.

"No. I need three. Move a date around and fix it."

Everyone nods in response, but I'm not sure who exactly is responsible for rescheduling.

"So … is that my job?" I ask. The last thing I need is for them to expect me to do something and it doesn't get done.

"No. I've got it," Max answers. "Your job is Knox. It's my responsibility to keep track of dates and arenas. I'll get it changed, but you'll most likely have to drive overnight to the next city since we've already sold tickets for the dates."

"That's no problem. I'd rather do that and be able to spend time with my family. If you guys need anything else, contact me or Rose—preferably Rose because she's much better at this shit than I am. I only show up and perform, then leave the rest to you guys," Knox says.

Max gets up and slaps him on the back. "That's what we're

here for, buddy."

Thomas stands up next and says good-bye, and the two guys disappear from the dining room.

Knox looks right at me as soon as we hear the front door close. "Are you sure you're okay with this?"

Why do I feel like he keeps asking me this same question? For someone who's portrayed as being a selfish asshole, he sure makes it his mission to check that I'm okay with stuff.

He frowns at my nod. "No, you're not. I can tell when you're lying, and I don't want you to do something you're not comfortable with."

I snort. "You don't know me well enough to know when I'm lying."

I don't want to give him the real reason I'm so nervous about going on tour with him. It's too personal. The last tour I went on with my dad was a nightmare and changed who I was as a person. I've never been able to fully come to terms with it.

"We still have two weeks before the tour starts. If you feel like I'm unbearable to travel with, you don't have to come. Don't come because it's your job. I can't be around someone who's miserable all the time."

"But it *is* my job."

"You're getting paid to travel the country and *sometimes* manage my ass and keep me out of trouble. If anything, you should be paying me for all the fun you're going to have."

"Good luck with that. I can't even afford rent right now."

"What happened with that? You obviously came from money. Where did it all go?"

"You seriously didn't look me up?"

"Briefly. I read the first paragraph on Wiki. It told me how old you are, where you were born, that your dad is some rock legend who has money problems, but I didn't go any further than that. I was hoping I'd get the truth from you—the real story because we all know Wiki doesn't have it."

"I don't feel like talking about it."

"How about this then? Every day I see you, we both have to reveal one thing about ourselves to each other. A secret a day."

"What are we, twelve?"

"We might be traveling thousands of miles together. I need to make sure you aren't one of those crazy people who chooses jam over jelly, eats their steaks rare, or trims their toenails with their teeth."

I roll my eyes. "First off, picking jam over jelly is a hate crime. Secondly, rare is gross. And never—and I mean, never—have I trimmed my toenails with my teeth." I shudder. "What kind of people do you hang out with?"

"Good to know you're not some jam-eating, toenail-munching freak."

I shove his arm. "You are seriously such an asshole, you know that?"

"We won't Google each other or read gossip magazines. Anything I learn about you, I hear it from your mouth. Deal?"

"No deal. I'd prefer we stay out of each other's personal business."

"I'll go first. I'm extremely attracted to you."

I throw my pen at him. "I'm out of here."

"What? What do you mean, you're out of here? I have rehearsal for the LA show."

Fuck. "I thought I told you I had to get off early today."

He shakes his head, and with everything going on, I probably did forget to mention it.

"Crap. Then, I meant to."

"Is it important?"

"Kind of, but it's not a big deal. I'll cancel."

"What is it?"

"A *personal* day."

"Am I going to get a doctor's note?"

"You can't be serious."

He laughs. "Go ahead, but try to get all of your errands done today. We have a packed schedule ahead of us."

He has rehearsals for his tour today, but I didn't think he'd need me for it. They've already hired all of the backup dancers and picked out wardrobe, but Knox has to go back through all the choreography and make sure he's comfortable with everything.

"Got it."

I've never been to a prison, and to be honest, I never thought I'd have to go to one.

I've watched plenty of documentaries on them, but the real thing is so different. I walk through the front doors and start to think about kids who've had to do this for years because a parent received decades-long or lifelong sentences. It's sad, and I can't even imagine how I would feel if my dad had been put in here when I was young.

My dad only added a few people to his visitation list, including Thomas, his bandmates, and me. My mom wasn't added—for good reason, considering neither one of us has heard from her in years.

"Hey, honey," he greets, smiling.

His hair is pulled back into a clean and combed ponytail, and his beard is a little longer. His prison uniform doesn't cover even half of the tattoos that trail up his arms, and I eye his right hand, where my name is scrawled along his fingers.

He doesn't look terrible, but he's in a federal prison. I've heard it's more for white-collar crimes, almost similar to a country club, except you're a convict who can't leave and you have rules.

"Hi, Dad," I reply, scrunching up my nose. "This place doesn't look too bad."

"It could be worse. I have to look on the bright side—it's only temporary. I've already scheduled interviews for when I get out to start paying the government back. I even have an offer for a book deal."

"Good. I can't wait to have you home."

"So, how have you been, my girl? Thomas said he got you a job, working with one of those pretty-boy types."

I laugh at him referring to Knox as a pretty boy, considering The Gravediggers performed their shows with faces full of makeup. My dad does his eyeliner better than I do.

"I'm working as his personal assistant, and he's even more high maintenance than you were."

He chuckles, and I hesitate before telling him about the video and decide against it. I'll break the news over the phone.

"We're going on tour."

His blue eyes widen, and he runs a hand over his face. That sentence has changed the entire mood of the visit. "Tour? You know tours aren't a good idea for you."

"That was years ago. I've grown up. I'm smarter. Not to mention, the pay is great, and I need the money."

I see the guilt form on his face. "I'm sorry about this. I promise to pay you back every cent you have to pay of your tuition. It's my responsibility as a father to provide your education."

"Don't stress about that, okay? You've supported me for twenty-three years. It's about time I do it myself."

"A father never stops stressing about his child," he mutters. "I feel like I failed you, spending all that money on booze and women when I should've been saving it."

"Five minutes until visitation is over," a voice says from the ceiling speakers.

"I guess that's our cue," he says. "Be safe on that tour, you hear me? And keep in touch."

"You know I will, Dad."

"I love you."

"I love you too."

A few tears slip from my eyes on my way back to the Jeep.

13

Knox

"No matter how many times I've performed here, I fall in love with this stadium every single time," I say, turning around to look at Rose and walking backward. "The first time was when I was fourteen. Thomas somehow convinced a singer to let me open up for her. Playing in front of thousands of people was way different than doing it on the streets. I was so nervous that I pissed myself."

"You're lying," Rose says, laughing.

She walked in a few minutes ago, but I've been here for hours, rehearsing for my opening show at the Crypto.com Arena tomorrow night. I want to start out with a bang and for everything to be perfect.

"I'm being completely honest. Good thing I did it before I got onstage and Thomas was smart enough to make sure I had backup clothes. Pissing yourself at fourteen is embarrassing enough, but pissing yourself in front of thousands of people would've been mortifying. I would've quit right then, moved to a different country, and started to raise sheep or some shit."

"Oh, don't be so dramatic. I bet the girls would have still loved you, piss pants and all." She snaps her fingers. "Those pants would probably sell for thousands on eBay, so if you have them lying around anywhere, I'd be more than happy to take them off your hands."

"Oh, Rose, I knew you secretly wanted to get your hands in my pants."

"Or I want to make money off them."

I point down to my dick. "You can take these and sell them … if you unbuckle them with your teeth."

"Is it okay if I bite?"

"That's not nice." I shake my head, chuckling, and then turn back around so she can follow me. I gesture toward the buffet table loaded with food that's set up in the back room. "I had breakfast catered in for everyone. Help yourself."

"Thanks. I'm starving."

We load our plates with waffles and bacon and sit down at a table in the middle of the room.

"So, do you have a doctor's note?"

"Nope, and you're not getting one," she says, stabbing into her waffle with a fork. "And thanks for letting me leave early yesterday."

I tear into my bacon, savoring the taste because I know my trainer is going to be watching everything I eat while I'm on the road. "Guess what time it is."

"What?"

"Secret of the day," I sing out.

"I told you, we aren't playing that stupid game."

"Yes, we are."

"I hate the idea."

"And I love it."

"Fine," she groans. "But you're going first."

I lower my voice to tell her something I haven't shared with anyone. "I'm terrified of fucking this tour up. All eyes are on me, and I've never had this much pressure in my life. I feel like this is going to mend or break my career. One or the other. There's no in-between."

An unexpected amount of tension falls from me.

Damn, it feels good, getting that out.

She takes a long chug of her orange juice and swallows it down with a sigh. She's shocked by my honesty. "I visited my dad in prison yesterday. That's why I needed to leave early."

I know her telling me this is a big deal to her, and I'm surprised Thomas didn't spill the beans about her dad being in prison.

"Damn, babe, that sucks. I wish you'd told me that. I wouldn't have given you such a hard time. I feel like a jackass now."

"Don't. You let me go, didn't you? That's all that matters. You would've been a jackass if you'd refused to let me leave."

I lean back in my chair, stretching my legs out, loving that she's opening up to me. "What's he in for?"

I'm technically asking for *another* secret, and she might not answer it, considering how guarded she is, but it's worth a try.

"You really don't know?"

"I told you, I stay far, far away from the tabloids."

"Tax fraud." She pauses. "He's in prison for tax fraud."

"Not fun."

If there's one thing my accountant has always stressed to me, it is, don't fuck with the IRS. I pay millions in taxes every year, but I don't mind. Taxes and the welfare system once fed me and put a roof over my head.

"Is that why Thomas is always throwing out the fact that you need money?"

"Yes. The IRS liquidated everything—his three homes, including my condo in the Hills, and our cars—and they froze our bank accounts. They wanted their money and didn't give a shit about how we were going to pay for our next meal. My dad took a plea to spend eight months in prison, and thankfully, Claire let me move in with her."

"Thank you for telling me that. I've always wondered why Thomas keeps throwing out that you need money. It's not cool that he does that."

"I've known Thomas my entire life. He's not saying it to be rude. He gave me this job as a favor, and he knows my degree is one of the most important things to me."

I nod. "I get it, *but* I think they took your car for the sake of public safety."

She narrows her eyes my way but cracks a smile. "For someone who complains about my driving so much, you sure want to ride with me all the time."

"I told you, I hate your driving, but love your company." I shrug. "Plus, I can do business in the car when you're driving. If you need any more days off to visit your dad again, let me know, and I'll make sure you're open."

She nods, although I'm not sure if she actually will. She gets up, grabs our plates, and starts heading toward the trash.

It makes me feel good that she's opening up to me, but I'm not sure why I want in so bad.

14

Rose

I chew the last bite of my sandwich and look across the couch at Claire. "So, I have some news," I tell her.

She drops the chip in her hand. "Oh my God, you're pregnant."

"What? No. Why is that the first thing that comes to your mind when I say I have news? Who do you think knocked me up? My vibrator?"

"I don't know," she says, laughing. "You've been jittery as hell all day and then say you have news, so I assumed it was something serious—either dying or pregnancy. I would obviously prefer pregnancy over dying, so I made it my first choice."

"To ease your mind, I'm not *dying or pregnant*. I'm going to be gone for a few months." I think the reason I waited to tell her is because I wasn't sure if I'd bail, and I knew if I told her in advance, she'd force me to go.

"Okay … and where are you going?"

"On tour with Knox."

I wait for it.

Her eyes widen, a smile hitting her lips. "You shut the hell up!"

I shake my head as she jumps up and throws her arms in the air.

"You're going on one of the biggest tours of the year with the hottest pop star in the country. You're seriously so damn lucky."

Lucky? No.

"I don't even want to go, but Knox insisted he needs me."

"Of course he insisted he needs you. He wants to screw you."

I give her a look. "Don't start with that again."

"I think you want to screw him just as much."

"I don't want to screw him or anyone else right now for that matter."

"You know, it's very insulting to our friendship for you to lie straight to my face."

I pick up a pillow and toss it at her, hitting her in the face. "Would you rather I hit you in the face?"

She throws the pillow back at me and gives me a serious look. "I can't wait to tell Dixon. Do you think you can get us the hookup on some good tickets to the show here?"

"I'll see what I can do, but I'm pretty sure you're not hurting to pay for them."

"Why do I need to pay for them when I'm best friends with the girl he wants to screw?"

I grab my phone when it beeps.

> Knox: What time are you going to be here tonight?

> Me: Whatever time you want me there.

I reread my text after sending it.

Whatever time you want me there?

If that doesn't sound suggestive, I don't know what does.

> Knox: I like it when you say things like that.

Me: Didn't we talk about sexual harassment?

I almost hit Send but decide to change the subject. I erase that and start typing something else.

Me: My roommate wants to know if she and her boyfriend can tag along with me tonight. I promise they won't be in the way, and I'll do my job 100%.

Knox: Sure, it's no problem at all. Call Max and make sure their names get put on the list for tickets.

Me: Thank you.

Knox: I got you, girl.

I drop my phone and look over at Claire. "You'd better start getting ready because you're going to the concert tonight."

She skips over to wrap her arms around me. "You're seriously the best friend ever. I need to call Dixon and then shower." She turns around and starts to head up the stairs while throwing an, "I love you," over her shoulder.

I arrive at the stadium three hours before the show starts.

Knox has been here since this morning, rehearsing. He's been working his ass off to make sure this is perfect, and I hope everything goes well tonight.

The security guard lets me through when I show him my badge, and music is already playing in the background. Thomas waves me over to ask if I have any questions about the tour. We talk for a good thirty minutes before he tells me he'll see me when the show ends.

Knox's dressing room is my next stop. I knock on the door

and wait for him to call for me to come in before opening it. He's sitting on the couch, and he sets his phone down on the table when I walk in and shut the door behind me.

"Hey," I greet. "Do you need anything before going on?" I feel sorry for not asking this sooner.

He grins from ear to ear. "A good-luck kiss or even a *screw* would be nice." He laughs at the dirty look I give him. "Fine, fun sucker. If none of those is an option, then I'm good for now, but can you make sure I have plenty of water throughout the show?"

I smile. "I already have a case in the cooler behind the stage."

"You're the best. You do a much better job at this than my mother did when she worked for me. She never asked me if I needed anything before a show. I either did it or Thomas had it set up."

I smile. "I'm only doing my job."

"And killing it. I know I'll be in good hands this tour."

I'm on the side of the stage, watching Knox perform, and, damn, can he put on a show. He's amazing up there. He has no reason to worry about the tour hurting his career. It's only going to get better from here.

Sweat is dripping down his forehead as he sings. I watched him rehearse a few times, but it's different when he's performing for the crowd. You can see how much he truly loves what he's doing.

I have to watch him perform night after night and try to keep my panties dry. I make a mental note to add *vibrator* to my list of things to bring with me.

"That was freaking awesome," Claire screams, skipping my way and wrapping her arms around me.

Max gave her and Dixon front row tickets and backstage passes.

"She's been Snapchatting the entire performance," Dixon says, coming up behind her and tightening his hands around her waist. "Please tell her it's better to enjoy the experience live. I'm not usually a fan of this genre of music, but the dude definitely has talent."

"He does," I reply, and I wish he were more recognized for it.

"So, are there any plans now? Like a big after-party?" Claire asks.

"I have no idea. Even if there is, I'm not going. We're leaving in less than a week, and I still have to make sure everything is in order." I'm not only responsible for making sure all my ducks are in a row, but I'm also in charge of Knox's.

Claire frowns. "Bummer."

Her frown turns into a shriek, and I turn around to see Knox behind me, a water bottle in his hand and sweat dripping from almost every inch of his skin.

"So, what did you think of your first Knox Rivers concert?" he asks.

"You did amazing," I say, smiling.

"You rocked it," Claire answers and then points to Dixon. "You convinced my boyfriend to join your fan club."

Dixon laughs, pushing his hand forward to shake Knox's, and thanks him for the tickets.

Knox points to Claire. "I take it, you're the roommate?"

Claire grins. "Present and accounted for." Her face goes serious. "I expect you to take care of my girl while on tour."

"She's in good hands," Knox says. "It was nice meeting you, and I'm glad you had a good time. The shower is calling my name." He squeezes my side before giving them a wave and walking away.

Another squeal releases from Claire's throat. "Oh my God, did you hear that? He said you're *in good hands*!"

"Get your mind out of the gutter," I say.

"I swear it sounded sexual."

"It wasn't. Do you think the *Allstate* commercial sounds sexual when they say that?"

"There's a difference between the way *they* say it and how he did. He's got something for you, I swear."

15

Rose

Knox is waiting for me when I walk through his front door the next morning.

"Come on. I have something to show you," he says, excitement beaming through him.

He tilts his head toward the hallway, and I follow him into a theater room that I've never been in. I slowly walk in and sit down after he falls down on the couch and pats the spot next to him.

"Are we watching a movie?" I ask.

He shakes his head and holds up the remote. A large screen at the front of the room lights up.

He peeks over at me and throws his hands out, gesturing to the screen. "Say hello to the world's hottest music video."

My mind starts spinning, and the urge to jump up and flee the room itches at me. I've been scared of this day, and I honestly don't even want to see the final product.

"I know you've blown me off every time I've tried to show you clips, but you're going to stay here and watch it even if I have to make you sit on my lap so you can't move." He nudges me with his elbow. "Especially since you're the star of it."

I snort. "I doubt anyone will even notice me, considering you're shirtless and all."

He chuckles and hits play. "We'll see about that."

I hold in a breath when the music starts.

We don't say a word, and I can't drag my eyes away from the screen—away from *us*. I tap my fingers to the beat, trying my best to settle my nerves.

"Sunshine, they are definitely going to be noticing you. This video is amazing. *You* look amazing." His eyes focus on me. "And don't you dare try to deny it. You might want to rip my head off sometimes and talk about how you're not attracted to me, but there is absolutely no question that we have sexual chemistry."

"Maybe I'm a good actress," I say, using the same excuse I did last time even though I completely agree with him.

The video is steamy, and if the actress were anyone other than myself, I would've sworn they were definitely screwing. And that's exactly what everyone is going to assume about us.

I'm suddenly reminded of every emotion I felt and how aware my body was of his as I watch him pin me against the wall. My face is flushed, my eyes burning with need. Knox is right. It's definitely the hottest music video I've ever seen.

My heart nearly stops when our lips meet on the screen. I'm into it—*so damn into it.* You can see my desire for him crashing through me like an eruption, and it only gets stronger when he takes me to the bed. I want to slam my eyes shut, but I can't stop staring at us, at our connection and how beautiful it is.

I shiver, remembering how captivating his soft lips felt against my bare stomach as he kissed his way up my chest before briefly hitting my cleavage.

He got me that worked up from just kissing me. I can only imagine how talented he is in a real bedroom.

"Delete and reshoot it," I say, my face serious, when the video ends.

His jaw goes slack, and the remote falls from his fingers into his lap. "Are you being serious?"

I wait a few seconds before cracking a smile. "I'm kidding."

He bumps my shoulder with his. "You're always trying to break my heart."

Now, I have to get myself ready to fight off the rumors that I'm banging *People's* Sexiest Man Alive.

This is probably the hundredth time my phone has gone off since the video released today.

So far, I've been able to keep myself from looking at the comments and reviews on it. I turned off Google Alerts to Knox's name and have been ignoring every text message in fear of people's reactions.

Now, it's time I put my big-girl panties on.

I open Claire's text first. I didn't give her a heads-up that the video was coming out today.

> Claire: OMG! OMG! The video is so fucking hot that I had to take a cold shower. I've already watched it 10 times!

I laugh.

> Me: You're so overdramatic.

> Claire: Lol. I can't wait until you get home and give me all the details.

I look up from my phone to find Knox's gaze on me. He raises a brow in interest, and I blow out a breath.

"It's Claire. She watched the video, and I'm positive that's all she's going to talk about during dinner tonight," I say.

She'll want to know how he tastes, how he feels, how he breathes.

Every single damn detail.

"Do you want to talk to her about it during dinner?" he asks.

"Not particularly, especially since her parents are going to be there."

Claire has a weekly dinner with her parents, and I usually join them because I have nothing better to do, but I always wonder what they think about me staying there for free. I offered to pay rent once I started working for Knox, but they wouldn't accept it.

"Then, come to dinner with me," he offers.

"What?"

"The video release dinner is tonight. I told you about it the other day, but you said you were busy. The crew and everyone will be there. It would only be right for the two stars to be present."

I hit the Reply button before I talk myself out of it. I'd rather sit at a dinner with Knox than explain to her parents why I'm half-naked on YouTube.

> Me: Sadly, we'll have to wait for that talk. I'm going to dinner with everyone to celebrate the video release.

> Claire: Boo, you suck. Don't worry. We can talk about it all night when you get home. I'll wait up.

I set my phone down and look up at him. "I need to go home and change before Claire gets there and won't allow me to leave until I give her the whole scoop. I'll change and then meet you back here."

"I want to wear something new tonight. Let's go shopping."

"Why do I need to go with you? You have a stylist."

"True, but sometimes, I like to go and pick out my own shit.

We deserve to get out a little. We're the most watched video on the internet right now." He walks around the island and stops in front of me. "We'll go by your place on the way back, so you can change and all that shit. We won't be too long."

"Better not be," I grumble, getting up from my stool. "Because if I don't make it out by the time Claire gets home, there's no way I'll be at dinner."

We're in a private shopping room in Neiman Marcus with Knox's stylist, Mallory.

I've been sitting in this chair for the past hour, watching her go through the rack of clothes before she has Knox try different stuff on. I check my watch. I have no idea why I'm here. I don't even know what I'm wearing tonight, and I want some time to get ready. I'll be in one of the city's most elite restaurants, hanging out with the big shots in the industry. I want to look decent.

Knox is standing a few feet away from me in a loose white shirt and a black leather jacket. Expensive jeans are buckled around his waist. This look is hot—*panty-dropping hot.* He'd better buy that jacket.

He looks back at me and raises a brow. I give him a thumbs-up, and he smiles in return.

He leans down and whispers something in Mallory's ear. She nods a few times and disappears from the room.

"Do you not like any of this stuff?" I ask.

"I do. What do you think? This leather jacket kicks ass."

"I like it. It's definitely you."

He hops off the fitting platform and sits down next to me. "Do guys in leather jackets turn you on?"

I scrunch up my face. "That's a weird question."

"Not really. What is your type, Rose Graves?"

I shift around in my chair, uncrossing my legs and then crossing them back. *Why is he asking me this?* I'm not some contestant on *The Bachelor*.

"I don't think I necessarily have a type."

"Oh, come on. Everybody has a type even if they don't think they do." He grabs on to the lapels of the jacket and spreads it out, giving me a glimpse of his T-shirt. "So, answer. Leather jackets, hot or not?"

"Hot. Definitely hot. You happy now?"

"So, your type then?"

"Yes, my type."

"Remind me to let Mallory know I need a few of these."

"Since we're on the subject, what's your type?"

"I don't have a type."

"Why is it okay for you to answer that, but not me?"

"I like women with sass. It doesn't matter if they have dark hair, light hair, *or pink hair*. I like women who know what they want and aren't afraid to say it. My type is a woman who doesn't give a fuck that I'm famous or is only interested in riding my dick for an actual *free* ride. It's not only looks for me. It's character and the quality."

"Your answer definitely sounds better than mine, so I'll go with, I agree with you and change my answer to that."

Money has never been something that's important to me when I've dated men. I can take it or leave it.

"Okay," Mallory says, bursting back into the room with a handful of dresses draped over her arm. She stops and bends down at the waist, catching her breath. "The fangirls are rampant and on the loose. They must've found out you're somewhere in the building. I guess they stalk you enough to know I'm your stylist." She laughs, straightens up her blonde hair, and looks at me. "You look like a size eight, but if I'm wrong, I'll grab some more." She starts to hang them on the rack. "I think these dresses will look stunning on you, especially with that great figure of yours."

Knox's eyes follow me up and down. "She does have a gorgeous figure. I've learned to appreciate it with each passing day."

I ignore his comment—I'll slap him for it later—and look at her. "I'm sorry … what?"

"Your dress for tonight," she answers, looking between Knox and me.

This is so his doing.

"I appreciate you getting them, but I don't need a dress. We're only here for Knox."

My gaze flits over to the pain in my ass who is now getting up from his chair. He walks over to Mallory to help her unload the dresses from her arm onto the rack, like it's no big deal what he had her do.

"Try on the dresses, Rose," he orders.

"I have plenty of dresses at my house," I argue. I did sell most of my expensive clothes on eBay, but there were a few pieces I couldn't part with. I planned on wearing one of them tonight. "I can't afford to buy new clothes right now." If this were six months ago, I would've been humiliated to say that to someone, but for some reason, with him, I'm not.

"I'm paying for it."

Oh, hell no.

I push my shoulders back and shake my head. "These dresses are crazy expensive. I can't accept that. You've done more than enough for me already."

He sifts through the dresses, and tags start fluttering down to the floor as he rips them off. "Pick a damn dress. Don't worry about the price. As your boss, I'm demanding it."

"No."

He grins, enjoying my challenge. "Pick one, or I will." His lips spread into a mischievous grin. "And I can guarantee it'll be the one that shows the most skin *and* cleavage."

"Ugh, fine," I groan. I slowly drag myself out of the chair dramatically.

He grins in victory and stuffs his hands into the pockets of his jacket as Mallory starts handing me dresses. I take them into the dressing room until I find the one. I step out and stand on the platform.

"Fuck," Knox hisses.

My stomach flutters when he moves in closer.

"You look gorgeous. This one is my favorite." His eyes stay on me. "Mallory, be a doll and find some heels to go with this."

"On it," Mallory replies, grinning.

"Knox," I say, starting my argument.

"Stop right now, or I'll buy you more shit."

16

Knox

I clasp my watch around my wrist while taking a final look in the mirror before leaving my bedroom. I head down the hallway and stop at the door to my best guest room.

"You almost ready?" I yell, knocking.

"Yes!" Rose calls back from the other side. "Give me five minutes!"

"No problem. I'll meet you in the kitchen."

I smile with each step down the stairs. Mallory found Rose the perfect heels, and I somehow convinced Rose to let me buy her makeup so she could get ready here since we didn't have much time to run back to her place.

Why did I do all of this tonight?

I'm still not sure.

I'm not one of those guys who spoils random chicks. I don't want my money to attract them. The only other women I've taken shopping are my mom, my Grams, and Stella.

Nate is in the kitchen with a drink in his hand when I walk in.

"Hey, cuzzo," he greets. "I saw the video. It's fucking kick-ass. All the chicks at work have been texting me, asking if you're coming to Emeralds to celebrate tonight. *Ecstasy* is your best album yet. Another Grammy is on its way. I'll put my money on it." His compliment is laced with pride.

"Let's hope so," I reply, opening up the wine cooler and grabbing the best bottle to start making us a drink.

"And your assistant ..."

"Rose," I say.

He snaps his fingers. "Yes, Rose. People have been asking me who she is. She's definitely going to be getting a shit-ton of attention from this. What made you choose her over a model?"

"It wasn't planned. The model was a no-show. We had to improvise."

"And she was happy to volunteer? You don't think she's doing all this for her own benefit? You did have her sign a nondisclosure, right?"

"Rose is the last person I'm worried about. We had to practically beg her to do it, and I'm not sure if she's even comfortable with it now. She hates the spotlight, but she did it for me."

"She definitely picked the wrong dude to work for if that's the case."

We go quiet, our jaws dropping, when Rose comes strutting into the kitchen. She's not trying to look like sex in heels, but, *fuck*, she does. She looks phenomenal. My cock jerks in my jeans, and I notice Nate sliding his tongue between his lips.

The fiery red dress is sexy as fuck yet modest at the same time. It clings to her thighs and flows out from there. It's sleeveless, jewels line the neck, and the back is bare. Her hair is down and parted in the middle—a different look for her—and her lips are a bright red, nearly the same color as her dress.

Shit. I'm in trouble.

I don't want to go to dinner anymore unless she's the main course. All I'm thinking about is flipping her over my shoulder, throwing her on my bed, and taking my sweet time in undressing her.

"Damn, girl, you clean up nice," Nate says.

My hand itches with the urge to punch him. I wanted to be

the first one to compliment her. I want to be the only man who compliments her.

"Where are you two headed?" he asks.

Rose nervously runs her hands down the length of the dress. "The video release dinner," she answers.

Nate's gaze swings to me. "There's a release dinner?"

I nod in response.

"Am I invited?"

"Were you involved in the video?"

He shakes his head.

"Then, no."

I don't take Nate out with me much because he tries to get jobs and take selfies with anyone famous. It's annoying and embarrassing as hell.

"I have to work anyway," he says with a shrug. "So, I wouldn't want to go to your lame dinner even if I were invited."

"Cool. Have fun at work," I respond. I grab both of the wineglasses and stalk over to Rose. "You ready to go?"

She starts to rummage through her purse and nods. "Yep, as soon as I find my keys."

"You're not driving."

"Well, you're sure as hell not driving. I have a feeling there's going to be alcohol served, and you can't be drinking and driving."

"My driver is here."

She stops to look up at me. "Why?"

"I have a feeling there's going to be alcohol served, and you can't be drinking and driving," I repeat.

"Smart-ass. What am I supposed to do with the Jeep?"

"You have the day off tomorrow. I'll make sure it's back to your condo by the morning."

I hand her the glass of wine and then gently tap mine against it. "Here's to a good night."

"Here's to a good night," she says shyly, which is the cutest fucking thing I've ever seen.

"Let's get going."

I don't miss the curious look coming from Nate when I rest my palm on the small of her back and lead us out the front door. My driver, Willis, is already here, leaning back against the SUV and talking with George, my bodyguard. I don't always go out with George, but I have Rose, and I want to make sure she feels safe.

"Hello, Knox," Willis greets.

I introduce Rose to both of them. He opens the door, and I slide in when Rose makes it into her seat and is buckling her seat belt. George jumps into the passenger seat. Willis looks back at me after he starts the engine, and I give him the nod that we're ready.

I scoot in closer to Rose. "You ready to make your big debut?"

"*Debut?*" she repeats. "Absolutely not. It was either I endure this or a conversation with Claire's parents about faking an orgasm while you're on top of me."

I raise a brow. "Would you tell them you enjoyed it?"

She slaps my arm but laughs.

"This will be more fun, I promise. What I can't promise is that you won't be asked about the video. My phone has been going off all day with questions about you."

"Mine too. People who haven't talked to me since my dad's whole situation are wanting to hang out now."

"Welcome to the entertainment industry, sunshine. They love you when you're up and snub you when you're down."

"The exact reason I try to stay away from it."

I lean in closer, the intoxicating sent of her perfume drifting up my nostrils. She shivers when my lips go to her ear.

"Will you kill me if I tell you how incredibly sexy you look right now?"

She levels her breathing before answering. I love that I have this effect on her. "*Sexual harassment,*" she whispers back.

"I didn't know it was sexual harassment to compliment a

woman, and you're not my employee tonight. We're celebrating the video you costarred in. You're off the clock, and you don't have to lift one finger for me tonight, so technically, no sexual harassment here." I run my hand down her smooth leg, watching goose bumps form in its wake, and I'm surprised when she doesn't brush me away. "You can even come home with me, and we won't act like we crossed that line. It's *our* night tonight —no labels, no jobs—just two people who are attracted to each other, celebrating."

Her pouty pink lips part, and she bites into the bottom one. I want to pull it with my teeth and suck on it.

"Which entrance do you want to go through?" Willis asks, breaking us away from our connection.

Bad timing, man.

I look out the window, noticing paparazzi everywhere. "The hounds are probably at both. We'll use this one."

George looks back at me from his seat. "How do you want me to handle this?"

"You stay with Rose. Make sure she gets in the building. I'll be fine."

He raises a brow. "You sure?"

"Positive." I grab Rose's hand in mine. "Stay with George. He'll get you in there with no trouble. I'll be right behind you."

"Okay."

She feels safe with me. I can tell.

George jumps out of the car and opens up her door. He stands over Rose, shielding the cameras from getting a good shot and most likely pissing them off. They can get thousands of dollars for a good photo. She keeps her head down as she moves through the crowd, doing a decent job at dodging them.

I slide out of my seat and am right behind George.

"Knox! Are you and Rose an item?" a guy yells, a camera glued to his hand.

I have to hold myself back from flipping them off or pushing them away from me.

I'm pissed. This is supposed to be a celebration, not an interrogation. They're ruining our night before it's even started.

"Rose! Have you visited your father in prison?" another one asks.

"Has Knox visited him in prison?"

We rush into the restaurant that was chosen because it thrives on privacy. Paps and reporters aren't allowed in, and everyone on staff has to sign a confidentially agreement upon hiring.

I grab Rose around the waist and turn her around as soon as the door is closed.

She blows out a breath and brushes a few flyaway strands from her face. "I can't believe they're making such a big deal about us going to dinner with a group of people. They act like we're walking into an orgy."

George laughs at her comment. "Now, that would be a kickass story."

17

Rose

Dinner is in a private room in the back of the restaurant. There are at least thirty people in here, everyone from the producer to Knox's management team, all celebrating the release.

Knox made a toast before the appetizers were served, thanking everyone for doing such a great job, and Thomas made the night even better by telling us the video has already hit twenty million YouTube views in *one day*.

I think I'm more shocked than anyone. People have watched Knox practically dry-hump me twenty million times.

Which reminds me … I forgot to tell my dad. *Oh fuck.*

No one wants to hear about that from a prison inmate.

Everyone is not only congratulating Knox on the success, but they're also saying it to me. A few nosy ones have subtly tried to ask if we're secretly boning or if we have some secret relationship going on, which is annoying.

I have Thomas on one side of me, Knox on the other, and am on my third glass of delicious champagne. I can feel the alcohol starting to work through me, making me feel more comfortable with everyone.

If all else fails, get wasted, and then no one will intimidate you.

The drunk ones are always the most comfortable people in the room.

Thomas looks my way when I tap on his shoulder.

"Did you tell my dad about the video?" I whisper.

"I did," he replies. "I asked if you told him about the video you shot last time you visited, and he said no, so I broke the news to him, you little chickenshit."

I scoff. "I was waiting for the right time."

"He's in prison. There's no right time." He laughs. "And you're happy I did it for you. Say thank you, and let's move on to the dessert they're about to serve." He runs his hands together in excitement.

"Fine. *Thank you.*" I am grateful he did the hard part for me.

My mouth starts to water, and I understand why Thomas was so excited for dessert when a chocolate cake, drizzled with raspberry sauce and garnished with fresh strawberries, is set down in front of me. I lick my lips, take the first bite, and swallow it down with a low, appreciative moan.

Knox dips his head down to whisper in my ear. "For the love of God, Rose, please don't moan like that, or you're going to kill me."

"Why? It's freaking delicious." I look over at him, noticing the brooding look on his face. *What the …*

I take another bite and moan again, louder this time, before swallowing it.

Heat hits my cheeks when he scoots his chair closer. His warm lips linger at my ear. "The more you moan like that, the more excited my cock gets." A rugged laugh escapes him. "So, go ahead, keep moaning, but FYI, you're going to be the woman who has to walk out with the guy sporting a big-ass boner."

My fork bangs against the plate when it falls from my fingers. "Sexual harassment," I hiss.

"You're the one over here, having an orgasm over a damn cake."

"Me enjoying cake shouldn't turn you on. You might want to see a doctor about that."

"You're right. You *enjoying* the cake doesn't turn me on. Your moaning and that sexy-ass look on your face are what's turning me on. It's hot as hell."

My heart batters against my chest. "Then, I'll stop." I pick up my fork and shove a giant bite into my mouth, sans moan. "Is that better?"

He shakes his head. "I didn't say I didn't enjoy the moaning. My only wish is that it were my cock you were moaning around instead of that cake."

I choke on my bite.

Knox chuckles as he starts to pat my back.

Asshole.

"That's not the only way I can cause you to choke."

Is he kidding me?

I rest my hand against my chest, trying to settle myself down, and he grunts when I ram my heel into his shin.

"You okay over there?" Thomas asks, looking over at me in concern.

I nod, my body moving in sync with my head as I try to regain my composure. Knox looks over at Thomas and leans back in his chair, making himself look innocent.

I bite into the edge of my lip in curiosity. I want to climb under this table and see if he's actually sporting a boner, but I have a feeling people will think I'm a damn weirdo.

Which I am, considering I want to crawl around on the floor and go boner hunting in the first place.

"I think I'm going to head home," I say when I gain control of my breathing. "It's been a long day."

Knox tosses his napkin on his plate. "Me too. I'll text Willis and let him know we're ready." He snags his phone from his pocket.

Thomas gives him a satisfied look. "I'm glad to see you're

deciding to stay out of trouble," he says to Knox before looking my way. "I knew you'd be good for him."

"Oh, she's most definitely good for me," Knox chimes in, texting on his phone.

Thomas must not pick up on Knox's sexual innuendos because he slides his chair out and gets up. "I need to talk to a few people about business. Congratulations on the video again."

"You don't need to worry about taking me home," I rush out as soon as Thomas is out of earshot. "I heard some people talking about an after-party. I'm sure you don't want to miss that."

"I don't give two fucks about an after-party," Knox says flatly.

I open my purse and start to hunt for my phone. "You should. I'll book an Uber or have Claire pick me up."

"Why? I'm going home. You're going home. Let's conserve gas, save the environment, all that good shit."

"Fine," I groan. "But no more moan talk ... or sex talk ... or whispering in my ear."

"Why do you like to take all the fun out of everything?" He leans in closer and whispers in my ear again. "Does that turn you on?"

I swat him away. "No!"

He chuckles. "Liar. If my tongue at your ear turns you on, you have no idea the other shit I can do with it, sunshine."

I gulp.

I'm in big trouble.

"You want to stop and get a coffee or something?" Knox asks after we climb into the backseat of the SUV. He scoots in close, giving me no personal space, and relaxes his shoulder against the leather seat so he can look straight at me.

The paparazzi are still outside. They snapped shots as we made our way to the vehicle, but George did a great job of blocking them from me. I can still see the flashes coming our way, most likely trying to get a shot of us in here.

"I don't think coffee at midnight is a good idea," I answer.

His face falls. "Good point." The ride goes quiet with the exception of the radio softly playing in the front. "What about a movie? We can watch something at my house. I have access to every movie out there, even the ones that haven't made it to theaters yet."

I fake a long yawn. "I'm pretty tired. It's been a long day."

I'm three glasses of champagne in, his words from dinner are still swirling through my head, and I can't stop staring at him in that leather jacket. If I go back to his house, I'm not sure whose bed I'll end up in tonight.

Therefore, my plan is to evade any situation where clothes can come off and sex can happen.

I suck in a deep breath when he rests his hand against the exposed skin of my thigh, right below the hem of my dress. He slowly starts to drum his fingers to the beat of the music.

"Are you sure?" he whispers.

I scrape my teeth over my lips and nod.

"You know us fucking won't make you any less professional."

"I beg to differ. Conflict of interest, buddy."

Not only is it unprofessional, but sex also complicates things. The whole *no strings attached* idea never ends well.

"The only conflict I see right now is that my dick is hard as a rock and I'm positive your panties are drenched."

I shiver when he starts to caress my bare skin.

"I want to kiss you, Rose. I want to do more than kiss you so damn bad. You have no idea. Ever since we shot that video, I can't stop thinking about you."

"You're drunk."

He wouldn't be saying this if alcohol wasn't flowing through his system.

"I'm not even close to drunk. I had one glass of champagne, and believe me, sunshine, I feel the same way when I'm completely sober. And so do you. I see the way you look at me. The feeling is mutual."

I let out a loud breath. "Obviously, I'm attracted to you, but that doesn't mean I want to screw you. We can't cross that line, and we both know it."

"Then, what do you want to do with me?" He pauses. "Or better yet, what do you want me to do with you?" He inches his hand up, moving underneath my dress. "This?"

I can feel myself sweating. *Did someone turn the heat up in here?*

I briefly look up to see if Willis or George is paying any attention to us. Both of them are looking forward, minding their own business—or at least pretending to.

I part my legs further without even thinking. My body wants it, wants him. The common sense in me is fighting it but losing.

He inches forward. "Is that an invitation? Do you want me to play with you, Rose?" he questions, sounding more serious than I've ever heard him.

I straighten my back up, the internal fight I'm having with myself still in action.

"I'm not doing anything until you tell me you want it. Say no, and I'll move my hand. Say yes, and I'll play with your pussy until you get off on my fingers."

"Yes." The small word stutters from my lips.

He swiftly slides my panties to the side and pushes a finger inside me. His mouth goes to my ear. "So fucking wet for me. I knew it."

My lips part, and everything around me grows hazy when he adds another finger, dipping them in and out of me.

"We ... we shouldn't be doing this," I whisper.

My actions don't match my words because I'm slowly pumping my hips up to meet his touch. *Fuck*, he's strumming his fingers inside me, giving me all his attention, just like he does his guitar.

Apparently, I don't want to fuck him, but I have no problem letting him finger-fuck me in the backseat of an SUV with two strangers in the front.

Sorry, Dad. This man has caused me to throw all of my morals out the door.

"I beg to differ," he says with a strangled voice.

I push away the voices in my head, telling me how bad of an idea this is. I already know that, and right now, I don't give a shit. All that's on my mind is how good he's making me feel.

He presses his free hand over my mouth as I let out my release.

Knox slides his fingers out of me and places them in his mouth, slowly sucking on them. "You sure you want to go in there?" he asks when Willis pulls up to the condo.

"I'm sure."

What do I say now? Thanks for getting me off? See you later?

He grabs my bag of clothes. "I'll walk you to the door."

I snatch it from him. "I … I got it. I'll see you later."

I grab the door handle and jump out as soon as it opens. No one even has a chance to stop me.

I take deep breaths as soon as I make it into the condo.

"Damn, girl, that dress looks amazing on you," Claire says when she sees me. She's snuggled on the couch with Dixon, watching some chick flick. "How was it?"

"It … it was good," I stutter out.

Her forehead creases as she looks at me in confusion. "Are you okay?"

"I'm fine," I rush out. "Just exhausted. I'm going to bed. You guys have fun."

I don't wait for her response. I dash upstairs to the bathroom, take off my makeup, and then head to my bedroom, still not thinking straight from the mind-blowing orgasm Knox just gave me. I grab my phone to put it on the charger when I see I have a text message.

> Knox: You let me know when you change your mind. When you're finally ready to come around, to see me as more than some stupid celebrity man slut, come to me. I promise, you won't regret it. Good night, Rose. We have some fun months ahead of us.

18

Knox

Thomas is relaxed in the chair behind his big-ass desk when I walk into his office. He called this morning and asked me to meet him here to talk some last-minute tour business.

I look around the room. Billboard charts showing off his clients' success—a few of them with my name—cover the beige walls. A picture of us when I won my first Grammy is set up on the bookcase behind him.

"What's up?" I ask.

He signals for me to take a seat, like I'm in the principal's office. "I want to talk to you about Rose and the tour."

"What about it?" I tense up in the chair. "Is she bailing?"

I pushed her too far after dinner. I'd never planned to have my fingers in her pussy. It just happened, and I honestly was surprised as fuck she let it.

He leans back in his chair, crossing his arms. "No, she's still in, but be easy on her *and* keep your hands to yourself. I know how you are on the road. You get needy and moody." He chuckles, shaking his head. "Although I don't think she'll fall for your charm anyway. I gave Rose this job because she's a strong woman who's done a terrific job of handling crazy tours like yours, but that doesn't mean every experience has been a good one for her.

She's nervous—I can tell. I'm going to trust you with her. Don't make me regret it."

"What do you mean, she knows how to handle tours like mine?"

"She used to go on tour with her father. I was his band's manager for over a decade. She had to deal with crazy fans and out-of-control, dirty-mouthed rockers for years."

Ah, yeah. I forgot Rose's dad was some rock legend because she doesn't act like most people I know with famous parents. She doesn't throw his name around to get free shit.

"Second question, what do you mean, they haven't all been good experiences?"

"That's not my story to tell, and Rose would probably quit if I did. We both know we don't want that to happen. So, don't ask and be good."

"If you're so worried about me corrupting her, why didn't you give her to someone else?"

"She knew how to deal with her dad in his rough times. I think maybe she can work her magic on you."

I grin.

"Not that kind of magic."

"I'll keep an eye on her. I promise."

"And?"

"And I won't try to sleep with her."

"Try again."

"Fine. I *won't* sleep with her."

"Now, go out there and show them what a kick-ass performer you are. If you need anything, give me a call, and you know I'll be on the first jet there."

19

Rose

Tomorrow is the day.

The day we leave for the tour.

And I'm one nervous-as-hell woman.

I'm almost done packing when my phone beeps. I grab it from my nightstand and read the text.

> **Knox:** Your bags packed and ready to go?

> **Me:** About to zip up my suitcase.

> **Knox:** Did you do what I said?

> **Me:** No. It's not necessary for you to buy me shit to take on tour.

> **Knox:** I was only trying to help you out. If you don't need anything, it's cool.

Why do I feel like a bitch for not accepting his offer of using his credit card to buy my necessities for the tour? I did have to take a chunk of the money I'd been saving up to purchase everything I needed, but the pay raise Knox promised will pay that back and more.

My phone vibrates in my hand again before I have the chance to reply to him.

> Knox: When are you going to be here to help me pack?

Help him pack? That's not in my job description.

> Me: Don't you have people who do that for you?

> Knox: Yes, you.

> Me: Fine. I'll be there in an hour.

This will be my first time seeing Knox since the whole backseat-fingering situation I got myself into—or better yet, when he got himself into me. I want to blame it on the champagne, but my raging hormones were the culprit. I haven't gotten laid in six months.

How is he going to act?

Will he bring it up or sweep it under the rug so shit doesn't get awkward?

I have my fingers crossed on the rug sweeping.

Shit. Fingers.

That only reminds me of how well he knows how to work his.

He brought me to a harder orgasm than I'd had in a while with just his hand.

I hit the garage door opener and park the Jeep inside. I find Knox lounging on the couch, shirtless, with his feet resting on the coffee table. I try to hold back from focusing my eyes on the water dripping from the top of his chest onto his lap, but I can't.

Please, heart, do not let me catch feelings for this man … and if I have already, please help me get rid of them.

The sooner, the better.

"Why aren't you wearing a shirt?" I ask when I finish eye-fucking him. I keep my distance, casually leaning against the arm of a chair. My nerves are going crazy.

He grins, amused at my reaction. "Relax, boss woman. I finished my swim a few minutes ago." He points to his swim trunks. "My dick is covered." He lowers his voice. "Although, from the way you're looking at me, I think that might be why you're so upset."

"Don't flatter yourself," I mutter.

He chuckles. "You can pretend you're annoyed with me all you want, sunshine, but you can't pretend that I didn't make you come the other night."

Tingles sweep up the back of my neck. "I don't know what you're talking about. I was faking it so you wouldn't feel bad."

He scoffs. "Oh, please. You were soaked, and your pussy was clenching against my fingers, begging for more. It was sexy as fuck, by the way." He gets up from the couch. "But I can tell that talking about how great I played with your pussy makes you uncomfortable, so I'll cut it out. Let me know when you're ready for seconds." He walks toward the foyer and looks back at me. "Now, come on. We have to get my shit packed."

I start following him up the stairs. "Is this some scheme to get me into your bedroom?" I call out.

He turns around and winks. "Something like that, sunshine. Will it work?"

"Definitely not."

"You take the fun out of everything, Graves." He holds his hands up and wiggles his fingers. "I promise I'll keep these bad boys to myself."

"You'd better, or I'll bite them off."

"Why? So you can use them to pleasure yourself without having to deal with me? That's some twisted shit."

"You're seriously incorrigible."

"And you're seriously slacking at your job. Come on."

I groan and curse with every step up. I'm being overly dramatic, but the more he talks about what happened in the backseat, the more I want it to happen again.

I need to keep my distance from this man. But that's going to be completely unrealistic, considering I'll be with him every day for months.

He waits until I meet him at the last door down the long hallway and pulls out a key to unlock it, gesturing for me to go in first.

The bedroom is huge with an expensive bed taking up most of the space. The bed is black and covered with dark bedding. The walls are painted a light gray, giving it some brightness to the dark furniture, and a big screen TV hangs on the wall across from his bed with a dresser underneath it.

It screams masculinity from every angle. The pleasant scent of mint and pine drifts through the air.

Five platinum records are hung up on one wall with a guitar that looks like it's seen better days below it.

"Is that *the guitar*?" I ask, walking over to it.

I know my fair share about guitars from being around my dad's band, and this guitar isn't expensive. It's cheap, beat up, and the only reason someone would keep something in this terrible of condition is if it meant something to them.

He looks from the guitar to me and nods. "That's the guitar that changed my life."

I want to reach out and touch it because of the sentimental value it holds to him but hold myself back, feeling like he's the only one allowed to do that. I'm not sure if he catches on to my hesitation, but I tense up when he walks over to me. He slowly drags his hand back and forth over the face of the guitar.

"I will keep this for the rest of my life. I have guitars that are worth thousands of dollars, but this is my most prized possession."

The look in his eyes when he talks about this guitar is hypnotic. You can't help but fall in love with it too. The passion. The love. This cheap piece of wood is what gave him the life he has now.

I suck in a breath before gaining the courage to run my fingers over it, feeling all the chipped pieces and wear and tear from over the years. I wonder how many other music lovers learned to play their favorite songs on this instrument.

I look over at him when I feel his finger graze the side of my hand. He's staring at me in a way I've never seen before. There's no cockiness. I'm not sure exactly what it is, but it reminds me of a mixture of nostalgia and tranquility.

His large hand folds over my slender one before he weaves our fingers together. The air in the room goes heavy, and the scent of fresh chlorine hits me as he guides our connection over the strings.

Warmth rushes through my body when he starts to play, using the tips of our fingers. The strings feel coarse against my skin. Our eyes are locked, and I can't force myself to look away.

"This is the first song I learned to play," he says quietly.

He starts to sing, and I swear if his hands weren't on mine, I would lose my concentration on what we're doing.

It's no lie that he can sing, and he does it so beautifully that I get caught up in his spell. His voice is sensual and masculine, and it runs through my veins like silk. I could stand here and listen to it all day, especially when he's giving me my own private show.

" 'House of the Rising Sun'?" I ask.

He squeezes my hand. "It was my mother's favorite song. She'd listen to it on repeat, and somehow, I ended up catching on to the beat. It's not perfect, but it's what shaped me into who I am. The lyrics hit pretty close to home."

He starts to sing again, and I never want him to stop. I can't take my eyes off him. I feel like he's giving me something he's never given anyone else. Or maybe I'm hoping he is—that he's never opened up himself like this to anyone but me. I want to be the only woman he's given this incredible personal show for.

"Wow," I whisper when he finishes.

Our hands are still enveloped, and my fingertips slowly slide along the strings.

"It always will," he says, slowly releasing my hand from his.

He takes a step back, and we stare at each other in silence.

What is going on?

I came here to help him pack, not to eye-fuck him and develop an even stronger attraction.

He closes in on the small space separating us, and I know in this second, it's going to lead somewhere if I don't stop it.

I fake a laugh and distance myself. "We'd better start packing before it gets too late. I have a feeling you're going to be high maintenance."

I'm trying to joke, but there's no confusion in what I stopped.

He forces out a chuckle, shaking his head, and points to the French doors on the opposite side of the room. "Closet and bathroom are over there."

I start to move in that direction while keeping my head down. *Please don't let him see the blush rising along my face.*

"And, Rose?"

I turn around at the sound of his voice and look at him even though I'm terrified to.

"I might be high maintenance, but I can tell you, that's not the case in the bedroom. I make sure I take care of others before myself."

I gulp before answering him. "Thanks for the info."

He says things that make my imagination run wild. *Why am I thinking about his hands on me?* He's the last person I should want touching me.

"From the sexual tension that just happened, I'd like you to be well informed."

Oh my fucking God!

I turn around and stumble a bit on my way into the bathroom. The room is as incredible as the rest of the house, and my favorite part is the claw-foot bathtub that I know would be amazing to soak in. It's my dream tub. I walk through the bathroom and straight into the closet.

Yes, I lived a pretty privileged life, growing up, but there is no doubt that Knox has more money than my father did … or he spends it more wisely and doesn't pour it into women and partying.

I walk back into the bathroom and poke my head out the door. "Do you have your packing list?"

"Shit, it's downstairs. I emailed it to you. Do you have your copy?"

"It's in my purse. I'll grab it." I go back into the bedroom and rummage through my bag. I start to separate the papers folded together until I find it. "Here it is."

I don't get the chance to stop him before he grabs a fallen paper from the bed.

"Is this yours?" he asks, his eyes trailing down my itemized list.

Oh. My. God. I want to die. Like, I'm seriously debating walking over to his balcony and jumping off.

I dart forward and try to snatch it from him, but he sprints across the room, grinning.

"Vibrator is number ten and underlined multiple times," he says. "Damn, I'm traveling with a bad girl."

How do I lie my way out of this? "I didn't write that. Claire did."

"It's in your handwriting."

I want to smack the smug smile off his face. He's eating this up.

I decide to just admit to it so we can move on. "Oh, shut up. A girl has to release herself sometimes."

"Why can't you use me as your release? I guarantee you, I'm better than any toy you can buy. Don't pleasure yourself with plastic." He looks down at his swim trunks–covered cock. "The real thing is always better."

"I don't want the real thing." I can't believe we're having this conversation. I'm so pissed at myself that I was stupid enough to let that get out. I should've thrown it away when I finished packing.

The amusement of my humiliation is still evident on his face. "So, you're saying you prefer artificial stimulation? I can tell you one thing for sure: there's no way I'd prefer artificial pussy."

"Have you ever even tried *artificial pussy?*" *And why the fuck are we saying artificial pussy?*

"Fuck no. Never have. Never will."

"Don't knock it until you try it."

"I think you'd look at me differently if you walked in on me fucking a fake pussy."

He does have a point there.

"Probably, but I prefer using a vibrator because I don't have to worry about it giving me the clap or any other venereal disease. I stay clean with my orgasm machine."

"Did you just say orgasm machine?"

"It's better than saying artificial cock!"

"I'm traveling across the country with a pervert."

I scoff. "No, buddy, I think it's the other way around."

He throws his head back and groans. "Do you know how bad it's going to kill me to know you're in the room next door, pleasuring your pretty little pussy with some cheap imitation? Let's make a deal."

"Let's not."

"If you feel like you're in need of an orgasm, you call me. You won't even have to worry about taking care of me. I prom-ise. I'll come in, do my job, and then leave."

The excitement on his face as he talks about pleasuring me is mesmerizing, and I can feel myself getting wet between my legs.

"How about no?"

"I swear, if I see said vibrator, I'm burning that sucker."

We need to move on from this conversation.

"Has anyone told you that you're annoying?"

"No, but I have been told I'm phenomenal in bed, *much better* than some ridiculous vibrator." He shrugs. "Maybe I'll steal your batteries and you'll get desperate enough to come knocking on my door."

He's so wrapped up in our conversation that I catch him off guard when I snatch the paper from his hand. "We need to get to packing because I can't stay long."

"Why? Do you have a date with your vibrator?"

"Say vibrator again, and I'm leaving."

"Fine." He laughs. "One more thing though."

"What?"

"We haven't done our secret of the day yet."

I roll my eyes. "This is the wrong time for that discussion. We have packing to get done."

"My secret is that I'm positive I'll be up all night, thinking about you pleasuring yourself."

"My secret is that I've changed my mind and the vibrator is staying home," I lie.

"Looks like you might be in need of my services after all."

20

Knox

I wasn't lying yesterday.

I did jack off to the mental image of Rose using a vibrator to get herself off last night … and then I did it again in the shower this morning. I should feel guilty about it, but I don't.

She's breaking through my barriers. I can't get her off my mind. I planned on having whoever my fling of the month was come over last night for a good-bye fuck. She texted, but I never replied, changing my mind because I couldn't get Rose out of my thoughts.

I drag the bags Rose helped me pack down the stairs. There's not much in them because I don't keep personal shit with me when I travel.

I head into the kitchen, grab a bottle of water, and open up the sliding glass doors to find Nate lying by the pool. I pluck the sunglasses off his face when I reach him.

"I'm about to head out," I tell him. "Take care of my house. No throwing parties." I point his glasses at him. "And I'm not kidding. I have people watching the place and tattling on you every second."

He squints at the bright sun and scrunches up his nose. "You throw parties here almost daily," he argues.

I knew I had to have this talk with him to lay down some ground rules.

"And? This is my house. I can do whatever the fuck I want to do in it because I pay the bills. Not you. You want to buy the house from me and throw parties? Cool. Until then, no parties. I don't want my house trashed, my shit stolen, or people lurking around here."

He snatches the glasses back from me. "Yeah, yeah. I got it. I'll be a good boy."

I'm not sure if I believe him or not, but it's too late to find him a new place to stay. I'll have Rose look for rentals while we're on the bus. Nate has been working long enough to start paying his own bills, and I don't give a shit if my family gets pissed about it. It's not my job to take care of everyone.

I head back into the house and pull out my phone to text Rose.

Me: You almost here?

I gave her a hard time about the whole vibrator thing and hope she doesn't decide to bail on me for it. I contemplated texting her and apologizing last night but decided against it.

My phone beeps with a response.

Rose: About 5 minutes out.

I open up the front door to find most of the crew already outside, waiting to leave. My chef, Marvin, personal trainer, Lucas, and barber, Andre, are loading their bags onto their bus. I don't keep a large staff on tour with me or do the outrageous shit, like cigar rollers or foot massagers, but I keep my barber, trainer, and chef with me.

When I first started, I didn't bring a chef. I thought I could count on my mom to cook for us, but she bailed on that idea, and I hired Marvin so I don't eat like shit the entire time.

I talk to them until I see the Jeep roll up. Rose gets out, wearing another one of her dresses, and unloads her bag from the back before I get a chance to help her. I notice a small paper bag shoved underneath her armpit as she wheels her suitcase toward me.

She hands me the bag, and I grin as I open it up.

"You brought me an Egg McMuffin?" I ask, pulling the breakfast sandwich out.

"I did. I know your trainer is traveling with us, and I have a feeling he's not going to let you get your hands on these very often."

"I know I didn't hear you say McMuffin," Lucas yells from across the driveway.

I hide the bag behind my back. "Nothing to see here," I holler back. "Move along." I tilt my head toward my bus and look at Rose. "Come on. Let's get our shit in here."

She leads the way and turns back to look at me when we make it inside. "This is seriously your tour bus?"

I nod. "Go big or go home. I like to be comfortable when I'm traveling."

My bus is the most kick-ass one I've ever seen, and I paid a pretty penny for it. There's a full kitchen with granite countertops and stainless steel appliances. The sectional couch provides plenty of sitting room, and the flat screen TV will help keep us entertained. In the back, there's a bathroom with a nice-sized shower and a master bedroom that doesn't make you feel claustrophobic.

"Do I stay in here with you or on the bus with the others?"

"You're my personal assistant. You stay with me."

"But those guys are your *personal* chef and trainer."

"They make me run and prepare my food. If I ask them my

schedule, they have no clue. If I ask them to take care of something business-related, they can't do it. You're the most important person to me on tour, so I need you by my side."

"Knock, knock," Thomas yells, coming up the stairs. He looks straight at Rose before acknowledging me. "You ready for this?"

"What am I?" I ask. "Chopped liver?"

"I think so," Rose answers him. "It's definitely going to be a more peculiar experience than what I'm used to."

"If there's one thing I can guarantee about this tour, it's that. Knox can be a handful, but he keeps his bus clean and doesn't allow groupies on it, and you don't have to worry about walking in on guys snorting cocaine off the bathroom counter. You'll be safe in here."

"That's good to know."

I keep my eyes on her, and she doesn't seem fazed with Thomas talking about cocaine on bathroom counters. *Damn, maybe her dad did give her a rough time when she traveled with him.*

Thomas is right though. If I hook up with someone on tour, I take her to my hotel room. There's something personal and sacred about my bus. Magazines have offered thousands to get pictures of the inside, and I always decline. It would take away the sanctuary of it all.

"I'll keep in touch with both of you and try to make it to as many stops as I can. If anything important comes up, call me immediately," he goes on.

We both nod in response and then wave good-bye to him when the driver tells us it's showtime.

"So … what do we do now?" she asks, plopping down on the couch.

Tours are pretty damn boring, to be honest. You're stuck on a bus for thousands of miles and countless hours. We thankfully have Wi-Fi, cable, and plenty of movies, but that can only keep you entertained for so long. Maybe that's why this is where I get my best writing done. I don't have shit else to do.

"We can make out on the couch?" I suggest.

She picks up a pillow and launches it at me. "We haven't even left yet. You can't start pissing me off this early."

21

Rose

I haven't wrapped my head around this yet. I'll pretty much be with Knox seventeen hours a day, every day. I scheduled myself to stay at a hotel after every show, but sometimes, that isn't realistic. If the show gets delayed or we're running behind on time, we'll have to crash on the bus while the driver gets us to our next destination. Some of his shows only have a day between them, so we'll be pressed for time.

"First stop, Vegas," I say.

He's playing at the MGM Grand Garden Arena tomorrow night.

"First stop, Vegas," he repeats, sitting on the other end of the sectional.

He doesn't seem excited about going to Vegas, like most people are. I'm personally not a big Vegas fan either, but that probably has to do with the fact that my dad would go out and have a good time while I stayed in the hotel, bored out of my mind.

"Where's your favorite place to perform?" I ask.

"Houston."

"That's where you grew up, right?"

"It is."

"Why is it your favorite?"

"I feel like there's a personal piece of me still there, you know? I used to go back to the spot I was playing when Thomas discovered me. It seems surreal to go from that to *this*." His hands go out to gesture to the massive bus we're in. "It was my favorite spot to think, although it's a bit hard for me to go there now without people asking for autographs." He pauses, scraping a hand through his hair. "Secret of the day: I bought ten acres outside of the city there for when I finally decide to retire."

"Really? I can't see you giving up the limelight to hang out in the middle of nowhere."

"I'll keep my house in LA but go to Houston when I want to clear my head from the madness. If by crazy chance I end up having kids, that's where I want them to grow up. I don't want my children growing up in LA. I've partied with too many trust-fund babies to know most of them end up being privileged brats."

His words hit me like a slap in the face. *Is that what he'd have thought of me if my dad hadn't lost everything and still paid my bills?*

"Not all kids who grow up with wealthy parents are spoiled brats."

"You're absolutely right. I've spoiled my little brother—well, at least tried to—and he doesn't act entitled at all. He's studying law, and he likes to stay out of the spotlight. Instead of asking me to buy him expensive shit and to take care of him the rest of his life, all he asked me to do is help with his education, which I'm happy to do."

I'm surprised his brother isn't trying to ride his coattails.

"I didn't know you had a brother." I feel dumb, not having known this. "He sounds like a great guy with a good head on his shoulders."

"He is. Mason is five years younger than I am. You'll meet him when we're in Houston. I tried to get him to come on tour with me, but he's taking summer classes, and he doesn't want to leave his girlfriend. What about you? Any brothers or sisters?"

"Not that I know of."

He gives me a look, waiting for more of an explanation.

"I wouldn't be surprised if my dad has illegitimate children running around that we don't know about, but as far as right now, I'm an only child."

"What about your mom?"

"She hasn't been around since I was four. She was a D-list model that assumed having a baby with my dad was her meal ticket to a fabulous life and fame. It didn't go according to plan. She tried to screw him in child support and then spent the money on plastic surgery and clothes. My dad got pissed and took her to court for custody. As soon as the checks stopped coming in, she stopped coming around." I shrug.

I had dreams she'd come back when I was younger, but I've given up on that idea. She didn't even bother getting in touch when the news broke about my dad's tax troubles and his prison sentence.

"What about your dad?"

"Similar story to your mom's. He's been CLAIRE for as long as I can remember. I don't even have his last name. When he was around, he was drunk and used to beat my mom. He didn't claim me until I became famous. He even went to magazines and sold his story to them. He got in contact and started asking for money. I paid him off to keep his mouth shut and stay away from me."

"Oh, the joy of having opportunistic parents."

He raises his beer bottle in the air. "To those of us with fucked up parents."

I laugh and do the same, except with a glass of wine. "To those of us with fucked up parents."

We both finish off our drinks, and Knox gets up to grab another. "You want a refill?"

I shake my head. "What should we do now?"

"We can watch a movie? Or Netflix?"

I look at him with excitement. "Let's Netflix binge!"

"Netflix what?"

"You've never heard of Netflix bingeing?"

He shakes his head.

"It's when you start a new show with, like, a gazillion episodes and watch them nonstop."

"Oh, you mean, kind of like *Netflix and chill?* I've heard of that before, but as far as I know, that's code for fucking."

"We're not Netflix and chilling. We're Netflix bingeing. Two totally different things."

"With the same result?"

"Negative."

"I like Netflix and chill better."

"That isn't happening." I grab the remote. "So, what do you like? Cheesy? Drama?"

"Put on your favorite."

"You sure about that?"

"Positive. Show me how Rose Netflix binges."

I turn on *Friends*, and we start to Netflix binge.

I'm not sure how many episodes I make it through before dozing off.

My eyes flutter open, and the only light is a faint one coming from a desk lamp. I softly yawn and blink a few times while I make out the figure sitting behind the desk.

"What time is it?" I ask, stretching. *How long was I out?*

Knox raises his wrist to look at his watch. "A little after two."

"Why are you sitting alone in the dark?"

"I'm doing some writing." He grins. "And looking at you. I've decided you're my muse for the song."

I cover my face with my hands. "Well, stop looking at me." I can only imagine what I look like right now. *Did I snore?* With my luck, I probably snored, slobbered, and talked about him in my sleep. "You need to get to bed. You have a show tonight."

He shakes his head and keeps scribbling on the paper. "I'm on a roll right now with this new song, so I'll be up for a while. You can have my bed if you want."

"No, this couch is pretty comfortable."

"You're lying, but that's okay. You're the one who's missing out on the giant, comfortable bed with sheets that smell like this rock star."

I roll my eyes. "Dear God, it probably smells like BO and herpes, so I'll have to pass."

"You know what I like about you?"

"My boobs?"

"Those are fantastic, yes, but I like that you're straight up with me. Not too many people are. They tell me what I want to hear, which can get old at times."

"I'm sure it's a very complicated life, having people constantly kissing your ass."

22

Knox

Rose hands me a towel, and I start wiping the sweat dripping from my forehead. Next comes a bottle of water from her, and I chug down the entire thing. Damn, I forgot how exhausting and demanding being on tour is. It's been two years since my last one.

I pull off my damp shirt and toss it on the couch in my dressing room. Adrenaline spreads through my chest when I watch her eyes skirt up and down my body.

I stroll over to the clothes rack and pull a T-shirt from its hanger. "Two down, dozens more to go," I say, pulling it over my head.

"I honestly don't think I've heard that many fangirls screaming in my life," she says, shaking her head and sitting down. "I thought my dad's fans were overdramatic, but they're like mimes compared to yours. I swear they almost burst my eardrums."

"All the ladies love me," I say, falling down next to her.

She gives me a brooding look when I lean over and ruffle my hand through her soft hair.

"Including you, sunshine."

"Speaking of the ladies loving you." She jumps up from the

couch, skips over to her bag, rummages through it, but doesn't pull anything out. "Guess what I found."

She's excited, eager, and I know she has something up her sleeve.

"I can only imagine," I answer, rubbing my chin. "But I'm hoping it's a pot of gold or some World Series tickets."

She whips it out, and it's me looking at me. I groan. I insisted they quit selling them ten years ago, but people still put them on eBay and Amazon. My mom and Thomas talked me into doing it when I first became famous.

She holds it up in the air and waves it back and forth in front of me. "It's you … only as a doll. I can't decide who's more handsome—you or Ken—but I'm sure you both fought over Barbie." She can't hold in her laughter, and even though I'm the butt of the joke, the sound of it is intoxicating. I have to figure out more ways to get her to laugh even if it means embarrassing myself in the process.

I run my hand down my chest. "Barbie chose me, obviously. There's no competition." I stand up and grab the doll from her. "And it's an *action figure*. Where did you even find this thing? They quit selling them years ago."

"Some woman brought it with her to the concert. She wouldn't give it up when I first tried to buy it from her, which is weird, considering she was my age."

"Yet *you* were trying to buy it from her."

"Fair point."

"So, how did you convince her to hand it over?"

"I gave her a strand of your hair in exchange for it."

"You're shitting me."

She blows out a breath and flops back down next to me. "Fine. I gave her fifty dollars and your fake phone number."

I hold the doll back out to her. "You only wanted it so you could sleep with me at night."

"Absolutely not."

I pat her leg. "Rose, you don't have to lie. We've known each other long enough now that you can tell me you not only have a kinky obsession with dolls, but you also have a kinky obsession with dolls that have my face and body."

"I so do not have a kinky obsession with anything that has your face on it."

"Right," I draw out. "And I don't wish I could get you out of that dress right now."

She gets up and points my way. "Sexual harassment." She opens up one of the drawers in the kitchenette and pulls out a knife.

"What the hell do you plan on doing with that?"

She doesn't answer me. Instead, she sets the doll down and proceeds to cut off his head—or *my* head, to be more exact.

"Ah, man, that isn't cool."

She grins and tosses the decapitated *action figure* to me. "What are you planning on doing after this?" she asks after I throw mini me in the trash can. "Do you want me to order you room service, or are you going to an after-party? I know some of your friends came to see your show."

"We can order something to eat, and then we're going out, probably to gamble."

"Okay, have fun and stay out of trouble."

"I said, *we* are going out."

She holds her hand up. "*We* are not going anywhere, especially gambling. You can, but I'd prefer to sit in my room without cameras in my face and people asking me if we're secretly banging."

"Fine. You're such a party pooper." I get up from the couch. "Just have something sent up to my room—whatever you're ordering is fine. I might need you to do some stuff for me, so keep your phone on and text me your room number."

She opens her mouth to most likely tell me it's not necessary to give me her room number, but I leave before she has the chance.

Will she text me her room number?

Probably not, but considering I'm paying for it, the front desk will tell me.

I'm standing in front of Rose's door, and I can hear the TV blaring on the other side. I made sure to tell her to book our rooms on the same floor at every hotel we're staying in.

I pull my phone from my pocket, hit her name, and can hear her phone ringing over the TV.

It goes to voice mail.

I redial.

Voicemail again.

I pull my hand up and bang on the door.

The TV volume decreases, and the door suddenly swings open. Rose stands in front of me, wearing only tiny pajama shorts and a tight little tank top. What she's not wearing is a bra. Her hair is pulled up into a messy ponytail, and her face is makeup-free. I stand there for a few seconds, staring at her fully alert nipples.

My gaze swings up at the sound of her cough, and she crosses her arms over her chest, blocking my fantastic view.

"Are you ignoring my calls?" I ask.

"No," she answers, moving her bare feet back and forth across the carpet. "My phone is on silent."

Dirty little liar. "Really?" I raise a brow at the same time she nods. "I just heard it through the door."

My sweet view of her nipples comes back when she throws her hands up in the air. *"Fine.* Yes, I'm ignoring your phone calls because I want to sit in this room for the rest of the night and binge on some obnoxious reality show. Not go out, like you want me to do."

She takes a step back in surprise when I walk through the doorway.

"Too bad. We're going out."

"I already told you no."

I head into the room and spot her open luggage. She gasps when I start to go through it. The door slams shut, and she comes stomping over to me.

"Could you be any more annoying?" she asks.

I drop the shirt in my hand when she grabs my elbow and pulls me across the room, away from her shit. I turn around to look at her.

"You pick something or I will." I clap my hands together in a pleading motion. "Come on, Rose. We have miles of being on the road ahead of us. Let's get out, do something fun, live a little. We can't hide in fear of the cameras the entire time we're on tour. Fuck them."

"For the hundredth time, *no*."

"No one will notice us, I promise." I nudge her with my elbow. "You don't think I have connections?"

"It's almost one in the morning."

"Vegas never sleeps, sunshine."

"But I do, or I'm one cranky bitch."

"You have all day on the bus to sleep."

She stays silent.

"Secret of the day."

"What?"

"If you say no, I will cry."

She slaps my shoulder. "You're seriously a pain in my ass, in case I haven't told you."

"Tons of times. Your favorite pain in the ass, who you're about to go explore the city and do tourist shit with."

"The only *tourist* shit available at this time are strip joints and prostitutes."

"I promise there will be no hookers."

She bites into the corner of her lip. She wants to come—I can tell—but she's too proud to admit it.

She groans and points her finger in my face. "Fine, but you'd better not be lying."

"I would never," I answer dramatically and hold my hand over my heart.

She stomps back to her suitcase and starts pulling clothes out. "So, what exactly are we going to be doing? I have to know so I can dress accordingly."

"We're going out and having fun. That's all you need to know, and you don't need to worry about what to wear."

Her clothes are going to be coming off anyway.

She grabs her stuff and goes to the bathroom, slamming the door shut behind her. I sit down on the bed and take a look around when something hits me.

Is it in here?

I slowly get up and tiptoe back over to the suitcase. There's no way she'd leave it on the bus, so it has to be in here. I unzip it and feel around. Nothing. I look in the front pocket. Nothing. I continue my search, fully aware it's wrong, but I'm curious. Just as I'm about to give up, I find a small bag crammed in the corner and open it.

Jackpot, baby.

I slip it in my pocket and rush over to the bathroom door.

"Hey," I yell through it. "I forgot something in my room." I snag the key card to her room from the dresser, just in case she tries to lock me out. "I'll be right back."

"Got it. I'll be done in about ten minutes," she answers.

I dash two doors down to my room, swipe my key card, and ignore the people inside as I go to my bedroom and cram the bag into my suitcase. Let's hope no one else finds it, or they'll think I'm into some kinky shit. I make it back to her room before she's out and sit down on the bed, acting all innocent and shit.

"Does this look okay?" she asks, stepping out of the bathroom.

My eyes roam down her body, and my dick stirs underneath

my jeans. I gulp. *Please don't let me get a boner in front of this chick right now.* She'd kick me out of her room and probably quit. I take in a few deep breaths and try to talk my dick down.

"You look perfect," I answer.

She took her ponytail out, and her straight strands hit right above her breasts. Her tight black dress shows off her toned legs and cleavage. Her tits would fit perfectly in my palms. It sucks she's not going to be wearing that tonight. She'll be changing as soon as we get to my place.

"You don't look so bad yourself," she says, grinning.

"You only make me want you more when you say shit like that."

"We all know I'm not Knox Rivers's type."

"I already told you, I don't have a type. Why would I only want to explore one pond for the rest of my life? Give me something different. I *love* different."

And that's exactly what Rose is. She's not a model, walking the runway, with a million Instagram followers. She's not an actress who has high expectations for every date we have. She's real.

"You ready?" I ask.

She blows out a long breath. "I guess."

I grab her hand. "You're going to love this."

23

Rose

I'm bitching the entire time Knox takes my hand and leads me down the hallway.

I'm in Vegas, and all I want to do is collapse on my bed and relax. Gambling, drinking, partying—I don't want to partake in any of that.

I'm close to panicking when we stop only two doors down—at *his* suite. He has something annoying up his sleeve—I'm sure of it.

I can hear music playing in the room while Knox slides his key card into the slot and opens up the door. I stumble forward when he snags my hand again, pulls me through the doorway with him, and leads me straight into the living room.

What the …

There's a group of guys with drinks in their hands, crowded around the furniture. When they see us, they all grin, throwing their hands up and cheering, like we're the stars of the party.

Okay, Knox technically is.

But that's not the weirdest part.

None of them look like they're about to have a night out in Vegas—or how they did at Knox's show earlier. They're wearing cut-off jean shorts, sporting American flag and beer advertisement apparel—on their shirts, pants, and bandannas. A few of them have mullet wigs on.

I blink a few times, noticing two of the men are Marvin and Lucas. I glance over at Knox, then to his friends, and back to Knox, waiting for someone to give me an answer as to what the hell is going on.

Knox laughs, obviously loving my confusion, and claps his hands. "You ready to have some fun, sunshine?"

Everyone's attention goes straight to me.

Fan-fucking-tastic.

I don't want to act like a bitch in front of his friends, but fun … or whatever the hell this is … was not in agenda for tonight. I had a grand plan of eating Cheetos and FaceTiming Claire to talk shit about the latest *Real Housewives* fight.

"I told you, I don't want to be bombarded by paparazzi," I answer, trying to keep my voice low so the others don't hear my lame excuse.

"There won't be any," Spencer says, moving toward us. He's one of Knox's friends and the apparent leader of the pack.

I grimace, my face turning red. I guess I was louder than I thought.

"Because they won't know it's you," Spencer adds.

"What do you mean?"

A door opens, interrupting us, and a woman walks out, wearing short shorts, a red tube top, and cowgirl boots with her hair teased to the gods. Even while she's dressed in that outfit, I know who she is—Yasmine Ulta, one of the hottest supermodels in the world right now.

She looks directly at me, her red lips forming a smile. "It's like playing dress-up," she starts to explain. "We put on these disguises so no one recognizes us and go have fun. We do it all the time, and surprisingly, no one has caught on yet." She skips over to us, grabs my hand, and drags me farther into the living room. "Knox asked me to bring a few options for you."

There's a large suitcase opened on the floor next to the

couch, filled with clothes similar to what everyone else is wearing.

"I have the perfect idea for you," Yasmine says. "You and Knox should dress up like a couple that's eloping. That would be awesome."

"I love that idea," Knox says, coming up behind me. "Do you think we should do the whole wedding dress and tux thing or act like it's spur of the moment and unplanned?"

"Spur of the moment," Yasmine answers. "Those are the best." She bends down and starts to rifle through the suitcase. "I did throw a few wedding dress options in here—nothing too crazy. I mean, you can't go to Vegas without packing an emergency wedding dress."

"She carries them with her everywhere we go—you know, in case I ever propose," Spencer says.

"You've proposed to me three times, Spencer, and I've told you we're waiting every single time," she argues.

I stand there, paralyzed in place, struggling to find the right words to tell them I don't want to fake elope Knox.

I grunt when Yasmine shoves a handful of clothes in my arms and points down the hallway. "Bathroom. I left some of my makeup in there if you want to use it."

I nod and head to the bathroom because I haven't come up with a plan on how I'm going to get out of this yet.

Do they really think we can get away with this?

People know Knox is here tonight and are most likely going to be looking for him.

I shut the door and go through my outfit options.

The first one is an '80s-inspired wedding dress with ridiculous shoulder pads.

Hell no.

The second is a pair of shorts that resembles Yasmine's—complete with red stars sewn into the denim. I toss them to the side. I'm not usually insecure about my legs, but there's a supermodel in the other room, wearing the same thing. That's not happening.

Next.

I try on a blue sequined dress. It's short, only hitting a few inches below my ass, but it's the best option I have. Sequins aren't my thing, but the other choices are a no-go.

I poke my head out the door and call Knox over.

"If we're supposed to act like we're married, what's my new husband wearing?" I ask when he reaches me. I can't believe I'm actually asking him this question.

"I haven't decided yet." He peeks in through the opening. "Whoa ... that's the look of my future bride? *Yes!*" He yells for Yasmine, and I suddenly regret asking him. He pushes the door open when she joins us, now wearing a black wig. "What should the groom wear with this look?"

"I have the perfect cowgirl boots to go with that, Rose. Here's your wig. You have to wear that." Yasmine hands it to me and then looks over at Knox. "And I'll find you something."

She pulls Knox away, and I shut the door again. I finger the blonde wig in my hand. The strands are crimped and frizzy. I sigh before putting my hair up and pulling the wig on over it. I open Yasmine's makeup bag and add some mascara to my lashes. I take one last glance at how ridiculous I look and go back into the living room.

Knox is changed, and I can't help but burst out in laughter. He's wearing a T-shirt that looks like a tuxedo and jeans with connecting suspenders, but that's not the best part. The best part is his long brown wig that's pulled into a low ponytail, complete with matching sideburns and a mustache. He looks ridiculous.

"Are you really going out like that?" I ask.

"Damn straight I am, and you're not going to be able to keep your hands off me, knowing we're celebrating our honeymoon tonight."

"There's no honeymoon tonight, so don't get your hopes up."

"Now, let's not make any rash decisions yet, my dear. Once

you hang out with me tonight and we go down to A Little White Chapel, you might change your mind about wanting to sleep with me."

"Stick to blackjack. Your chances of winning are much higher on that."

I shiver when his mouth hits my ear. "My chances of winning are always high."

"How about a pregame shot?" Spencer yells.

"I'm game," Lucas replies. "Let's get this party started. Not to mention, I love drinking expensive liquor for free. Once we get down there, it's fuckin' ridiculous."

I look around. "How are we supposed to drink without showing our IDs?"

"Glad you mentioned that," Yasmine says, grabbing something from her purse and handing it to me. "Here's your fake."

I look down at the ID.

It looks real—like it has my actual photo from my real one, but the name and address is different.

"My name is Belinda Jackson?" I ask.

Knox laughs and holds up his ID. "And soon to be Belinda Kettle when the night ends."

"You're really going to play up this whole *bride and groom* thing, aren't you?"

"Hell yes."

"And I almost forgot this," Yasmine says, handing me something. "This is for the bride."

I look down and play with it in my hands. "A Ring Pop?"

"I provide the best bling for my wife," Knox says.

"Dear God, this is going to be a *long* night."

"But a *fun* one. I can promise you that."

I'm taking slow steps as we make our way through the casino. *How is everyone else acting normal?* Even Knox doesn't seem fazed that someone might recognize us.

"Go with it, wife," he says, bringing me into his side. "You need to loosen up."

"I'm trying," I hiss.

"No, you're not. You look like we're plotting to rob the place." He takes my hand and squeezes it in his. "Act like I'm a regular guy that no one cares about. Forget about Knox Rivers. We can pretend I'm your polo-wearing club boy, *Joe*."

"*Josh* is not my boy, and we could've picked clothes that wouldn't draw attention to us. We look crazy."

He runs his hand down his shirt. "*Excuse me*, speak for yourself. I'm lovin' my look."

"There's an open table over there," Yasmine says. "Let's get to gambling."

We follow her to a blackjack table and take a seat. The dealer —Lou, who looks like he's peaking at seventy—doesn't look enthused at our arrival.

"Hello," he grumbles. "This is double-deck blackjack. Does everyone know the rules?"

"Sure do," Knox says. "We play it all the time on the farm, but we usually bet with beer caps and sunflower seeds."

"I won the lottery last week," Spencer says, his accent ridiculous. "Two million buckaroos—that's a helluva lotta money. I bought my mama a new home and decided to take my friends to the infamous Vegas to try my luck some more!"

I put my head down and cover my mouth, trying my best to contain my laughter.

"That's nice," Lou says, clearly not impressed.

"I'm going to sit this one out," I say.

"What? Why?" Knox asks.

"The minimum is fifty dollars. I suck at this game, and I'm not about to waste money I don't have."

"That reminds me." He pulls out two stacks of bills and slides one to me. "This is for you."

I shove it back his way. "I'm not taking your money."

"Yes, you are. Now, take it before we make a scene."

"Fine, but if I win anything, I'm giving it back."

"Whatever you want. Just take it, so we can start. You're holding shit up."

A waitress stops by to take our orders, interrupting Lou as he starts to deal the cards.

"Fireball for everyone!" Spencer yells to her.

"And a water for me, please," I add.

Spencer points at me. "And a Fireball for her as well." He pauses. "Correction: make it double shots."

Lou looks like he's ready to kill us. "Let's get started."

We play the first hand. I'm not much of a blackjack player, but I know the basics.

Lou wins.

We bet again, and the waitress brings us our shots. The sweet but rough taste of hot cinnamon flows down my throat as I take mine.

Lou deals the next hand, and I squeal in excitement when I hit blackjack.

Winning always makes things better, and, well, so does alcohol.

We play another round. Spencer orders more shots.

Knox wins the next round, and we order more drinks.

"We got married an hour ago," Knox tells Lou. He grabs my hand with the Ring Pop and holds it up. "Have you ever seen a rock this big?"

Lou rolls his eyes and releases an exasperated breath. "Can't say I have."

"The one in his pants might be a little bigger." My hand flies to my drunken mouth. *Oh my God. Did I really just say that?*

Knox looks at me in surprise but goes with it. "That's my girl. She loves her big rocks."

I can't stop laughing. I'm happy I didn't stay in my room. I'm actually having a good time. I'll forever remember this night.

We play a few more rounds and then decide to give Lou a break.

"Where are we off to now?" I ask.

"A club?" Spencer suggests.

"We're going to a club as normal people?" Yasmine asks. "I'm not trying to sound pretentious, but screw that. I can't stand lines and people rubbing up all over me." She shudders. "New idea."

"What about a *strip* club?" Spencer asks.

"What about I break up with you?" she fires back.

Spencer holds up his hands. "Guys, the strip club is a terrible idea. Who would even recommend that?"

"How about we walk the Strip?" Knox suggests. "I've never really been able to do that, but I've heard shit gets crazy."

"I like that idea. It's something we normally wouldn't do," Yasmine replies.

"We can buy a bunch of stupid shit and have fun," Knox goes on.

He looks over at me and raises a questioning brow.

I nod. "That's fine with me."

I love to people-watch, so that's right up my alley.

Knox grabs my hand and throws it up when we make it outside to the Strip. "Ladies and gents," he yells, "this chick and I got hitched. She agreed to be my wife, and I'm going to have sex for the first time!"

He grunts when I release my hand from his and shove my elbow into his side.

An older couple stops in front of us.

"Oh, young love," the woman says. "Congratulations. Would you like us to take a picture of you?"

"Sure," Knox says.

She takes his phone, snaps our photo, and they congratulate us again before walking away.

We have a blast on the Strip. I'm enjoying it more than when we were gambling. We go into souvenir shops and buy stupid stuff, take pictures with the best impersonators, and enjoy our time together with the help of our buzzes. No one even recognizes us.

Their plan is actually working.

I yawn and finally look at the time on my phone. "Wow, it's four in the morning."

"Damn, really?" Yasmine asks. "We were having so much fun that I lost track of time."

We head back to the hotel and crowd into an elevator. Everyone gets off on their floors. Knox and I are the only ones left.

"Admit it," he says when we reach our floor and the doors open. He drags me into his side and rests his arm on my shoulders.

"Admit what?" I ask.

"Admit you had fun tonight."

"*Fine*," I grumble. "I had fun."

"I knew you'd enjoy being my wife." He pauses when we reach my door and grins wildly.

Why does it feel like we're ending a date?

"Are you sure you don't want to consummate our marriage?"

I pull the Ring Pop off my finger and hand it to him. "We are officially divorced."

He moves in closer, the Ring Pop on the tip of his finger. "What if I don't want it to be over?"

I shiver as he runs his hands up my bare arms.

"What if I want this night to keep going?"

I gulp nervously, leaning back against the door for support. "It can't … we can't … and you know that."

"Why are you fighting this? I know I'm not the only one who wants it."

I shut my eyes, taking a calming breath. He's not the only one who wants it, but I have to be the one who thinks logically.

"I'm fighting this because it's not a good idea. I made a promise to myself to not get hurt again."

I clasp my hand to my mouth. That's not the argument I planned on saying in my head.

"What do you mean, get hurt again?"

Shit. How do I get myself out of this conversation? "Nothing. I'm exhausted and not thinking clearly."

"Too exhausted to invite me in?"

I rub my hands over my face and nod. I turn around and unlock my door without giving him another look. "Good night, Knox."

"Good night," he whispers behind me. He's still standing there as I close the door.

I'm tired, yes, but that's not my biggest problem.

I'm so ridiculously turned on that I can't think straight.

I open my luggage and head directly to it, but it's not there. I feel around, thinking I probably misplaced it, but find nothing. I start tossing everything out. My clothes hit the bed, the floor, even the lampshade as I desperately search for it.

It's gone.

What the fuck?

I'm positive I packed it.

I snatch my phone from the bed and hit Claire's name. Hopefully, she's not asleep.

> **Me:** Check my nightstand drawer and see if I left V.

I continue to look through my shit until my phone beeps with a response.

> **Claire:** Drawer is clear of V. Should I look anywhere else?

> **Me:** No.

Claire: Is V MIA?

Me: Apparently.

Claire: Go replace V with the real thing. I know exactly who you should ask.

Me: Good night.

She's just as bad as he is.

I throw myself down on my bed and let out a long sigh. I knew this was going to happen, which is the exact reason I put it on my packing list. There's no way I can survive months of Knox's flirting and not relieve myself.

My phone beeps. I check it, knowing it's most likely Claire telling me she found it.

I'm so wrong.

Knox: Are you missing something?

He wouldn't have. He couldn't have.

Me: What are you talking about?

He sends me a picture of my vibrator.
And I fucking lose it.

24

Knox

I can't fight off the grin on my face as I stare at the picture I sent Rose. I debated with myself on whether or not to go through with my plan. I was going to wait until we were on the road longer to break it out, but I have a feeling that's the first thing she went for when she got back into her room.

She was trying to hide it, but there was no doubt she was turned on in the hallway.

She hasn't texted me back yet, but the three dots on the bottom of our message feed tell me she's trying to come up with a response.

I wait another minute.

Nothing.

I decide to help her out.

Me: Why not come over for the real thing?

The bubbles stop … and then reappear … and I wait for it.

Rose: Why are you sending me a picture of a vibrator?

She's trying to play clueless.

> Me: I found it in the hallway and figured the owner might want it returned.

> Rose: You seriously stole my vibrator? You're evil. Just plain evil.

> Me: You're more than welcome to come and get it, but I'm demanding ransom. You have to spend the night with me.

> Rose: You've lost your damn mind!

I exit out of our text messages and go into my call log. I hit the FaceTime option next to her name. It rings a few times, and I'm shocked when she answers.

"What?" she yells.

I crack a smile at the grimace on her face.

"I have something you might like to have back," I say. I grab the vibrator and show it to her. "If you want it back, untouched, do what I say, and no vibrator will be hurt."

She pinches her face together, her blue eyes narrowing in on me. "Have you ever heard of invasion of privacy? I cannot believe you went through my luggage, creep. Did you smell my panties while you were at it?"

"No, I didn't have time to."

"Keep the vibrator. You probably need it more than I do."

"The hell I do."

"Good night," she sings out.

"Stop! What are you wearing?"

She tries to hold in her laughter but fails miserably. "You remind me of a little perv right now."

"Only for you, babe."

She rolls her eyes before hanging up on me.

Mission failed.

25

Knox

I'm not sure if Rose is going to answer my phone call this morning when I hit her name on my phone screen.

"I'm only answering because you're my boss and I don't want to get fired," she immediately says. "I ordered your breakfast. It should be there in about ten minutes."

She's being the professional Rose, not the spontaneous one I had an incredible time with last night. I need to break down those walls more to see that beautiful, carefree side of her.

"Did you order something for yourself?" I ask.

"Yes."

"Call room service back and tell them to deliver yours to my room. I need to go over some shit with you."

"Right now? We have an entire bus ride to do that. I mean, *hours upon hours.*"

"True, but I don't want to sit in here and eat breakfast by myself. So, get your ass over here and enjoy some waffles with me."

"Fine," she groans. "I'll be there in five."

I'm grinning from ear to ear as I drag myself out of bed and head to the bathroom to brush my teeth. I run some cold water over my face, and I'm still shirtless when I hear the knock. I walk through the living room and answer the door to find Rose standing in front of me, her hair wet and in a ponytail, and she's wearing another one of those long dresses, this one black lace and hanging loose from her shoulder.

I lightly chuckle, not missing the way her eyes roam down my chest before moving back up to meet my gaze.

"Morning," she says slowly. "Thomas wants to have a conference call, so I told him to call us in an hour. That will give us plenty of time to pack up and make sure we stay on schedule for the next city. That okay?"

"You're the boss, babe," I answer, resting my arm against the doorframe. "And have I ever told you how much I love those dresses you wear?"

Her baby blues narrow in on me. "It's too early for me to deal with your flirting."

I move aside, allowing her to slide into my suite. The door closes behind her, and I meet her in the living room.

"Are you still mad at me?" I ask, sitting next to her on the couch.

"I was never mad at you."

"You sure acted like it."

She shakes her head. "Not mad. I just need to keep in mind that you have sticky fingers, *thief.*"

I can't help but grin. "Babe, if you let me have you for one night, I'll show you how great it feels when my fingers are sticky."

She pushes forward to slap my shoulder. "You went through my bag, Knox, and took something of mine. That's an invasion of privacy. You're lucky I didn't report you for stealing."

"Go right ahead." I hold my phone out. "Tell them you need to make a police report for your missing vibrator."

She swats it away. "It's also too early to deal with your bullshit. I'm sleep-deprived."

I get up from the couch and start to head toward my bedroom. "If you want it back ..."

She jumps and runs after me. "No! It will be humiliating if you hand me my vibrator right now." She grabs my elbow, drags me back into the living room, and pushes me down on the couch.

"Then, how exactly do you expect me to give it back? Mail it to you?"

She throws her arms out, shaking her head. "It's not like I'll need it for the next few days. Slip it in my bag or something when I'm not looking." She gives me a cold glare. "And don't take anything else."

I stick my lower lip out. "You're ruining all my fun. I was planning on making a shrine of you. I've been saving up all your used bubble gum and water bottles."

She flips me off.

"Another question."

"No more questions if it involves anything having to do with a vibrator."

I hold my finger up. "One more question, and I promise I'll stop."

She falls back onto the couch. "Fine, one more."

"Do you have anything kinkier in that little suitcase of yours?"

I grunt when a pillow flies toward me and smacks me in the face.

"No," she screeches. "I like vibrators. They get the job done without any commitment."

"What the hell? I can do the same job." I stop and clear my throat. "Let me correct myself. I can do a *better* job without the commitment. What's the difference?"

"There's a big difference. I can't develop feelings for my vibrator. My vibrator can't develop feelings for me. When it's time for me to part with it, it'll be easy. Vibrators give you the benefits of a relationship without the hassle and heartbreak."

"Wrong. It gives you an orgasm. That's not the only advantage of being in a relationship."

"You know what I mean."

"One of these days, you're going to let me in, Rose Graves, and I mean, let me in, in *a lot of different ways.*"

"Not happening."

"Life is too fucking short to be afraid of doing things you want to do. I'll leave it at that." I decide to drop it. It's not going to go anywhere right now, and I don't want her to think I'm trying to push her too much. "What time do we head out?"

"Two hours—after Thomas's call. I've already scheduled to have your bags brought down. Our next stop is Seattle."

"Sounds good."

Rose is sitting on the couch with her computer on her lap when I walk up the stairs to the bus.

"Looks like we made headlines again," she says.

Fuck. Here we go.

If *we're* in the news, that means she's going to pull away more.

"Good news or bad news?" I ask.

She turns the laptop around so the screen is facing me and starts scrolling down the page. There's a picture of us sitting at the blackjack table. My hand is resting on her knee, and we're staring at each other, laughing.

Our chemistry and attraction bleed through the photo.

I shut the door and let out a deep breath. "We've been doing that trick for years—*years*—and have never been busted."

She turns it back around and starts to read the article out loud. "Some of them are even reporting that we actually eloped!"

I pull my phone from my pocket. "I'll fix this right now." I log in to my Twitter account and start typing.

"What exactly are you doing?"

"I'm tweeting that it was all fun and games last night and I'm not a married man."

Her eyes are wide. "You don't want me to make a statement?"

"You can if you want, but it's a waste of time. If I tweet it, it's pretty much a statement in itself. Anyone who cares about what I'm doing follows me on here."

She shuts the laptop, sets it on the floor, and rests her head against the couch cushions. "I wish it had been that easy when I was dealing with my father. You couldn't just tweet the truth back then."

"It has its ups and downs. There have been plenty of mornings that I've woken up, wishing Twitter didn't exist because I drunk tweeted some stupid shit."

She snorts. "I know what you mean."

I sit down on the other side of the sectional. "What's the worst thing you've tweeted?"

She shakes her head. "No way. I am so not going there."

"Come on. I'll tell you mine."

She shakes her head again.

I grab my phone and turn on the camera.

She jumps when I take a picture of her.

"What are you doing?"

"Tell me your worst one or I'll tweet this picture and tell them it wasn't a joke and you are my new wife."

"Fine," she mutters. "You're seriously a pain in my ass."

"I like your ass, so we're even."

Her cheeks start to turn a soft pink. "It was my twenty-first birthday. My friends and I went out clubbing. I got completely hammered, and I don't remember everything that happened that night. What I do remember is waking up to a tweet of mine that somewhat went viral, asking who wanted to give me a screaming orgasm."

"You dirty girl, you."

"I was referring to the drink—a screaming orgasm—but

apparently, my tweet made it sound like I wanted someone to come over and actually give me an orgasm. My friends haven't let me live that one down."

I laugh. "Babe, you let me know if you ever need a screaming orgasm."

"I told you, enough with the sex talk."

"I was talking about the drink. I'm a pretty good bartender." She rolls her eyes.

"If it makes you feel any better, mine is pretty bad, but probably not *as* bad as yours because it wasn't me doing the actual tweeting."

"Then, that doesn't count."

"It does if it was on *my* Twitter. A girl I hooked up with somehow got ahold of my phone after we … *you know*."

"After you gave her a screaming orgasm?"

I snap my fingers. "Exactly. She tweeted like fifteen pictures of herself lying in bed with me passed the fuck out."

Her face gets redder before she bursts out in laughter.

I raise my voice to talk over her. "After that, I started having George lock my phone up when I was hooking up with a chick." I wait until she stops laughing before scooting toward her and nudging her with my elbow. "So, when you finally decide to let me give you another screaming orgasm, please don't take pictures and post them online."

"Trust me, you don't have to worry about either one of those things happening."

"Never say never because who knows when you'll be in need of a screaming orgasm?"

I grab my phone when it starts to vibrate and groan when I read the text.

Mom: You were supposed to be staying out of trouble on this tour. I'll be having a talk with Rose about her unprofessional behavior.

I'm not sure why my mom is so pissed about last night. She

should be proud of me for selling out every venue and excited that we're already in talks of adding more shows.

She's scared because she doesn't want people to quit being my fans. I don't know why she gets so damn worried. I have plenty of money to live a comfortable life even if I don't make another dime. I think it's because she's afraid of losing the spotlight. She developed a skin care line that sells on QVC and wrote a few books about raising me. She doesn't want those opportunities to go if people want nothing to do with me.

"What is it?" Rose asks, raising a brow.

"Nothing," I answer. "It's Spencer telling me about our marriage headlines."

I hit reply.

> **Me:** The hell you will. It was my idea. Don't say shit to her.

> **Mom:** I'm only doing what's right for your career.

> **Me:** You don't handle my career. She and Thomas do. You have no say.

My phone beeps again, and I'm glad this text isn't from my mom. It's from my brother.

> **Mason:** Dude, I'm pissed our whole dress-up game is ruined. I can't believe you got busted.

> **Me:** I know, but I'm surprised we got away with it for that long.

> **Mason:** I heard the tour is kicking off with success. Miss you, big bro.

> **Me:** Miss you too. I expect to see you when I make it home.

> **Mason:** You know I wouldn't miss it.

26

Rose

I knew the fun was about to end when I got on the bus this morning. I've memorized the schedule, and I am fully aware of how many shows are set up. Knox is going to be swamped.

What I was worried about happening happened, but I'm not as stressed out as I thought I would be. Sure, there are tons of articles about us, but most commenters say it looks like we're only having fun and enjoying a night out. The Ring Pop on my finger should tell anyone with common sense that it was all one big joke.

Knox is texting on his phone when mine goes off. I've been waiting for her text since I saw the pictures of us.

> Claire: I need an explanation ASAP.

> Me: I have no idea what you're talking about.

> Claire: Don't you dare try to play coy with me! I saw the pictures. Did you get married in Vegas WITHOUT ME THERE TO BE YOUR MAID OF HONOR?!

> Me: Do you honestly believe I got married last night?

Claire: Nope. I'm only giving you a glimpse of how dramatic I'll be if you ever do something like that.

Me: Noted.

"The best friend?" Knox asks, looking over at me.

I shake my head. "The new boyfriend."

His phone drops from his hand, and his eyes go wide. "What?"

"My boyfriend saw the pictures of us and wants to know if I'm cheating on him."

"Boyfriend?" His nose scrunches up in confusion. "Since when did you get a boyfriend?"

I probably shouldn't ask him this, but I do. "Are you jealous?"

"You know I'm jealous, *and* I know you're lying. It's the best friend."

I sigh. "She saw the pictures and was going to kill me if I got hitched without her being the maid of honor."

"Tell her you chose Elvira over her."

"She would probably come hunt us down and kill me."

"I don't doubt that. She seems a little high-strung, that one."

"We balance each other out. She's the crazy one. I'm the levelheaded one."

"Kind of like how you balance me out?"

"I guess so."

We both jump when the driver opens the door and walks up the stairs.

"You guys ready to head out?" he asks.

"Sure are," Knox answers.

"We've got some long days ahead of us, but I'll make sure you have a safe and comfortable ride."

"Thanks," I say.

He disappears, and a few minutes later, we hear the engine start up.

"Did you have your other assistants stay on the bus with you?" I ask. I know most musicians like to have company on the bus while others prefer to be left alone.

"My mom would usually stay with me on here when we were on the road, but I made sure we stopped and stayed at a hotel every night. She's on the high-maintenance side."

"Has she always been like that?"

This man, he's so easy to talk to that, sometimes, I forget that I work for him and we're not friends. I'm beginning to grow more and more comfortable with him.

"She hasn't. Fame changes people. One thing that worries me about her now is how she looks at the people who are where she was years ago. When I go to charity events, sometimes, she won't come with me. She acts like they're beneath her. It's sad, and I think that's why I've started to pull away from her. I will never forget where I came from or look down on someone who's in the position she used to be in."

I love his answer. Thankfully, my dad brought me up to treat everyone the same, no matter how much money they had.

"What do you think has changed the most with you?" I ask curiously. I don't like him asking me personal questions, but I want to know every single detail about what makes him.

He tilts his head to the side, his lips slightly parting. "Is this our secret of the day?"

I gulp. I hate this game. Okay, I actually like it when it's one-sided—when he's revealing stuff to me—but I hate it when it's my turn. *Is it worth opening up so I can figure him out?*

"It can be."

"My trust of other people," he immediately says, like the answer was on the tip of his tongue. "What do you think has changed since the whole ordeal with your dad?"

He opened up to me. It's only fair I do the same thing.

"Who I can count on and how truly ungrateful I was at times."

He nods in agreement, understanding where I'm coming

from. "I've lost that somewhat as well—my sense of appreciation. When I was younger, if someone did something, anything, for me, even give me a piece of bubble gum, you would've thought they had handed me a million dollars from how greatly I appreciated it."

"But you've given back. I see all of the charities you've donated to, how many people you've helped, how many sick children you've visited."

He releases a shallow sigh. "You want to know my favorite part of doing all of that?"

I nod.

"The way their faces light up, like me being there or what I've done is life-changing. It reminds me of how I looked at all the people who helped my mom, the ones at the food pantry or those who donated school supplies. That shit would make my day."

"I wish I could help people like that."

"I have some meets set up during my tour. Want to come along?"

"I'd like that."

He scoots in closer, puts his arm around my shoulders, and brings me into his side. "Now, my new wife, can we finally consummate our marriage?"

I'm unable to hold in my laughter as I push him away from me. "Absolutely not. I've already filed for an annulment."

He frowns. "First, I don't get laid. Now, you're leaving my ass. What's next?"

"I take half of everything you've worked for." I jump up and go in search of the remote. "Shall we watch *Friends*?"

He frowns. "Not exactly how I imagined I'd be spending my honeymoon."

27

Knox

We've been on the road for four weeks now, and it's been complete madness.

The tour schedule is jam-packed. I'm performing at least every other night, depending on how far apart the cities are. We hit one city. I do my show. I sleep. We leave and do the same thing in the next one. I also try to fit in radio interviews and promotional shit. If it wasn't for Rose, I'd probably be all over the place and stressed out.

But she makes sure I have everything I need and that I don't have to worry about a damn thing.

"What number are we on?" I ask, falling down next to her on the love seat in my dressing room.

She stretches out her legs and rests them on the coffee table in front of us. "You just finished your eighteenth show. You ready to retire yet?"

"Not even close. Being on tour gets me all hyped up."

"I can tell. You're doing a killer job. I've never seen stadiums so busy or heard screams so loud."

"Trust me, I can get louder screams."

She rolls her eyes at my response. "You have a few meet and greets after this."

"And then we're going to do something fun."

She raises a brow.

"Like hang out."

"We hang out every night."

"We hang out on the bus, Netflix binge, or discuss work. I want us to have fun and focus on stuff other than that."

"Do you not remember the last time we did that? People thought we secretly got married. I even saw stories that claim you knocked me up and your mom forced you to elope with me."

"We won't dress up or be in a busy place where people can see us. It'll only be you and me. You've been working your ass off. I want you to relax a little."

"I'm only doing my job."

"You're doing more than that. You're making sure my shit is straight from city to city. I think you work harder than I do."

My mom and Rose as my assistant on tour are night and day. I would've hired someone else years ago if I had known they would do what Rose does. She gets shit done. By now, she knows what I like and doesn't even have to ask me questions. She's a lifesaver and a breath of fresh air.

"We've had a long night," she says.

"This will relax you." I get up and pat her leg. "Put something comfortable on. I'll do this meet and greet, and then we'll get going."

28

Rose

I'm staying in Knox's suite tonight—in a different room, of course.

The hotel we're staying in didn't have any open rooms on his floor, and he insisted he didn't want me that far away from him. It's a two-bed, two-bath, so it would've been ridiculous for me to argue.

I'm relaxing on the couch in a pair of yoga pants and a T-shirt when he walks in after doing his meet and greet. I usually go to those with him, but he said he was fine on his own tonight.

"Nice shirt," he says when he sees me. "I look good on you."

I chuckle, pulling at the bottom of the shirt and looking down at it. It's one of his tour tees with his face on the front and all the show dates are listed on the back. "These things are comfortable as hell. I could wear them every day."

"Glad I'm also comfortable on you." He whistles on the way to his room and turns back to look at me before shutting the door. "I'm going to hop in the shower real quick, and then we'll get going."

"Where are we going?" I yell after him.

"It's a surprise," he shouts back. "You don't always have to know every little detail, Graves."

I frown.

Oh, yes, I do.

I watch TV, half-paying attention to it until he comes out, wearing gym shorts and a T-shirt.

"I tried to find one with your face on it, but unfortunately, I don't have one." He tugs at the bottom of the shirt, like I did with mine. "I think it's only fair I get one."

I get up from the couch. "I'll get right on that, boss."

I follow him out the door, down the hall, and into the elevator.

"Are you going to tell me where we're going yet?" I ask.

"You'll see."

The door opens right into the hotel's spa. I eyed the brochure this morning, and they offer some of the most extravagant services.

"My muscles are sore as hell," he says, opening up the door for me. "I need a massage and figured you could keep me company. I tend to get bored during these things."

A massage sounds damn good to me.

Two women are waiting for us in the empty lobby. They're older, most likely the best employed here, considering it's after hours. I'm sure Knox is going to be footing a nice bill for this.

"Hello, Mr. Rivers and Miss Graves," one says. "I'm Sabrina." She points to the other. "And this is Pat." She hands us each a flute of bubbly champagne. "Would you like to soak before or after your massages?"

Knox glances over at me. I shrug.

"We'll do after," he answers.

"Great," Sabrina says. "Follow me."

We're led down a narrow hallway and into a private room that's dimly lit with candles. Side-by-side tables take up the majority of the space, and lavender and mint flow through the air. There's no doubt this is a luxury spa.

Oh, how I've missed these.

Sabrina points to each side of the room. "There are two dressing rooms with robes for you. We'll give you some time to change."

We both nod, and they leave the room. Knox starts to head toward a dressing room, but I stop him.

"Don't come out until I tell you to," I say, causing him to whip around and give me a confused look. I let out a breath. "I'm obviously going to be naked underneath my robe. I'll change, get on the bed and cover myself up, and then tell you when to come out."

"So, I can't see you naked, but you can see me?" he asks.

"I'll cover my eyes up when it's your turn."

"You can look all you want. I don't mind. I encourage it."

He dips into the dressing room without another word, and I do the same. I strip out of my clothes and laugh to myself when I hang up my T-shirt. I never thought I'd be sporting anything with his mug on it.

The robe is warm and plush as I pull it over my shoulders and tie it around my waist. The room is empty when I walk back out. *Thank God.*

I drop the robe, hang it up, and tiptoe over to the table.

"Coast is clear!" I shout after I cover myself with the silky sheet.

The door flies open, and Knox comes out. His robe is loosely secured around his waist, giving me a glimpse of his muscular upper thighs. I gulp when he walks over to the hooks and drops it, giving me a beautiful full view of his toned ass.

My mouth falls open. I want to look away. I *need* to look away but can't.

"If you don't want to see my cock, you'd better turn around now," he warns.

I cover my eyes. "Let me know when it's safe."

He laughs, and a few seconds pass before he lets me know all is good.

I remove my hand and open one eye at a time. There's a knock at the door, and the ladies come scurrying in when Knox gives them the okay. I make myself comfortable while they get ready for our massages. A low, quiet hum of music starts playing, and I relax when a pair of soft hands lands on my back.

"This feels amazing," I moan out about halfway through our session. I can already feel the tension in my body start to disappear.

"It's well deserved," Knox says.

I turn my head to look over at him. "For me only being your assistant, you're pretty good to me."

"It's the other way around, sunshine. You're one of the best things that has happened to me on this tour."

My mouth goes dry.

I have no idea what to say back to that.

So, I gently smile and shut my eyes, ending our conversation.

I don't open them back up until the hands stop.

"Are you ready for your soak?" Sabrina asks.

I look over at Knox in question. I'm not sure how to answer. I've never soaked after a massage.

"Do you want to do it?" Knox asks.

I shrug. "Sure."

"We'll be naked," he clarifies.

"It's fine. We'll stay on our sides."

Wait. What the hell did I just say?

I just agreed to soak in a tub, naked, with him.

The soak is in what might be the most romantic environment in the world.

I wasn't exactly sure what I was getting myself into when I agreed, but it definitely wasn't anything like this. The only light source we have is candles. They've provided more champagne, and chocolates are added to the mix.

Now, I'm questioning myself on whether this was a good idea.

It definitely wasn't.

We haven't said a word to each other since we quickly dropped our robes and dipped into the tub. I was so concerned about him seeing me that I didn't get a chance to get a look at him.

"So … should we do our secret of the day?" Knox asks, shifting around in the bubbles and finally breaking the silence.

"Sure. You go first, as usual," I answer.

"I never cheated on Stella."

I rudely snort into my glass of champagne. "Oh, come on. I might be young, but I'm not that naive."

He makes eye contact with me before replying, "I'm not lying."

"There are pictures of you with other women. Straight evidence. You can't dispute that."

"That's true, but all of those were taken when Stella and I were broken up. We did that a lot—broke up and then made up. When I'd ask her to speak on it, she'd say she didn't want our relationship in the public eye. She wasn't the one who looked like a cheater. But *she* was the one who cheated on me once. I think that's when we started to go downhill and realized it was time to end our relationship for good."

"Wow. We didn't see it like that from the outside."

Whenever I heard the stories about their relationship, I always felt sorry for her and thought of him as the scumbag. I guess everyone has their masks they hide behind.

"It's hard to prove your innocence when she has everyone on her side. Girls felt sorry for her when she broke down during interviews. Guys bashed me because they wanted to be on her good side to get laid."

"Why don't you tell them about it now? Try to clear your name?"

"I don't want to hurt her. She's been through some rough stuff, and I'd never want to see her go through any more pain. So, instead of getting back at her, I decided to end things and move on. It's less messy that way. And to be honest, if someone wants to believe what the tabloids say, I don't want them in my life anyway." A few seconds pass. "Now, it's your turn, sunshine."

I lower my voice, like I don't want anyone else to hear my confession, and run my hands through the water as I start to open up. "The last tour I went on with my dad was when I was sixteen. There were a few bands that opened up for his show, and a guy named Adam was the lead singer of an up-and-coming one. I found him drunk off his ass in the bathroom one night and helped him. After that, we grew close and ended up having a secret relationship for a few months.

"I stupidly thought I was in love and gave him my virginity. Three nights later, I walked in on him railing a groupie against a dirty bathroom vanity. I was so irate and hurt. He chased after me. We got into an argument. One of my dad's bandmates over-heard it and told him.

"It all went to hell from there. He was twenty-two, and I was obviously underage. I had to beg my dad not to call the cops or let the press get any word of what happened. It would haunt me forever. He agreed but found other ways to ruin him. He kicked him off the tour and pretty much bad-mouthed him to everyone in the music world. It ruined his career."

"What a dumbass. Is that why you hate musicians?"

"I don't hate anyone. I don't *trust* musicians."

"Rose, we're not all like him. I can tell you right now that I've never fucked a groupie against a vanity in a dirty bathroom."

I snort. "So, you're going to sit here and tell me you've never hooked up with a girl on tour before?"

"Not on this tour."

I stare at him, my face going hard.

"The only woman I want on this tour is you."

"I told you, that can't happen."

"Then, why are you in here with me? You knew we'd be naked, alone, and in a romantic setting." He scoots in closer. "You knew that, didn't you?"

I gulp, nodding.

"What did you think was going to happen in here?"

"I … I don't know."

"The ball is in your court." He raises his hands up. "You want me? I'm right here. You don't? That's cool too. You're fully aware where I stand."

My body is moving faster than my mind, and before I realize what I'm doing, I'm on the other end of the tub, crushing my lips to his.

29

Knox

I thought my eyes were deceiving me as I watched Rose slide from her side of the tub to me. Reality shatters through when her lips find mine, and her wet, naked chest presses against me.

"Oh shit," she gasps, hastily pulling away before I have the chance to kiss her back. "I'm sorry … I was *so* not supposed to do that."

My arm shoots out to curl around her waist and stop her from moving any farther. There's no way I'm about to let this opportunity slip—or swim—away from me. Having her lips on mine was like a dream come true. She's what I think about before I close my eyes at night and when they open back up in the morning. She's the face I see when I'm jacking off in the shower and who I imagine in my future.

I've been craving her every second of every damn day.

And her reaction tonight proves I've been right every time I've said she's fighting her desire for me.

We need to stop this push-and-pull game we're playing.

"Don't apologize," I say, bringing her in closer. "Do it again."

She lets out a frazzled breath, her upper lip trembling, and stares down at me in contemplation. "This will change everything."

I bob my head in agreement. "You're right. I can guaran-fucking-tee that. It'll make everything ten times better."

I ease my hand around the curve of her neck and press my lips back against hers. She doesn't pull away this time. Instead, a groan escapes her as I cautiously slip my tongue into her mouth, massaging it against hers.

She tastes even more delectable than I remember—hints of chocolate and champagne hitting my taste buds.

I've never been this turned on in my life.

"You taste so fucking good, baby," I mutter into her mouth, my hands trailing down to her perfect, round ass. "You feel amazing." I squeeze each cheek and grip them in my hands. "I can't wait to be inside you and feel your pussy clench around my cock, like it did my fingers that night in the backseat. I can't wait, sunshine."

She hesitates, and I lose her mouth when she looks around. "Here?"

"Do you want to do it here?" I question.

She shakes her head, looking away shyly. "Not really. It's too public. I won't feel comfortable, knowing anyone can walk in here any second. Not to mention, we'll have to hold ourselves back, so we're not too loud."

I stroke my hand across her cheek. "Then, we won't. How about we have a little fun in here and leave the best stuff for the bedroom?"

"That sounds perfect."

My cock is aching to plunge into her, but I'll make sure I take my sweet time later. I want to see her let go with me. I want her to be so excited that she melts against my dick when I'm inside of her.

I glance down at her, transfixed. She's so damn beautiful. I press my lips to her chilly shoulder and use my knees to carefully nudge her legs open.

"Is this good?" I ask, waiting for permission.

She answers by bucking her hips forward, her pussy slightly brushing against my cock, and slams her lips on mine, her tongue sliding back into my mouth.

I chuckle. "Is that a yes?"

She eagerly nods, still devouring my mouth, and I ease my hand between her legs. I lose her mouth, and she buries her face into my shoulder when I hit her sensitive spot, slowly massaging her tiny nub.

"You ready for this?" I ask, moving my fingers to her entrance. I wish I could feel how wet she was for me.

"So ready."

Excitement is jumping at me when I'm about to slide two fingers inside of her tight pussy, but I'm interrupted by a knock on the door.

Motherfucker.

I have no damn clue what the person on the other side is saying. The only thing my ears are picking up on is the heavy panting coming from Rose, but I have a feeling it's a warning that our time is up.

I sigh in disappointment. "Rain check?" I ask.

She looks down at her wrist. "Can I cash that in as soon as we get back to the suite?"

"Hell yes. I'd be delighted to honor that." I kiss her one last time. "And there's no expiration date or any of that *one coupon per customer* bullshit."

30

Rose

Knox slams the door shut behind us, and I stumble back into his firm chest when he wraps his strong arm around my hips. I can feel his excitement pressing against my ass.

He's still hard from the spa soak.

Or it could be from the elevator, where we couldn't keep our hands to ourselves. I have my fingers crossed that no one tries to sell that video footage to some gossip site, but at that moment, I had not one damn care in the world about paparazzi or how crossing this line would impact our relationship and my job.

I throw my head back, lightly resting it on his shoulder, and stare up at him. I'm about to give everything to this man and hope to God he doesn't give me heartbreak in return.

"Shall I grab your vibrator and send you on your way?" he grumbles.

"Don't you even think about it," I say. "If I recall correctly, you were *very* adamant that you could do a much better job." I run my hands down his sides. "Let's see if you live up to your word."

He stares down at me with eager eyes. "Babe, I'll be doing much more than I promised. I'm going to get you off over and over again until I've exhausted every ounce of energy in your tight little body. Then, I'm going to fuck you so hard that you'll ache when you walk, and you'll remember how good I feel inside you with every step for days."

"Then, prove it," I challenge.

He lifts me up as if I were weightless, and I hook my legs around him, rocking against his erection, silently asking for more. He cups my ass with his strong hands and stalks straight for the bedroom.

He flips on the light and tosses me on the bed. "Never question my abilities, sunshine. I'll do more than prove it to you."

My nipples peak, and I lick my lips when he strips off his shirt. I lean back, leveling myself with my elbows, so I can watch him crawl up the bed, straight to me. He plants his lips on mine, tasting me briefly, and I whine at the loss of him.

He peels off my shirt, uses only two fingers to unsnap my bra, and throws them to the floor. His mouth moves straight to a sensitive nipple, lashing the tip of it with his tongue.

"Your lips taste delicious. Your tits taste amazing. I can't wait to get my mouth on your pussy," he mutters against my chest.

He rains kisses down my stomach and disposes of my yoga pants before tearing my panties down my legs.

All this happens before I even get the chance to catch my breath.

I'm naked, feeling the weight of myself trapped underneath Knox Rivers in his bed.

And we're about to have sex.

Hot damn.

My mouth suddenly falls open as a shot of excitement spirals straight through me. I must've been deep in thought of how electrified he's making me feel because when I look down, I see Knox's head between my legs. I don't even have time to prepare myself for the first flick of his tongue against my heat.

He's not wasting any time tonight.

He starts off slow, caressing me with his skilled tongue, but as my breathing gets deeper and my moans grow louder, he speeds up the pace. I reach down and delve my fingers into his soft hair, tugging at the roots uncontrollably as I writhe beneath him.

He doesn't even seem fazed that I'm on the verge of nearly scalping him. He's lapping me up, using both his tongue and fingers to pleasure me, hitting every sensitive spot until I can't take it anymore.

It's coming.

I'm coming.

I shake, coming undone and flying off the rails of the roller coaster ride he's taking me on, and cry out my release.

It takes me a few minutes to gain control of my breathing before I can say anything.

"Jesus Christ," I blurt out. "How in the fuck do you do that so well? What are you, some orgasm magician?"

He kisses each one of my thighs and takes one last lick before looking up and shooting me a confident grin. "What did I tell you? I'm much better than anything *or anyone* you've ever had."

I shiver when he slides his hands back up my thighs.

"And for my next trick, I'm going to get you to scream my name."

"I'm excited for the show."

He chuckles, watching me with a hooded gaze while he moves back and steps off the bed. "Not as much as I am to perform."

I prop myself back up with my elbows, and excitement buzzes through me at the anticipation of finally getting to see him naked.

I've heard the rumors.

He has a massive cock that he knows how to use well.

And the rumors are true. My mouth falls open when he

drops his shorts, his thick cock springing forward, and steps out of them. My elbows nearly give out as I fixate on the perfection that is Knox Rivers.

I crawl over to him, and his stomach muscles tense when I wrap my hand around his shaft. I stroke him a few times, loving the soft curses flying from his mouth, and duck down to wrap my lips around the swollen head.

"Fuck, Rose," he breathes out when I take him in my mouth.

He pumps his hips up, meeting my lips, and I take him in deeper.

I peek up, and the sight of him throwing his head back in ecstasy only turns me on more. "Yes, suck me, just like that."

I inch my hand around his waist, digging my nails into his ass, dragging him closer to my mouth. I groan when he pulls away, stopping me.

"That's not how it's going down tonight, sunshine," he tells me, his voice stern. "When you make me come for the first time, it's not going to be in your mouth. I want to be inside you, taking you in long, deep strokes. I want you to feel what I've been trying to tell you is right all along."

A rush of heat barrels through me when he bends down, picks me up from underneath my armpits, and places me on my back against the crisp sheets. He goes to his bag lying on the couch in the room, unzips a side pocket, and pulls out a box of condoms. He tears one off and sets the box on the nightstand.

"We're not going to need *all* of those," I say with a laugh.

"I like to be prepared," he answers.

I watch him, unblinking, as he opens the condom and slides it over his cock. The bed indents when he comes back to me.

"You positive you're ready for this?" he asks.

"I'm more than positive," I answer, squirming underneath him and opening my legs wider—a way to tell him to hurry the hell up.

His face scrunches up as he situates his cock in front of my heat and slowly glides it inside me. I gasp, and he gives me a second to adjust to his large size.

"You're so damn tight, sunshine," he mutters. "I haven't even started yet, and you already feel like heaven."

I come alive at his first thrust, closing my eyes to savor the experience.

He starts out slow, his pace gentle and unhurried.

So good. So hot. I need more.

"Harder," I pant, meeting his strokes. "I thought you were going to fuck me so hard that I ached for days."

"Your wish is my command, sunshine."

He carefully withdraws, and I arch my back when he drives back into me with no warning. I dig my nails into his shoulders, begging for more until my body starts to tremble.

"Knox! *Oh my God,* Knox," I scream out, my orgasm shattering through me.

He starts fucking me harder, and I continue to pant his name while he finds his release.

He collapses on top of me, his chest rising and falling with rapid breaths against mine.

"Shit," he breathes out. He balances himself on his elbows and dips his head down to kiss me. "That was even better than I'd imagined." He presses his lips against my nose and then gets up, removes the condom, and goes to the bathroom to throw it away.

He's grinning from ear to ear when he slides back into bed, drags me over to him, and positions me at his side, his arm resting on my stomach.

"This is like *Friends*," he says. "When Ross and Rachel finally give in to their desires."

"You're right," I mutter, my eyes feeling heavy.

He damn sure wasn't lying about draining all the energy out of me. The last thing I remember is his lips sinking into my hair before I drift off to sleep.

"I'm in your bed," I whisper into my pillow as the bright sun starts to shine through the thin curtains. "Holy shit. I'm in your bed."

I fucked Knox Rivers.

I also sucked his cock.

And I want to do it again.

This is exactly what I was afraid would happen—that I'd start to get consumed by this man and keep wanting more and more of him.

I hear a deep laugh behind me, and the white sheets slide down to my waist as strong arms wrap around my stomach. He pulls my naked body into him, my back resting against his front, and I can feel his morning glory against my ass.

"Fucking finally," he replies. "I've been trying to have a morning like this for months."

"Thomas is going to flip his shit if he finds out."

And so is every Knox Rivers fangirl. I saw the way they treated Stella. They were brutal, commenting on her social media pages, telling her she was ugly and Knox belonged to them. I don't need that kind of drama in my life.

"It was bound to happen."

I lose the warmth when I turn around to face him. *Damn, he looks amazing first thing in the morning.* I can see the damage my nails did to his shoulders last night. I nearly assaulted the man. His hair is wild, most likely from my fingers pulling at the roots while he went down on me.

"What do you mean?" I ask.

He signals between the us. "You and me ... *this* ... it was going to happen sooner or later. We have something, Rose, and your mouth can mutter out all kinds of denial, but your body is throwing something else out. Your heart isn't agreeing either."

"You don't know that. Maybe you only turn me on. It had been a while since … you know."

"Since you had dick as good as mine?" He pauses. "Actually, that's never happened, considering the way you tore me up last night."

I sigh. "I guess we got each other out of our systems."

"Trust me, I did not get you out of my system. If anything, what happened last night only makes me want more of you. I want to know what it feels like inside you in every position possible."

I fight with myself to restrain from moaning when he rests his hand on my hip and scoots in closer to me. He rubs his erection against my heat, making my argument harder as *he* gets harder.

"I don't know if that's a good idea."

"It is a good idea. Turn around, sunshine."

I do as I was told and look back at the sound of him opening up a condom. He grunts as he slides it onto his erection. I tremble when his chilly hand reaches down and slips between my legs.

"And you're soaked for it." He wastes no time hitching my leg over his waist and sliding his manhood inside of me from behind.

I moan, feeling every inch of him as he starts rocking back and forth. I tilt my hips up, meeting his long strokes, and shiver when he swipes my hair from my shoulder to whisper in my ear.

"Out of your system, my ass. I want you on top, riding my cock, showing me you'll never get enough of it. That you'll never have me out of your system."

Heat curls up my spine when he pulls out of me to collapse onto his back. I'm aching at the loss of him as I eye his erect cock, now soaked with my juices.

"Maybe I need to work a little bit harder then," I say, licking my lips.

"Then, get to it."

Oh, fuck it.

Like Knox said, it was bound to happen … and him lying there, offering his cock, makes me bound to ride him, right?

I stroke his cock once before nervously lowering myself down on him. He fills me perfectly, like we're two puzzle pieces destined for each other, and I start to ride him.

He controls my pace—slow and passionate—until we both lose control of ourselves.

"I just realized something," Knox says, staring down at me. He's sitting up, his back against the headboard of the bed with me resting against him. "And I feel like a self-centered jackass for not asking earlier."

Three hours have passed since our morning screw, and we've been in bed, talking, laughing, sharing stories. I've probably never enjoyed myself more. There's none of that morning-after awkwardness. I feel so damn comfortable in his arms and his bed.

"What is it?" I ask nervously.

Knox lives for heart-to-heart, deep-in-your-soul talks. Me? Not so much.

"What are you going to school for?"

I relax my shoulders. Easy question. "Social work."

"Why social work?"

"We had a housekeeper, Marilyn, who worked for us for years. She was one of the most selfless people I've ever met. Aside from working for us, she was also a foster mom, and I'd sit there while she made dinner, listening to her tell me story after story about the children she took in. I couldn't believe some of them. They were horrible, like a sad movie but it was someone's real life. These children were born to drug addicts. They were malnourished and neglected. My dad would invite them over for the holidays, so they'd have Christmas presents and Easter baskets. I decided that when I grew up, I was going to be like Marilyn and help make a difference in kids' lives."

"Wow, that's amazing. *You're* amazing."

"Trust me, there's so much more I could do, but you have to start somewhere, you know? Eventually, I want to be able to create a home for them, give them some stability."

He scrubs his hand over his face. "I think I had it rough sometimes, but when you hear stories like that, it hurts. I was one of those children, wishing for new shoes or even extra money for a cookie at lunch, but at least I had a parent. At least I had a roof over my head. It might not have been much, but it was something." He squeezes my side. "You'll change people's lives. I'm sure of it."

"That's my plan." My throat clenches when it hits me, and I try to force a smile on my face. I've tried not to think about this because it kills me every time.

"What's wrong?"

I slam my eyes shut, shaking my head. "It's nothing."

"What's wrong, Rose?"

"Talking about it reminds me of what I wanted to do. I planned on using my inheritance money to open up a home for foster children who haven't been placed yet. It's difficult for some, especially older kids, to get put into a decent place. I even met with a realtor and found the perfect home, but that fell through when my dad lost his money. I wanted to change children's lives, and I feel like I'm letting them down in a sense." Sadness grips my chest, and I try to hold back the tears.

Knox grabs my hand, brings it up to his lips, and kisses it. "You're going to change lives with or without that money, Rose. You've already changed mine for the better, and I won't be the last. You bring sunshine everywhere you go."

"So, you're meeting up with your brother later?" I ask Knox.

We're sitting across from each other, eating a late lunch. We're in Houston, and Knox made a three-day break in his schedule, so he can spend time with his family while he's here.

"That's the plan," he answers.

I nod and am about to ask him if he needs me to do anything for them, but my mouth clamps shut at the sound of a loud knock on the door.

"I heard Knox Rivers is in there! Let me in!" a man shouts on the other side. "Hello! I'm here to have Knox Rivers sign my chest. I paid the security guard fifty dollars and made my girl-friend flash him, so I demand I get that signature!"

What the fuck? I mouth to Knox so the crazy person behind the door doesn't hear me.

He shrugs. "Sounds like another stalker to me."

"A *male* stalker? You have those too?" There's more loud banging. "Where the hell is George?"

"I told him he could go out on the town for a while."

I throw my hands up. "Great. You have a stalker banging on your door, and your bodyguard is gone. Maybe we should call the police?"

"Just open the door, Rose."

My finger goes to my chest. "Me? You're the one they want."

"You're acting like there's a serial killer on the other side of that door."

"There might be."

He laughs, and I tuck my legs underneath me when he gets up from his seat. I hold my breath when he opens up the door. Knox is usually cautious about dealing with crazies, so I can't believe he's about to face this lunatic.

A man comes barreling in, and his hand goes straight to his mouth. "Oh my God! Knox Rivers! I am your biggest fan," he says, jumping up and down. He looks over at me. "Are you his girlfriend? I'm sorry, but I'm going to have to end you."

Knox is standing to the side, watching the guy with an amused smile.

What am I missing?

I tense up when the guy gets closer and shoves his hand my way. "Mason Rivers," he says. "Nice to meet you." He has a country drawl to his voice, which is surprising because Knox has no hint of an accent.

I look from him to Knox and then back to him. "You're Knox's brother?"

Mason nods. "The good-looking one. The smart one."

"The one who likes to do stupid shit," Knox says. "I knew it was him from the sound of his voice."

"And you didn't think it would be nice to tell me that?"

"No, it was too entertaining, watching you freak out." He looks over at Mason. "You should've brought a knife and looked scarier."

I flip Knox off. "Hilarious."

"This is Rose, my assistant," Knox introduces. "As you can clearly see, she's extremely professional with me."

"Oh, I've heard plenty about you, Rose," Mason says, a wild grin on his face.

"Good things, I hope?" I ask.

"Very good things."

"You two don't look alike."

They only have a few similar features. While Knox is tall, Mason is on the shorter side with lighter hair. A few freckles are sprinkled over his nose.

"Same mom, different dads," Mason answers. "Our mom was obviously smarter the second time around—choosing someone handsomer, who could pass his looks down to me."

"Go piss on a power line, asshole," Knox says.

"I'm going to shower," I say, taking my last bite of eggs and getting up from my chair. "I'll let you two catch up."

I give them a smile and then scurry to my room in relief.

Mason showed up at the perfect time. I need to think about the whirlwind that's happened in the past twenty-four hours.

I'm going to have a few days away from Knox while he's with his family, so that'll give me time to figure out where I want to go with this and if I made a mistake.

31

Knox

"I see someone has a crush. Very cute," Mason says, cracking a smile while taking Rose's abandoned chair.

"What the hell are you rambling about over there?" I grumble.

"You like her."

"Who?"

He gives me a dumbfounded look. "Rose, dipshit."

Do I lie or tell him the truth?

If I tell him what happened with us last night, he'll either try to play matchmaker or run her off, depending on how he feels about her. He and my grandma like to think they can pick and choose the women I date.

"She's my assistant. We work together every day. I can't exactly be an asshole to her."

"I said it then, and I'm saying it now. You *like her*, like her."

He called me after the video released and grilled me about Rose when I divulged that she wasn't an actress, but my assistant.

"Is it supposed to be more serious if you say it twice?"

"Don't be a smart-ass. Do you need me to point out the fact that she's wearing your clothes, your hair looks like it was pulled at the roots all night while you pleasured her, and it smells like sex all over this place? I think it's obvious she's into you, considering she's screwing you. Ask her on a date or something."

"You're joking, right?"

"No."

I stretch my legs out in front of me. "She'll say no. She's already made it clear she doesn't want anything to do with guys like me."

Rose will let me touch her, but there's no way she'll step into the feelings zone with me or let me claim her. She wants to screw me and then not leave her number on my nightstand.

"What if we all do something together?"

"No."

I don't want Rose to start pulling away because I'm pushing her too much, especially with Mason. He thinks he has a degree in matchmaking.

"If you don't ask her, I will."

"Prepare to get shot down, brother."

"She'd be good for you."

"Girls aren't good for me, period. Do you remember my last serious relationship? It obliterated my reputation and almost fucked up my entire career. I'm happy with what I'm doing now. If Rose wants to fuck around, I'm game. But don't be trying to plan a wedding or some shit."

Mason has been with the same woman for three years, and he'll probably end up marrying her. She's good people, and they're perfect for each other. So, now, he thinks that I need to settle down and do the whole domesticated thing, like him.

"You can keep hooking up with all these random girls all you want, brother."

"Thank you. I'm glad you're giving me permission," I say sarcastically.

He holds up a finger. "But don't be upset when the party is over, the booze is gone, and no one is there to love you."

"Don't try to pull your psychoanalyzing bullshit on me."

"No psychoanalyzing bullshit, only telling you the truth. I obviously know you've had sex with her, but it's not only lust and sexual chemistry I see. You want more. You might be trying to hold back because she doesn't, but I know you better than anyone."

Like she knew we were talking about her, Rose's door opens, and she walks out with wet hair and wearing a robe.

"Question," she says. "I know you planned on staying here tonight and Mason's the next few days, but do you want me to change anything since he's here now?"

"He's going to stay at my place tonight," Mason answers for me.

"Got it. I'll book me a room here. Let me know if you need anything. You guys have fun."

"Why don't you come have a good time with us?" Mason asks. "We're having dinner and game night at my place tonight. I have a guest bedroom you can crash in. It beats staying at another hotel, *and* you get to hang out with the coolest brothers in the world."

He flashes her a bright white smile, and I'm hoping she falls for it.

She shakes her head. "No, it's okay. I don't want to interrupt your whole brotherly bonding fun."

"You won't be. My girlfriend lives with me, so she's going to be there." He throws his thumb over to signal to me. "You'll actually be saving this guy from being the third wheel."

She nervously looks over at me, silently asking for permission.

"You know I'm always game for hanging out with you, sunshine," I say.

"I guess it is better than hanging out by myself." She runs her hands through her hair. "Let me blow-dry my hair real quick, and I'll get ready."

I nod, and she disappears back into her room.

Mason looks at me with a smug grin. "Date time, brother. I

told you she'd want to come. Now, get your bags, and let's get the hell out of here."

"You go ahead. I'll get a car and meet you at your place in a while."

When he leaves, I go to my bedroom and change, putting on a ball cap and a jacket in an attempt to disguise myself. Mason hasn't let it slip that we're related to any of his neighbors, so we're still trying to lie low. Mason's girlfriend probably wouldn't be thrilled if groupies started showing up at his door.

And trust me, they'd fuck him just to meet me.

They've already tried.

32

Rose

"Mason seems nice," I comment next to Knox in the backseat of the SUV.

We're on our way to his brother's house after switching vehicles twice to steer away from any possible paparazzi or fans. Knox said Mason doesn't want people to know where he lives.

"So, what are the plans for tonight?" I take in a deep breath and squirm in my seat.

What did I get myself into?

I not only agreed to hang out with Knox and Mason tonight, but I also agreed to spend the night with them. I hate being put on the spot.

"Most likely pizza and games," Knox answers, raising his arm and resting it at the head of our seats. "We always lie low while I'm here. His girlfriend would kill me if chicks started hunting him down to get their claws in me."

Understandable. I like her already. "That sounds amazing, to be honest. We need a low-key night."

He laughs. "I think that's what we do daily on the bus. Eat and Netflix."

I look out the window when we stop in front of a brick ranch house in what looks like Houston suburbia. Knox lowers his hat, covering his eyes, and ducks down as George pulls in the driveway. The garage door opens, and Knox waits until we're parked inside and the door shuts before getting out. George opens his door and helps us with our bags.

"Go have yourself some fun," Knox tells him, slapping his back. "We're going to stay in for the night."

"Thanks, boss. Let me know if you need anything," he answers. "I'll wait until you get inside before leaving."

The door flies open, and Mason is standing there with a bright smile and gleaming eyes. My chest warms at the love and adoration he has for his older brother. I'm glad Knox has someone like him in his life. From what I've heard about his family, most of them look at him as opportunities and dollar signs.

I grab my bag, and Knox trails behind me as we walk through the door and into the house. We land straight in the kitchen, and my stomach grumbles at the delicious scent of garlic and pizza.

"Long time no see," a woman says, walking into the kitchen with a glass of wine in her hand. Her burgundy-red hair is pulled back in a loose ponytail, and a pair of black-framed glasses takes up the majority of her face. She looks over at me with a genuine smile and holds out her free hand. "Hi, I'm Gretchen. I'll admit, I was a little terrified when Mason told me Knox was bringing a girl with him tonight, but he gave you a good endorsement, which is surprising, considering he can be a judgmental asshole at times."

"Hey!" Mason yells. "I only want the best for my big brother."

Gretchen laughs. "That's what I was trying to say." She sets her glass down. "Come on, Rose. I'll show you our guest room." She goes to turn around but stops. "Are you both staying in there? Or is someone crashing on the couch?" She holds up her hand. "Not trying to make any assumptions here."

"I'll take the couch," Knox says, stopping me before I have the chance to offer.

"No," I rush out. "I can. I'm the one who's barging in last minute, and it's your brother's house."

Knox's eyes dart my way. "I'd be an asshole if I made you sleep on the couch."

"He does have a point." Gretchen leans forward to slap Knox on the back. "And who would've thought this guy could be a gentleman?"

"It's when you find the right woman," Mason says. "I was an animal until Gretchen tamed me."

Gretchen rolls her eyes but cracks a smile at the same time. "He's still an animal. Now, let's go get rid of those bags."

I look around as I trail behind her to the guest room. The house is nice, but not what I was expecting. Knox wasn't lying when he said Mason didn't accept much, except help with his tuition. The house is filled with feminine touches—flowers in colorful vases, furry pillows, and candles everywhere. I have a feeling Gretchen makes all of the design decisions here.

"Bathroom," she says, pointing to the door as we pass it. "And here's the guest room." She flips on the light. It has a nice-sized bed, a TV, and a dresser. "There're towels and extra blankets in the closet."

"Great. Thanks so much for having me," I say.

"No problem at all. They usually outnumber me when we choose movies or which game to play, so I'm happy I won't be stuck watching some ridiculous man flick."

A knock on the door catches our attention.

"I'm going to jump in the shower real quick," Knox tells us, a stack of clothes in one hand.

"You know where everything is," Gretchen says.

Knox salutes her and disappears into the bathroom.

"Gretchen made her homemade pizza," Mason says when we get back in the kitchen. "Is veggies and pepperoni okay with you?"

"I thought I smelled something delicious," I say. "And, yes, that's perfectly fine."

"Wine?" Gretchen asks.

I nod and thank her after she hands me a glass.

"So, what's going on with you and my brother?" Mason questions.

I choke on my sip of wine.

He sure cuts to the chase.

"Seriously?" Gretchen asks. "She just walked through the damn door."

"I can't ask her in front of Knox, so it was now or never."

"I work for your brother, and we've developed a friendship while on tour." My answer sounds like I'm making a public statement.

"I'm a smart man. I know attraction when I see it, and I can promise you this: I've never seen my brother look at a woman like he does you."

"What about Stella?"

"At the beginning, yes, but it was puppy love between them. He was young and dumb, but they were so familiar with each other that it was hard to move on. They started to grow apart and realized their love was only temporary. Knox is cautious about who he opens up to now, but I can see he's starting to with you. That means something."

I fake a playful laugh. "I think you're seeing things."

"I'm not, and he might kill me for telling you this, but not only do I see it, but he also confirmed it."

"What?" I stutter out.

"He likes you. He told me himself."

The wineglass in my hand nearly drops from my fingers.

33

Knox

If Mason thinks he's sly by talking to Rose when I leave the room, he's damn dumb. The walls are thin, and the bathroom isn't far from the kitchen. I can hear their every word.

I wrap my hand around the doorknob, debating with myself on whether I should go out there or not. I hesitate and then drop it, deciding to eavesdrop instead. If I join them, it'll stop the conversation, and I won't get to hear Rose's answer. I lean my shoulder against the door and place my ear against it.

"Yes, I know your brother is attracted to me, but that's all," Rose says.

"He's attracted to you more than just physically," Mason counters. "He doesn't only like you for your looks. He likes everything about you. He trusts you, and that's very rare for him. Shit, sometimes, I'm not sure if he even trusts me."

Yes! Go, little brother.

He's going to law school, so there's no doubt in my mind that he's trying to work Rose like he would a jury.

"Babe, she's only been here for ten minutes," Gretchen cuts in. "Let's not interrogate her before feeding her." She laughs. "I apologize for my overbearing boyfriend."

"It's fine," Rose replies. "I don't blame him for being curious."

"Just tell me one thing," Mason says. "And then I'll leave the conversation alone. Are the feelings mutual?"

Everything goes silent for a few seconds, but it feels like minutes.

"They are," Rose finally says.

I back away from the door and punch my fist in the air like an idiot. If I can't bring her to say those words, at least my little bro can.

This night just got a helluva lot better.

I feel lightness in my chest as I put my ear back to the door, not wanting to miss a word of their conversation.

"But we can't do anything about it," Rose adds. "It'd be too complicated."

"Relationships are always going to be complicated," Gretchen says. "No matter who you date. You only trade one problem out for another. We won't keep bothering you about it, but think about how you feel when you're with Knox and how it'd feel to lose that." She laughs, and I hear the cork of a bottle of wine popping. "Now, how about a refill?"

Shit, a point for Gretchen too. I knew I liked her.

"That sounds perfect," Rose says.

Their conversation goes in a different direction with Rose talking about being on tour, and I finally undress and get in the shower.

Tonight is going to be a good night.

"Did you guys miss me?" I ask, strolling into the kitchen, freshly showered and in a delightful mood.

Rose is situated in a stool at the island, and Gretchen and

Mason are standing on the other side of it. Everyone is sporting a smile as they sip on their wine.

"No, we're only happy you took your monthly shower," Mason answers. "You were getting pretty ripe there, brother."

I chuckle, flipping him off, and pull out the stool next to Rose to sit down. "They're not interrogating you too much, are they?" I ask her.

Her fingers curl around her wineglass, and she takes a big swig before answering. A light blush creeps across her cheeks. "No ... not at all," she replies into the glass. "We haven't even brought you up."

I'll let her get away with that response for now, but I'll definitely be bringing up her admission when we're alone later.

"You're not always the center of attention," Gretchen says, most likely covering up for Rose. She opens up a cabinet, pulls out a glass, and pours red wine into it.

"We're not going for the hard stuff yet?" I ask as she hands it to me.

"Absolutely not. Last time you two idiots got wasted, you decided to see who could eat the most slices of pizza." She stabs her manicured finger into her chest. "*I'm* the one who not only had to deal with your dumbasses, but also got stuck cleaning up your mess. We're saving the good stuff for the games later."

"Games?" Rose asks. "As in drinking games?"

"Yes," I answer. "What were you thinking? We were going to spend the night playing an intense game of Chutes and Ladders?"

I grunt when her foot rams into my ankle. "I'd actually prefer Candy Land, thank you very much."

"Eh, I don't think there's a way to incorporate whiskey with Candy Land. It just doesn't seem right," Mason says and then shuffles across the kitchen to open the oven. "And since there is four of us, I think Would You Rather is the perfect choice."

Rose groans. "Nope, too personal."

I dip my hand down and run it along her thigh. "There's nothing more I'd rather do tonight than get personal with you."

She stares up at me, shyly biting into her lower lip.

Mason pulls out the pizza. "Time to eat!"

I slide off the stool and hold my hand out to Rose. She grabs it and allows me to pull her up as Mason starts cutting the pizza.

"I've got the plates," Gretchen tells us. "You guys go ahead to the dining room."

"Why are you acting so nervous?" I ask Rose before anyone joins us.

"I'm not nervous," she rushes out before lowering her voice. "Did you tell your brother we had sex?"

"No. I don't fuck and tell."

"He seems to think we did."

"Incorrect. He thinks I have a thing for you, which I do. He has no idea you've also let me taste you."

"We aren't talking about this right now," she hisses at the same time the others make it into the room.

We scarf down our food while Mason and Gretchen catch me up on everything happening in Houston. Mason tells me our mom hasn't called him in over a month, which doesn't surprise me since, last I heard, she rented some yacht for her and her piece-of-crap boyfriend to spend the summer on. My mom likes to be a cougar and spoil her men … on my dime.

Rose helps Gretchen clear the table and load the dishwasher while Mason and I start dragging out the bottles of alcohol.

"Rule number one," Gretchen says, "no one is getting wasted. When it looks like you've had enough, you're cut off."

"Fine with me," I say, turning the cap off a bottle of tequila. "Grams will kill me if I show up hungover tomorrow."

"She will kill any of us who show up hungover tomorrow," Gretchen says. She hands everyone a shot glass, a pad of paper, and a pen. "Does everyone know the rules?"

Mason and I nod. Rose shakes her head.

"You've never played this game before?" I ask her.

"Sure, I've played with my friends, but we've never done it as a drinking game. What are the rules?"

"Someone asks a *would you rather* question, we write down our answers, and whoever is in the minority has to drink."

She shrugs. "Sounds simple enough."

"Great," Mason says. "We'll let the guest of honor go first." He looks over at me with a shit-eating grin on his face. "Rose, what'll it be?"

"Asshole," I mutter.

Rose taps her nails against the table, scrunching up her nose. "Would you rather have no fingers or no eyes?"

We all write down our answers.

Everyone chooses no fingers.

"No one drinks," I declare. We need to make this more intimate and creative. I want to break Rose out of her shell. "I'll go next. Top or bottom during sex?"

We write down our answers and hold them up.

Rose chooses bottom.

I, along with the others, choose top.

We all look at her as she picks up her shot glass.

"What?" she asks with a shrug. "I think it's hot to have a guy on top of me, feeling the weight of his body and showing me how much I turn him on."

She downs her glass, and I fucking love her answer.

We keep going, and I focus all of my attention on Rose's answers.

She'd prefer sex on the beach instead of grass. I don't agree with that one. I'm not trying to eat pussy and choke on sand at the same time. That shit gets everywhere.

She'd rather pay for sex than get paid for sex. I agree.

We both prefer long-term relationships.

Hours fly by as we run through question after question, taking shots periodically, but surprisingly, we choose the same answers most of the time. Maybe this will show her we are more compatible than she thinks.

"It's our bedtime," Mason declares with a yawn, sluggishly getting up from his chair.

Gretchen does the same and looks over at us. "Good night. You guys make yourselves at home. Knox, you know where everything is."

"Sure do," I answer. "Thanks for letting us crash here."

I sprawl out in my chair when I hear their bedroom door shut. "You do know the game isn't over," I say, fixing my eyes on Rose.

She tilts her head to the side. "Oh, really?"

"Yes, really."

"Then, it's your turn."

"Would you rather kiss your boss or have him kiss you?"

Her chest moves in as she inhales a long breath. "I'd rather him kiss me." There's no doubt, no confliction, in her voice, only hunger and anticipation.

I'm craving to feel her again, to be back inside her, and to taste her sweet pussy on my tongue.

I rise up from my chair, offering my hand out, and she allows me to pull her up. She stares up at me, her baby blues fringed with long lashes, and I take her chin in my hand, smoothing my fingers along her soft cheeks.

"I love that answer," I mutter.

She immediately opens her mouth when I slide my lips along hers. Chills run through me as she brushes her tongue against mine, and I savor the delicious combination of her mixed with strong tequila. I lock my arms around her waist to push her against the wall.

"Would you rather share your room with me tonight or force a desperate man to sleep on the couch?" I rasp out.

She grins wildly. "Sharing is caring, right?"

I grunt when she slides her hands down my back to my ass and drags me into her. I'm close to exploding when she starts to grind her jean-covered pussy against my erection.

Fuck. I need her again. My cock is begging for it.

I haven't even gotten her naked yet, and I'm hard as a rock.

"Would you rather me fuck you against this wall or the bed?" is my next question.

"Bed," she pants out. "The last thing I need is someone walking out and finding us fucking against their dining room wall."

"It'd be a beautiful sight."

She yelps when I throw her over my shoulder and walk us through the dimly lit hallway to the guest room. I gently set her down on the bed and shut the door. We immediately start stripping off each other's clothes.

I drink up the sight of her waiting for me on the bed. We're both butt-ass naked. She's staring at my cock, hungrily licking her lips, and the only idea running through my mind is how I'm going to taste her … and then take her.

"What if they hear us?" she asks.

"They won't."

"They're in the very next room," she hisses, jutting her finger toward the wall with each word.

"I'll cover your mouth when you get off or you can bite into my shoulder. You can use me any way you want."

"You promise?"

I nod. "Now, for your next question. Would you rather me climb between your legs to eat your pussy or you sit on my face?"

"Sit on your face," she whispers. "I've never done that before."

"I'd be honored to be your first."

She brings herself up and pushes me onto my back, and her pussy is right above me, begging to be pleasured. I oblige, pulling her closer to my mouth, and plunge my tongue into her hot pussy.

I'm picking up on every moan from her as she squirms above me and flip her over when her legs start to wobble. I add my fingers, pushing them in and out of her heat with the same intensity as my tongue to finish her off. As promised, I reach up and cover her mouth when her back arches and she reaches her peak.

I draw back to look at her. She's panting underneath me with hooded eyes.

"You want me on top?" I ask, remembering her answer from earlier. "You want to feel dominated and see how much you turn me on?"

"Yes," she begs. "Show me. Prove it to me."

My heart nearly stops when I grab my cock, stroke it a few times, and hold it against her tight entrance before carefully pushing myself inside her.

I can't pull my gaze away from the gorgeous sight. There is nothing more captivating than her mouth opening into a gasp when I fill her up.

Nothing.

What she's giving me is more satisfying than winning any award, making any amount of money, or having a million groupies on my dick.

I plant myself deep inside her, slowly pull out, and then slam back in. I move in and out, adding more force with each thrust, and she tilts her hips up to meet me. I'm relishing in the sensation of our connection, and I never want to come down from this high.

I know she's close when her arms dart out and she digs her heels and nails into the sheets. I bend down, giving her my mouth to drown out her screams, but she shoves her face into my shoulder, biting into the skin, and shudders out her release.

I slam into her three more times until I can't take it anymore. Waves of pleasure roll through me as I bust inside her.

Oh shit.

We forgot a condom.

I look down and know she's thinking the same thing.

"It's okay," she breathes out as we both come down. "I'm on the pill."

I collapse next to her.

I've never had sex without a condom. Not even with Stella.

"Are you mad?" she croaks out, turning to look at me.

"Of course not, babe. I'm the one with the dick. It was my responsibility, so I'm sorry."

"How can I be mad at you after you got me off like that?"

I give her a peck on the lips, grab a washcloth, and head to the bathroom to run it under cold water. She lets out a breath of relief when I come back and start to clean her up.

"Keep some of it," she says. "I like you being inside me."

I grin.

I could spend every day of my life with this girl and be forever happy.

I flip the light off and love the feel of her snuggling into my arms.

"I think I have a new favorite pastime," she says into the darkness.

"What's that?"

"Sitting on your face."

I chuckle. "I think that mixes well with my favorite pastime of devouring your pussy."

This is where I belong. She's where I belong.

I'll do anything to keep her.

34

Rose

"I still don't understand why we couldn't ride with Mason and Gretchen," I say.

Knox is in the driver's seat of a rented SUV, and we're on our way to his grandmother's house. Instead of riding with Gretchen and Mason, he chose for us to drive separate.

I tried to get out of the grandmother visit by insisting Knox didn't need me intruding on his family time. I had other stuff I could do—explore the city, people-watch, read an erotic romance where the virgin tames the man-whore, anything that didn't involve the pressure of the grandma interrogation. From what I've heard, she's the biggest parental figure in Knox's life.

"Well, I still don't understand why you keep asking that," he fires back. "We obviously could've, but I didn't want to."

"Why not?"

"I want us to talk, and I know you wouldn't feel comfortable doing that in front of them."

"What do we need to talk about that's not okay to say in front of other people?" I'm well aware that's a stupid question, but I'm trying to play it coy over here.

Knox stayed in the guest room with me last night, and I

know it wasn't lost on Mason and Gretchen exactly how he ended up there … or what took place in that bed.

I'm falling for Knox, undeniably, and the damage he could cause to my heart petrifies me. I've opened it up before, only to have it obliterated at the end. It killed me, making me the cynical person I am, and the infliction Knox could cause would be more painful than ever. I wouldn't recover.

He keeps one hand on the steering wheel and looks over at me when we hit a red light. "So, you're telling me you'd be comfortable talking about you riding my face as I ate your pussy in front of them?"

I look down at my lap, biting my lip.

"Don't play shy with me now, sunshine. You weren't shy when you were begging me to fuck you harder. I'd like to think we're beyond the shy and *this can't happen* stage. We're progressing. Sooner or later, you'll let me hold your hand in public with the same one I used to play with your pussy the night before."

His words.

He's a songwriter, and he knows how to hit you with all the feels. A man who can talk dirty is my biggest weakness.

"Maybe this isn't the best conversation to have while we're on our way to visit your *grandmother.* She'll probably think I'm some loose tramp."

"I told her we were banging months ago. She's cool with it."

"You're so lying."

He shakes his head.

"Turn this car around right now."

"Sunshine, I'm a grown-ass man. She knows I'm not a virgin."

"That doesn't mean I want her to think I'm screwing you."

"Relax. I'm kidding. I love my Grams and all, but I don't share sex stories with her."

"I can't relax. Now, you have me all nervous. Why am I nervous?"

"Because you like me." He shrugs when I narrow my eyes at him. "You don't get nervous about meeting someone's family unless you want them to like you because you see a future with that person."

I scrape a hand through my hair. "Or maybe I don't want to get the granny wrath."

He pats my leg. "There will be no granny wrath." He doesn't move his hand, instead deciding to rest it there the entire ride, and I'd be lying if I said that little gesture doesn't send sparks through me.

"This house is seriously adorable," I say when we pull up the drive of a charming bright yellow two-story cottage that's shaded by giant oak trees. It reminds me of where Snow White lived with her little dwarves.

Knox cuts the ignition. "You ready to go in?"

"Ready or not, there's no way I can walk back to the hotel."

I open up the door, noticing Mason's car is parked next to us. Knox gets out and walks around the SUV to wait for me. He takes my hand in his and leads us up the slate path with colorful flowers along the outside.

I'm hit with the scent of fresh cookies wafting through the air when we walk inside. It's homey and inviting with yellow walls and vibrant colored furniture. All the trim and bookcases look like they were handcrafted, and family photos flood the walls.

Knox squeezes my hand, like he's afraid I'll pull away, and walks us into the kitchen. He's making a statement. He's telling his grandmother what I am to him—more than an assistant. Everyone is in the kitchen with cookies in their hands.

"There's my other grandson," an older woman shouts.

She's short, and her white hair is pulled back with sparkly butterfly clips. She heads straight for Knox, wrapping him in her arms. Knox rests his arm over her shoulder when he pulls away and kisses her on the cheek.

"Rose," Knox says, turning so they're both facing me. "This is my grandma, Estelle."

I shake her hand, smiling. "It's nice to meet you. Your house is beautiful."

A bright grin takes over her face. "Thank you, honey. Knox surprised me with it years ago. I used to keep these old magazine clippings of my dream home if I ever won the lottery." She pats Knox's belly. "He snuck in one day and stole them to give to a builder so he'd know exactly what I wanted." You can't miss the pride and gratitude on her face. "He spoils me so darn much."

"You deserve it, Grams," Knox replies. "It's because of you I'm even able to do it."

"Nonsense. I only provided the guitar. You're where you are because of your hard work and talent."

Knox releases her from his hold and heads farther into the kitchen. "What's on the menu today?"

"Your favorite—fried chicken and all the fixings."

"My stomach is already growling."

Estelle pauses, as if something hits her, and looks over at me in concern. "Is that okay with you? I'm so sorry. I intended to call Knox and double-check, but it completely slipped my mind."

"That sounds amazing actually," I answer.

I help Gretchen set the table, and we make small talk over dinner. Estelle takes over the conversation, telling stories of when the boys were younger and some of the hardships they had while growing up. When Knox was playing music on the street, he gave every dollar he made to his mom to go toward rent. With everything I'm learning about Knox, I'm so glad I tagged along with them.

It's not until I'm alone with Estelle that she takes my hands in hers.

"I want to thank you, Rose," she says. "I have a confession. I was nervous for Knox to go on this tour. So much has hit him this year—relationship-, career-, and family-wise. But I've heard nothing but positive things from the news and him. Whatever you're doing, please don't stop. I like to see him happy. He deserves that and so much more."

"She likes you," Knox says when we get back into the SUV and start heading into the city.

He got a call after dinner that we have to leave tonight, a day earlier than scheduled, because a serious storm is headed to the next city and the driver thinks it might double the time we thought we'd need to get there.

Our mini vacation is over, and we're stepping back into reality with Knox being busier than ever.

"I have a feeling that woman likes everyone," I reply. "She doesn't have a bad bone in her body."

"I wouldn't say that. She can be a feisty one, believe me. Mason once brought a girl he was dating over, and Grams caught her playing hand grab with his dick at the dinner table. She kicked her out of the house, empty stomach and all."

"Now, that's just cruel. It was difficult, but I'm thankful I managed to restrain myself from crotch-grabbing you while gripping my fried chicken in the other hand."

"Appreciate it, but I want to make myself clear that any other time, it's completely acceptable." He leans back in his seat and points down to his cock. "Even right now."

"Settle down, killer. Not happening."

"Fine with me. I need you to have all of your energy for when we get back to the bus."

"Why?"

"Because I'm going to fuck you on every inch of it."

35

Rose

I'm staring straight at the first man who broke my heart. He looks different, but there's no mistaking it's him, and the way he's glaring at me confirms it more. His upper lip is snarled as he wipes the sweat from it with his arm, and his eyes narrow in on me, like he's ready to attack.

My stomach sinks when I watch him bring himself up from the stage and head in my direction. I turn around, my feet moving quickly, and rush toward the first exit I find. I push open the door and catch my breath when I make it outside.

Unfortunately, I stupidly chose the door that leads to a back alley.

I whip around at the sound of the door slamming shut and come face-to-face with him.

"Why are you here?" he hisses. "Are you following me to fuck up my life more?"

I bitterly let out a snort. "Don't flatter yourself, Adam. I'm definitely not here for you. I'm Knox Rivers's assistant."

Any attraction I had for him years ago is gone. The arms I used to love around me are now chubby with the same vibrant tattoos that covered them before. He promised to get my name tattooed on one when I turned eighteen. I laugh to myself at how naive I was. His hair is longer, a bit on the greasy side. There's no way he has girls begging to suck his cock like he did years ago. Those days of being the hot rock star are over.

"You're his assistant?" He snorts when I nod. "Assistant or fuck buddy? Because I could've sworn I saw his hands on your ass and your mouth on his earlier."

I cross my arms and take a few steps away from him. "That's none of your business. Why do you even care why I'm here?"

"I care because I fucking despise you."

The nerve of this man. "*You* despise me? I think we can both agree it should be the other way around."

"I didn't ruin your entire fucking life."

I raise a brow. *Do what?*

"Don't act like you don't know."

I continue to stare, not answering him. After the incident, my father and I never brought him up again. It was like it never happened.

"My band's reputation was destroyed by your piece-of-shit dad. He told anyone that would listen that I was a pervert who put his hands on teenage girls and couldn't be trusted. Do you know what that does to a man? My band kicked me out. I lost everything because of you."

"You lost it all because of me? Last time I checked, I didn't force you to take my virginity. You willingly fucked with my head, acted like I meant something to you, but in the end, you were only using me."

"It wasn't an act. I did like you."

"And you also liked the whore you were fucking in the bathroom, so I don't feel very special."

"I was drunk, high, and horny. She was there, rubbing all over my dick. What was I supposed to do?"

"Say no? Walk away?"

I'm pissed at myself at the feel of tears pricking my eyes. I thought I was over this asshole. I stopped thinking about him years ago, but I guess there's always a little place in your heart put away for the first person you loved.

"So, what? Now, you're back, screwing another guy on tour? Must be your thing, huh? I hope for his sake that you don't ruin his career too."

"Oh, *fuck you*," I yell. I don't need to deal with this shit. I give him one last look of disgust before making my way toward the door.

He lets out a sinister laugh. "You already have, sweetheart, and let's just say, I loved popping that sweet cherry."

I can't stop myself. I spin around, and the next thing I know, my fist is connecting with his face. I can feel the pain shooting straight to my knuckles. I've never punched anyone before.

"What the fuck, bitch?" he screams, his hand immediately flying down to stop the blood gushing from his lip.

I start to retreat backward, realizing what a stupid decision that was. I'm alone with this dude in an alley. He could kill me, for fuck's sake.

I jump when the door bursts open, and suddenly, George is at my side.

"Rose," he says, looking from me to Adam. "What the hell is going on here?"

I gulp, not exactly sure how to explain the situation.

George plucks his phone from his pocket without bothering to hear my explanation. "Meet me at exit B. We have a situation."

Adam is moaning in the background, calling me names and saying he can't wait to get his hands on me, but I know he won't do anything with George by my side. He can't be that stupid. George is at least six-five with muscles larger than anything I've ever seen, and he used to be a champion heavyweight body-builder.

"You'd better shut your mouth, asshole," George warns him. "She might pack a good punch, but mine is much more destruc-tive. I promise you that."

Adam points to me. "I want you kicked off the premises and a police report filed. It's your turn to have your life destroyed."

My pulse skyrockets. I never thought about the actual consequences I'd have from nailing him in the face. If he calls the cops, I'll most likely be fired *and* back on the news.

The door flies open, and Knox appears, nearly out of breath. He looks at me, then George, then to a bloody Adam. He does it again, waiting for someone to give him some answers.

I nod toward Adam. "He's an asshole, so I punched him in the face."

"And I want to press charges," Adam yells.

"You sound like a little bitch," George tells him.

Knox is working his jaw. "And why exactly did you punch him in the face, Rose?"

"He was being an asshole."

"She punched me because I told her how much I enjoyed popping her precious little cherry," Adam yells, holding back the pain to throw Knox a taunting smile. "But she might've enjoyed it more."

Knox gets to him before I even realize what's happening. Adam grunts at Knox's first punch and then cries out at the second one.

"Fuck," George says, rushing over to them. He grabs Knox around the waist to pull him away.

My stomach sinks when we he lets go of Knox to point at a man holding a camera between a hole in the fence.

"Motherfucker, give me that thing."

"We're all fucked," I mutter to myself.

"Get him. I'll stay with her," Knox tells George.

He nods, and the guy takes off running. I watch George jump the fence to go after him.

"This is going to be bad," I say to Knox.

"I don't give a shit," he replies and then glares over at Adam. "You say one more thing or even look at her again, I'll beat the shit out of you. Do you hear me?"

Adam holds up his arms in surrender and swipes his tongue over his bottom lip, capturing blood. "It's your career, not mine, man."

"Unlike you, I'll always choose her over my career and any groupie ho," Knox replies.

I stumble forward when Knox grabs my hand and walks me back into the building. He keeps his hold on my hips and turns me around to face him, backing me up against the wall.

"You okay?" he asks, sweeping my sweaty hair away from my eyes.

"I'm all right," I whisper.

"You swear?"

"I swear."

His hand traces my jawline, and he lets out a deep breath. "God, I wanted to kill that fucker. It tortured me to hear him talking about putting his hands on you … having you … you loving him. I hate that, Rose. I hate that you gave more to him than you have me."

"That's not true. I was a stupid teenage girl. I didn't give him anything, I promise."

His lips meet mine, sweet and soft. "Do me a favor," he says against them. "Let's not say anything to Thomas about this yet. Put your phone away and enjoy my show."

"Got it."

We both jump when the door swings open, sunlight beaming down the hallway, and George appears.

"The motherfucker with the camera got away," he says. "I tried to catch him, I swear, but he had a getaway vehicle. I might be fast, but not as fast as a BMW 750."

Knox pulls away from me to look at George. "It's okay, man. Thanks for trying and always having my back."

36

Knox

I'm nervous as hell.

My lungs are knocking against my chest while I walk to the middle of the stage, taking slow, deep breaths. This isn't how I typically start my shows. I usually have this kick-ass intro with lights and videos, but tonight, I'm doing something different. It has to be done even though I'll probably pay for it later.

The cheers from the crowd suffocate my thoughts as I grab the microphone from the stand. I gulp before holding it up to my mouth.

"Hello, Atlanta!" I scream. "How is everyone doing tonight?"

The audience screams louder. Their reaction is my favorite part about being onstage, seeing the excitement on their faces. I fucking love my fans.

I pause, waiting for them to settle down before going on and possibly creating career suicide. All eyes are on me as they wait for my next move.

"I'm sure many of you will find out about something that happened today, but I wanted to be the first to tell you and give you my side of the story. About an hour ago, I punched a guy." I hold up my swollen fist. "Battle wound."

The camera phones rise in the air, and I know I'm about to start live-streaming on thousands of social networks.

"The media will most likely report that I have anger issues or that I'm out of control, but that's not why I did it. I did it because I have a problem with men who disrespect women, especially women I care about."

Mouths drop. More phones go up in the air.

"If you care about a woman and someone does something terrible to her, defend her, and that's what I did. So, to all of my fellas out there, let your girl know she's appreciated."

The audience roars with cheers. If the guy who recorded us exposes me, I know my fans will still have my back.

Will the media twist the entire story? Probably.

Is it going to be breaking news? Most likely.

But right now, I don't give a shit. I'm ready to perform and then hang out with my girl.

I hold the microphone back to my mouth. "Now that that's done, let's get this show started!"

"How many do you have?" I ask Rose when I get back to my dressing room when the show ends.

I rip my sweat-covered shirt from my body and throw it down onto the floor. It's burning up in here. She grabs a towel, places it under cold water, and starts to run it down my neck. My mouth falls open as I let out a moan.

"I've been afraid to look," she answers, helping me cool off before grabbing her phone. "Fifteen from Thomas. Two from your mom."

"Time to see mine." I punch in the code to the room safe and pull out my phone. My stomach rolls while I scroll through all of the missed calls and text messages. "I win. I have eighteen from Thomas and twenty from my mom. That's not counting their texts either."

She falls down in a chair and runs a jerky hand through her straight hair. "They're probably on a flight right now to murder us."

I chuckle. "Doubt it. If I'm dead, they get no bread."

"True, so they're on the way to kill me then." She draws in a deep breath before slowly releasing it. "Thank you, by the way, for that." A light flush crosses her cheeks.

I grab her hand, and she allows me to lift her up from the chair. "Babe, you don't have to thank me for standing up for you. As your man, that's my job. I support you, care about you, and will always defend you." I run my lips up her neck until I hit the soft skin of her ear. "Although you do pack quite the punch, Rocky Balboa." I laugh and can feel her chest moving against mine. "You did some damage to that asshole."

She's smiling from ear to ear when I pull away.

Mission accomplished.

"He did deserve it."

"Damn straight he did."

She jumps at the sound of my phone going off.

I look down at her. "Should we answer it?"

She bites the edge of her lip, shaking her head. I laugh.

"Let's make 'em suffer."

"How about we make them suffer and I make you feel good?"

"Mmm ... I always love your bright ideas, sunshine."

37

Rose

"**D**o you think people will assume you're only here because of what happened last night?" I ask Knox.

We're in the backseat of another rented SUV, and George is behind the steering wheel. Knox looks out the window as we turn into the private entrance of the children's hospital. This visit has been on Knox's schedule since the very beginning, but I'm well aware of how the media twists shit. They'll make it look like it's a last-minute storyline to take the heat away from him punching Adam.

"Probably," he deadpans.

"That's sad."

"The world can be a sad place, and if that's the kind of person people want to think I am, let 'em fucking believe that. I'm done caring."

There's no missing his frustration. We had a long-ass night with phones going off nonstop. Knox ended up deactivating his social media accounts temporarily because of the backlash he'd been getting. His fans might support him, but those who aren't are making him out to be some hotheaded criminal.

Guilt crashes through me. I'm the one to blame for the entire situation, and not one video was posted of me hitting him. Adam is giving interviews right and left, trying to get in his twenty minutes of fame and look like the good guy, at Knox's expense.

"Maybe I should make a statement and tell them the truth," I say. "I'm the one at fault for what happened. Not you."

He snakes his hand out and captures mine. "I'm not letting them go after you. This bullshit will blow over in a few weeks, and that dude will go back to being some nameless asshole." He lifts our hands and presses his lips to my hand.

God, how did I manage to get someone this perfect? Someone who gives me this sense of security but makes me feel like I'm free at the same time.

There's no doubt he was being honest about Stella. He's protecting me, like he did with her. He'd rather put his ass on the line than see me get hurt.

"You're amazing, do you know that?" I ask, leaning forward to give him a kiss.

"You're the only person I need to hear that from," he replies.

"You two lovebirds ready?" George asks. "Or do you want to keep making out back there?"

I push his shoulder, laughing. "Yes, we're ready."

We get out, and a dark-haired man dressed in scrubs is waiting for us at the entrance. George opens the hatchback, and Knox helps him unload the gift bags we made last night. After the show, we'd raided the merchandise trailer and sent George toy shopping.

George drags out the red wagon stuffed in the back, and we load the gift bags onto it. Knox grabs the handle and pulls it to the door while George takes Knox's guitar and swings the strap over his shoulder.

The man extends his hand out to shake Knox's. "I'm Matthew. Thank you for coming. The children have been buzzing with excitement all morning," he says.

"I'm happy to be here," Knox tells him before introducing George and me.

Matthew punches in an access code, and we follow him through the door. Crayon-colored artwork and pictures of cancer survivors line the hallway walls. I'll be reading every single one of those on our way back.

Matthew leads us into a room that's filled with kids, parents, and staff. Pain grips at my heart, squeezing it roughly, when I see the children—some underweight, some with IVs connected to their bodies, some with pale complexions, some with no hair.

My mood lifts though as I watch the children's eyes light up when they see Knox. I stand behind him, and this might be one of my best experiences on this tour.

"Who are all of these rock stars in here?" Knox asks.

The frustration he had in the car has evaporated, and there is nothing but excitement in his voice now. It's not forced or fake. A fresh energy has burst through him. The smile on his face as he walks through the room is so damn genuine that I want to throw my arms around him, shower him with kisses, and whisper how phenomenal he is.

"I know you guys didn't get the chance to make it to my concert last night," he goes on, "so I thought I'd bring the show to you."

Everyone cheers in response, some clapping their hands, as bright smiles take over their faces. Knox grabs his guitar from George and takes a seat in the chair at the front of the room.

I stand to the side, resting my back against the wall, and watch as he starts to play. I'm taken to another world while listening to the children sing along with his every word.

The hairs on the back of my neck stand up. It's the most angelic sound I've ever heard. Tears prick at my eyes as I pull out my phone and start to record them. This will keep me going on my worst days. Whenever I think I'm going through something rough, I will pull this out as a reminder of how incredibly lucky I am.

They sing four songs together. The children that can get up

start dancing while others sway to the melody. The cheers erupt again when Knox finishes.

"Wow, I think you sound better than I do," he tells them.

They giggle in delight.

He slides his guitar off and sets it down. "I also brought you some goodies."

That's my cue.

Everyone's eyes go to me when I wheel the wagon over to him, trying to control my sniffles.

A tiny girl with glasses points her finger at me. "Is that your girlfriend?"

Knox laughs. "You'll have to ask her that, darling. I keep begging her to be, but she turns me down." He winks at the girl. "What do you think I need to do to convince her?"

"Kiss her!" the girl replies, and laughter along with some *yucks* follow her answer.

"Buy her diamonds," a boy says. "That always works with my mom. Dad says she loves the bling!"

"Get her a puppy!" another suggests.

Knox glances over at me. "What do you think, sunshine? Will any of their ideas help me win your heart?"

A blush creeps over my cheeks, and I nod, giggling. "You're doing very well on your own."

"Oh, make out already!" a kid in the back yells.

"Gross," a smaller voice shouts. "Girls don't want to make out with boys until they make them their wives."

Knox snaps his fingers at the girl. "Exactly. Maybe she'll agree to that one day, and I'll get that lucky kiss. But for now, how about we give out some toys?"

The mention of toys completely offsets their attention on my relationship status to Knox. We spend the next two hours handing out toys, playing with the children, and taking pictures.

You don't always see the real person behind all the headlines. *Why don't they write about this amazing man who visits children fighting cancer, who helps pay medical bills for those who can't afford treatment, or who agrees to every Make-A-Wish request?*

Knox is right. The world is sad.

What's even worse is, I would've never believed he was as charitable as he is had it not been my job to schedule and keep track of it all. I don't like being proven wrong, but in this case, I'll make an exception. I've been wrong about him since the very beginning.

When it's time to go, Knox waves Matthew over. "Before we leave, can we make a round through the rooms of children who couldn't make it? I'd like to surprise them as well."

Lord help me, every day, I'm falling deeper and deeper for this man.

I'm falling deeper and deeper *in love* with him.

"Do you want to know why I call you sunshine?" Knox asks when we get back into the SUV.

I've always been curious about it, but I assumed it was because of my hair. "Why?"

"When you walked into Thomas's office, I was having a shitty day. I was even thinking about pulling out of the tour and quitting it all. When I saw that I'd snapped at you instead of him, I felt like an asshole. You were there, giving off this positive light, and even though I didn't want to bring that light into my life, I knew it was the best for me. I gave you a hard time because I was trying to stay in my hole of darkness, trying to drown everything away with alcohol and acting out."

"You seemed fine to me. You were throwing parties and going out clubbing."

"Numbing your mind with booze and bullshit doesn't mean you're happy." He frowns, running his hand over his face. "This probably sounds stupid to you."

"No, I know from experience that's what men in the industry tend to do. They try to numb themselves. Do I understand it? Not exactly. But it isn't stupid." I grin. "And I love my nickname, now even more since I know what it means."

My phone vibrates, and I pull it out of my bag.

> Thomas: Tell Knox to answer his phone. We have a problem.

I hold my phone out and show Knox the text.

"I turned it off when we were at the hospital," he says, digging in his pocket. He turns it on, and the smile on his face fades into a frown as he starts to read the messages.

"What is it?" I ask.

He shakes his head, unable to look at me, and stuffs the phone back into his jeans. "It's nothing."

"It's obviously *something*. You look like you were told the tour is canceled."

"It's not important."

"Then, tell me," I push.

"One of my biggest sponsors withdrew their contract with me today."

"What? Who?"

"Netphase."

Netphase is the new up-and-coming cellular network that is making millions from using celebrity endorsements.

"But isn't that, like, a million-dollar contract?"

He nods, lifting his shoulder into a half-shrug. "It's not that big of a deal. Their loss."

"It is a big deal. You just lost a million dollars because of me!"

"I have plenty of money. It's fine."

I unlock my phone. "I'm calling Thomas right now to tell him to fix this," I snarl. "Better yet, I'm calling Netphase myself and giving them a piece of my mind."

He plucks my phone from my hand. "Don't. It's done." He sighs. "We had a good day today. Don't let this news put a damper on it. I lost some money. So what? It happens."

I lean back in my seat and nod even though the guilt is seeping in stronger. *How can he think I'm sunshine when I just cost him a million dollars?*

38

Knox

I rub the back of my stiff neck while following Rose into the bedroom. I've been holding in the words I'm about to say. Saying them will mean it's time for me to face reality, and reality isn't my best friend at the moment.

"This is it," I whisper. "Our last night together."

It's late, after midnight, and I'm wiped after tonight's show. My feet are killing me. My body is sore as fuck. But there's nothing that's going to stop me from staying up as late as I can to savor our time together. I tried convincing her to reschedule tonight's show, but she wasn't having it.

Typical Rose—more concerned with my career and her responsibilities over everything.

She flies home in the morning. My stomach drops while I think about how she won't be next to me when I wake up in the morning or waiting there with a water bottle in her hand as soon as I step off the stage after ending a show. Those small things I've become accustomed to with her are about to end.

It's going to hit me hard.

I don't want her to go, but asking her to bail on college and throw away her dreams would be selfish of me. She feels the same way about asking me to take time off from my tour and music.

We're stuck between a rock and a hard place—caring about each other too much to let the other miss out on something so important to us even if it means we're breaking our own hearts in the process.

It's bad timing.

And timing is so damn crucial in relationships. It's a cloud lingering over you, giving you challenges that can make or break your love, and you can only hope you make it to the sunlight.

She drops her bag and kicks off her sandals when I flip on the light. "I swear, it feels like time has flown by, yet so much has happened." She pauses, scrunching up her adorable nose. "If that makes sense?"

"It does, and I wouldn't change it for the world."

We've traveled thousands of miles together, gone through highs and lows, and we've grown closer and closer each day. Two weeks have passed since the fight with her ex and the bullshit backlash that followed, but the guilt is still with her—I can tell —even when she's lying about it.

She grins. "Me neither. This tour has been some of the most enjoyable months of my life. I'll never forget it." She raises her wrist to look down at her watch. "We have T-minus eight hours until I have to leave. How about I go out with a bang?"

She reaches down to grab the hem of her dress and pulls it over her head. I lick my lips at the sight of her standing in front of me, wearing only pink lace panties and a matching bra.

I dart over to her, nearly tripping on my feet. "Literally. I'll give you the best bang you've ever had, sunshine."

I capture the band of her bra in my fingers, unsnap it, and revel in the view of her tits spilling out. I take my time worshipping her, tasting each nipple, swirling my tongue around each one, and then sucking hard on the peak.

Her face is flushed, our breathing slow, when I gently lay her down on the bed and start to trail kisses over her chest and down to her stomach—wishing time would stand still each time my lips hit her soft skin.

I don't want to lose this woman who's changed my life in so many ways. She's made me want to be a better man.

Her legs part when I reach her thighs, and she trembles as I run my fingers along her pussy lips, feeling how drenched she is for me. I dive right in, devouring what I'm always starving for, and she whimpers underneath me, repeatedly begging me to give her my cock.

I focus on pleasuring her, ignoring her protests, and drive my tongue in deeper. She tenses up when I add my fingers to the mix, working her, lapping her up until she arches her back and lets go against my lips.

Fuck. I could spend forever eating her pussy.

I rise up and watch as she starts to level her breathing.

"My turn," she whispers, climbing forward.

I grunt when she pushes me on my back and immediately pulls off my shirt. The room feels hot when she starts to run open-mouthed kisses over my chest and circles her tongue around each of my nipples, tugging at them with her teeth. I tremble when she unbuckles my pants, yanks them down, and wraps her lips around my cock before even taking them off.

My needy fingers sink into her hair, guiding her how I like it, and she stops right before I'm about to explode—she knows my body that well. She licks her lips and then wipes her mouth with the back of her hand while grinning down at me.

"I want you on top," she says.

"Your favorite," I mutter. It's mine too.

"Show me how much I turn you on. Dominate me."

She smiles the entire time she drags my pants down my legs and tosses them off the bed. She's back underneath me as soon as they hit the floor, my weight hovering over her, and I put a condom on before positioning my cock at her soaked opening.

Everything feels right when I sink into her.

I rock my hips, and she meets my thrusts with a moan.

"Yes," she mutters. "You always know exactly how I like it."

"Fuck, baby," I rasp out, rearing my hips back to make longer strokes. "You feel so damn good. Nothing is better than this."

I entwine our hands, pushing them into the firm mattress, and rock into her. We go slow, giving each other everything we have as we say our good-bye.

She tilts her ass up, and I rest her legs on my shoulders so I can drive deeper into the woman I'm obsessed with, keeping my eyes on the breathtaking view of her the entire time until she cries out in ecstasy.

I shudder out my release three pumps later.

"I love you," I say, staring down at her and catching my breath.

The words had been at the tip of my tongue for a while now, but I held myself back from saying them in fear of scaring her off.

The room falls silent, and it seems like my confession ruined the moment. Alarm rings through me when she peeks up at the ceiling, avoiding my gaze.

I hit her with an orgasm and then smacked her in the face with love devotions.

Her reaction is only more evidence that time isn't on our side.

"You don't have to say it back," I rush out, collapsing next to her and squeezing her thigh. "I wanted you to know how I felt before you land in California tomorrow. I don't want you getting home, thinking this was some fling to me. You mean so much more to me than that."

It takes her a few seconds before she looks down. "The feeling is mutual. I love you too." Her hand grabs mine. "Sorry for the delay, but you startled me when you blurted it out. I can barely think straight right now. That was incredible."

I'm sure the smile I'm giving her is cheesy as hell, but I can't help it. "You have no idea how good it makes me feel to hear you say that."

She nods shyly, but her eyes still don't meet mine.

I get up to dispose of the condom and pull her into me when I crawl back into bed.

We made love tonight. It was passionate and emotional. But I'm afraid all of that passion is going to depart with her on the plane tomorrow.

Rose falls asleep before I do. Her breathing settles, her chest moving in and out against mine.

Sleep doesn't come to me.

I saw the truth in her eyes. There's love there.

But I also saw something else.

Doubt.

Rose's feelings are mutual, but they might not run as deep.

It's early, and the sun is already beating in through the tinted SUV windows as we're on our way to drop Rose off at the airport.

She asked me to stay in the car and for us to say our good-byes in here, so it could be private with no media attention. I offered to rent her a jet, even suggesting I go with her and fly right back, but she refused.

"I can send a plane for you on the weekends or anytime you have a break from school," I say, resting my hand on her leg. "We'll figure out how to make this work."

She pushes her dark sunglasses up her nose, sighing. "Knox, you know that's going to be too difficult and not going to work."

What the fuck? My chest starts to tighten, my mind already knowing exactly where this conversation is heading—into a dead fucking end.

"You're going to be swamped with tour stuff. I'm going to be studying my ass off. Neither one of us is going to have time to jet around the world. Not to mention, I'm going to be working part-time for Thomas, and I have my dad."

I keep shaking my head. "Don't do this, Rose."

"Don't do what?"

"Decide that it won't work before we've even given it a chance. Don't break things off because you're scared of a little distance. I might not have the best relationship track record—neither one of us does—but that doesn't mean we're incapable of commitment and love. Trust me, I was terrified to say it myself. There's only been one other woman I've spoken those words to, and that relationship went to shit. This time around though, it's stronger. I feel my love for you through my entire body, my veins, my heart, every part of me. I will do anything to make us work. I will fly to you every day I have off. I will bring you to me. *Anything.* Please don't do this." I'm rambling, but I only have a short time to plead my case before she has to go.

She shakes her head. "I'm not breaking anything off. All I'm saying is, our relationship is going to change drastically as soon as I get on that plane. We'll be in different times zones. My bedtime will be your showtime."

"We're both mature enough to handle minor shit like that. We can text, talk on the phone, FaceTime. Modern technology is a pretty kick-ass thing."

She stays silent.

"Why didn't you say any of this last night? Why are you springing this on me last minute, right before you're about to leave?"

"Because I didn't want to hurt you. I wanted us to enjoy our night together." She looks down at my hand, as if it shouldn't be there, and shakes her head. "Maybe I'm reading too much into it. I'm exhausted, and I know I have a long week ahead of me, trying to get everything in order for my classes."

My mouth turns dry as George pulls up to the airport entrance.

Circle around! We need more damn time!

He looks back at Rose. "You ready?"

She nods before ducking down and grabbing her purse from the floorboard.

"Call or text me as soon as you land, okay?" I croak out.

She nods, looking down at her lap. "I will."

I want to pull those sunglasses from her face and force her to look at me. It's the best way I can read her. I have a sick feeling in my stomach that as soon as she steps out of this car, we're over.

I inch forward and capture her chin between my thumb and forefinger and lightly press my lips to hers. She responds, grabbing the back of my head and strengthening our kiss.

It hits me when she slowly pulls away and breaks our connection.

This wasn't just a good-bye kiss.

It was *the* good-bye kiss.

It could possibly be the last kiss we'll ever have.

"Well ..." She pauses. "I have a flight to catch."

"I love you," I say around a rough swallow.

"I love you too." The words rush from her lips as she opens up the door.

She doesn't look back at me as George pulls her luggage from the back and hands it to her or when she strolls it behind her as she disappears through the airport doors.

39

Rose

"I have my roomie back, *la-la-la*. I have my roomie back, *la-la-la*," Claire sings as she comes skipping into my bedroom.

I got in a few hours ago and took an Uber home since Claire was going to be gone at a charity event with her parents all day.

I have my luggage unloaded, and the last load of laundry is in the dryer. I've been busy trying to unpack and get everything together for when classes start. I have a meeting with financial assistance in the morning to set up a payment plan.

During the flight, I went back and forth with myself on whether I should've accepted Knox's offer of flying with me, but I had to insist he stay. He's leaving the country in two days and going to need plenty of rest. Not to mention, it would've only made our good-bye harder, especially after I hinted that things between us wouldn't work out long distance.

My eyes welled up, tears biting at me when we pulled up to the airport, and I'm grateful I had my sunglasses on. I had to stay strong. I had to be sensible. I couldn't lead him into thinking everything was going to be the same after I left.

"Am I still considered a roomie if I'm technically not paying rent?" I ask.

I've offered to pay Claire for letting me stay here with her now that I have some money, but she won't take it.

She moves over a stack of folded clothes and sits down on my bed. "I don't pay the rent here either, so I guess we're both getting away with it."

I smile. That's why she's my best friend. Instead of making me feel like a loser, she makes fun of herself.

She smacks my bed. "Now, I want to know all the details about the tour."

"It was busy," I answer.

"That's all the details? You were busy? *Busy* working or *busy* in the bedroom?"

I stay quiet.

"Or both?"

"I know you're not going to let me off the hook, so both."

"Yay! She finally got laid, ladies and gentlemen. Now, I want to know everything. I want to know where your vibrator went, the truth about what happened with douchebag Adam because I know the shit posted online are lies, and how Knox is in the bedroom."

I spend the next hour giving her the scoop about the tour but try to stay away from talking about saying good-bye to Knox. I refrain from telling her that Knox used the vibrator on me a few nights when we were together, and that's how I got it back from him.

"Do you think you guys will stay together?" she asks, not letting me get away with it.

Her question hits me hard, and I can feel my heart pounding against my chest. "I'm not sure. I don't want to talk about it."

"Did he break your heart?"

I shake my head, a tear falling down my cheek. "No, I think I broke his."

Her face goes soft, and she wraps her arms around me. "Then, unbreak it. You obviously have feelings for him—strong ones."

"I love him."

"You can fix it. You can be with him."

"I can't. It'll never work out between us, and the longer it goes on, the harder the pain will be when it falls apart. He's on tour, Claire. He's traveling all over the world with girls throwing themselves at him every three seconds. Do you honestly think he's going to stay celibate and wait around for a girlfriend thousands of miles away, sitting in a classroom? I witnessed it happen with Adam, with my father, with all of his bandmates. Men who are musicians cannot stay faithful, especially on the road."

"Have you told him that's what you're scared of? Why you're running away?"

"I've tried explaining it to him, but he doesn't understand. He swears he'll stay committed and he won't cheat, but I can't trust his word, no matter how hard I try to talk myself into it. If I don't trust him, it'll never work."

I'm wiping tears from my cheeks when my phone beeps. I pick it up and can't help but smile.

> Knox: My new assistant smells like pickles and hot sauce. She also won't stop chomping on ice cubes. Would you get mad at me if I made her ride on top of the bus? It would be like a convertible.

My replacement is a woman in her thirties, who seems nice and organized. Anna has worked as an assistant for a few other celebrities, but her schedule has never been as packed as it is with Knox. I told her she might want to stock up on Xanax or something because she seemed like a nervous wreck when it was time for her to take my place. I knew it was going to be a big change for Knox when I left and that he was probably going to give her a hard time at first, like he did with me.

> Me: Be nice to her. She had great references.

Knox: She's not doing a bad job. She's just
not you.

His response tugs at my heart. *She's just not you.*
I could give it all up—quit my job, drop out of school—and
start working for him again, but then where would I be when things
went south? I'd be out of a job and a college dropout.

Me: If you get rid of her, they'll bring your
mom back in.

Knox: Shit. Good point.

My phone vibrates with another message.

Anna: You said I could text if I needed
anything. Do you have a happy pill anywhere
for this guy?

Me: Not a happy pill, but try Friends on
Netflix.

Knox: Did you really just text her and say to
put on Netflix like she's my babysitter, asking
how to control a cranky child?

Me: You are acting like a cranky child. Be nice
to her for me.

Knox: You want to know something that'll put
me in a good mood?

Me: Who knows with you?

Knox: Send me a sexy picture.

Me: I'm sitting in my room with Claire. She'll
think I'm a freak.

Knox: You are a freak, and I love it.

"Is that him?" Claire asks.

I nod.

"Be up-front with him right now. Don't lead him on if you're not sure what you want."

"I will."

At another time.

40

Rose

"Hi. I need to set up a payment plan," I tell the financial advisor, who I've had an appointment set with for months. "I have about a third that I can pay up front."

I've saved up almost every penny that I could, but only working for a few months still wasn't enough to pay for both semesters. It's something though, and every little bit counts for me right now.

The middle-aged woman shoves her glasses up her narrow nose and nods. "I need your ID, please."

I pull out my wallet and hand her my ID. She starts to type in all of my information.

"Rose Graves." She punches in a few more keys and then tilts her head to the side to study the screen. "It looks like your tuition is paid up for both semesters."

I lean forward in my chair. "What? I think there's a mistake." I point to my ID in her hand. "Did you spell my name correctly? Do you want to call and make sure there isn't a glitch in the system?"

"There are no glitches, your name is spelled correctly, and all the information matches your account. Your tuition is paid."

"By who?"

"It doesn't say. All it's telling me is that it was paid in full two weeks ago." Her slender pink lips form a smile. "Whoever it was, they are awfully nice." She pushes her hands together and rests them on her desk. "Anything else I can help you with?"

The office is packed with people. She wants me out of here, so she can move on to the next broke student.

"No, thank you," I say, getting up from my chair. I take my ID and leave her office.

My purse is hanging from my arm as I look through it to find my phone while I make my way back to the Jeep in the parking lot, which I still need to give back to Knox. When I asked when he wanted me to drop it off, he told me to wait until Nate was home. I have a feeling waiting until Nate is home is going to take a while.

> Me: Did you pay my tuition?

I unlock the doors and slide into the Jeep. I make it all the way back to the condo before my phone beeps with a reply.

> Knox: I have no clue what you're talking about. The tuition fairy must've done it.

> Me: I'm serious. Un-pay it.

> Knox: Hell no.

> Me: Then, I'm paying you back for it.

This is supposed to be my time to be independent, and Knox paying my bills for me is the complete opposite of that.

I throw my purse over my shoulder and stomp into the condo, like I'm three years old.

"He paid my tuition!" I yell.

Claire is sitting at the kitchen table, chomping on a bowl of yogurt and granola. "Good boy."

"No, bad boy. I wanted to do this on my own. I'm not one of his little charity cases."

She drops her spoon into her bowl and rolls her eyes. "I don't think he did it because he feels sorry for you or thinks you're a damn charity case. He did it because he cares about you, and I have a feeling he also did it because he's in love with you."

I haven't told Claire about Knox confessing his feelings for me, and I don't plan to. She'd really be on my ass about my pushing him away if she found out.

"This helps you so much," she goes on. "If you make more money in the future and it's tearing you up that bad, pay him back then. But you need to take all the help you can get right now, okay? You would be paying student loans off for the next five years had he not paid it. You have so much going on—required community service hours, your work, homework. You'd be stressed out, having to worry about paying for school on top of that."

My phone beeps when I sit down in the chair across from her.

> Knox: Are you mad? Sorry. I only wanted to help. I want you to focus on your degree and doing what you enjoy.

> Me: I'm not mad. It just took me by surprise.

> Knox: You're honestly one of the best people
> to ever walk into my life. When I'm old and
> write a tell-all about my life, you'll be in there
> as someone who changed me for the better.
> Everything you've done for me, every emotion
> you've made me feel, it's made me a better
> man, and I can't thank you enough. I want to
> thank you for giving me something so
> amazing by helping with your tuition. Please
> give me that. You're going to go out there and
> do great things. You'll be helping those less
> fortunate and taking care of kids whose
> parents haven't made the right decisions. I
> want you to be able to focus all of your
> attention on that, not student loans.

I suck in a breath as I feel my eyes start to water. I want to stop the tears, but I can't as they fall down my cheeks. *How can I fight him on this when it seems like it means so much?*

> Me: Thank you. You have no idea how much I appreciate this.

> Knox: I know you do, which is why I did it.

"Oh shit, the ugly-cry face," Claire says, startling me.

I was so wrapped up in Knox's texts that I forgot she was even there.

"Tears of joy or tears of fury?"

"Tears of joy ... gratefulness," I answer. I hold my phone out so she can read his text.

"Damn, girl, this man is so sweet for you." She punches her arm through the air. "We have a winner. My best friend finally has a good man."

I suck in a sniffle. "Whoa. Calm down, killer. He's not *my man.* We're not even *together*, together."

"Does he know that?"

"Yes, I made it very clear before I left that we couldn't be anything serious."

Claire's dark brows pull in. "Why? You have a good thing in your life, and you're throwing it away for nothing. I know you think men in those situations can't be trusted and it won't work out, but you're basing that belief off of two men. Your dad and Adam. Don't kill your entire love life off because one douchebag hurt you. Plenty of celebrities are in committed relationships."

"He has a reputation that matches theirs to a T, Claire. *To a fucking T.* I'd rather step away now than get my heart stomped on in a few weeks and an embarrassment is made out of me."

She lets out a long sigh. She doesn't like my answer, and I probably won't be hearing the end of this. "Let's go out to dinner tonight. We haven't celebrated your homecoming since you've been back, and I know as soon as school starts, it's going to be like pulling your hair out to get you to do something with me."

41

Rose

"**D**on't freak out," Claire whispers.

I look up at her as she twirls her dark hair around a finger and looks at me anxiously.

Since I've been home, Knox texts me every morning, and we talk throughout the day. He hasn't mentioned our relationship, but I think he's subtly trying to show me this is how we make it work—that we're capable of surviving a long-distance relationship.

I'm at lunch with Claire. She's trying to get in all the girl time she can before I get swamped with school and work.

"Don't freak out about what?" I ask.

We're sitting outside on the patio of one of our favorite restaurants.

"Right behind you, there're three men with cameras pointed directly at us."

"What?"

I turn around to see what she's looking at, and sure enough, there are three guys with expensive cameras plastered to their hands with the lenses focused directly on me.

I twist back around in my chair and let out an annoyed huff.

"See? This is exactly what I told you happens when you're dating a man in the spotlight … especially one as famous as Knox."

"So the fuck what? They'll take a few lame-ass pictures of you scarfing down your grilled chicken and asparagus. If that's the stress you have to go through to be with a great man, take it. You could have to wait months for him to come home from war or have to become a sister wife."

"Are you really trying to compare me being with Knox to sharing him with numerous other women?"

"Yes, and hopefully, it sinks into that thick-headed skull of yours that shit could be worse."

I grab my water and take a drink. "It's still not what I want to go through every time I decide to go somewhere. They'll post these pictures online, and all of his fans will call me ugly and criticize everything about me."

"And you're the one in his bed, so whether you're wearing an unflattering dress or you have a zit on your nose, you still win."

"Whatever. I'm done talking about it."

We finish our food, pay the bill, and make our way back to the Jeep. The jackasses with the cameras are still snapping photos and recording our every move. I pick up my pace when they start to follow me.

"Rose! Rose! How are things with Knox now that you're not on tour with him anymore?" one yells.

Another one gets closer. "Are you guys an official couple? Does he still have feelings for Stella?"

"Has he met your dad in prison?"

"Why did he punch Adam Dole? Are the rumors that you used to date him true?"

I twist around to look at them. "Please quit following me!" I yell. "Knox and I have decided to go our separate ways." The words leave my mouth before I realize what I'm saying.

Everyone holding a camera grins. I gave them exactly what they wanted.

I roughly pull open the Jeep door and jump in.

"I can't believe you said that," Claire says, getting in. "Are you crazy?"

"They wouldn't shut the hell up," I snap, attempting to shove the key into the ignition with my shaking hand but I keep missing.

She grabs it and does the job for me. "You need to call Knox and tell him about this. He's going to be livid and confused when it gets back to him."

I hate that she's right, but what's done is done.

42

Knox

I'm watching the clip Mason emailed me for the fifth time.

"Knox and I have decided to go our separate ways."

I refresh the screen.

"Knox and I have decided to go our separate ways."

I pause on her face. She looks beautiful. Fucking gorgeous. Her hair is swept back in a braid, showing off every color in it. I miss her so damn much, and it sucks that the first time I see her after leaving, she's saying this. I don't see a smile or any light in her eyes. There's only annoyance and irritation. But she looks breathtaking, even when she's driving a knife into my heart.

The feeling of betrayal pumps through my veins.

Why didn't she come to me first instead of blindsiding me?

Yes, she hinted at not wanting a long-distance relationship while I was on tour, but she's still been texting me. We talk daily. *How can you claim to go separate ways with someone that you're still in constant contact with?*

I feel like I'm the side dick—the guy she's trying to keep hidden from the world.

I pick up my phone and hit Thomas's name.

"Hey, can we make a break in my schedule?" I ask.

"What do you mean, make a break in your schedule?" His

tone is annoyed, which I don't blame him for. "You just got to Tokyo."

"Find time, okay? Even if it's only for a day, I don't care."

"What's going on? Where do you intend on going?"

"Home."

He blows out a breath. "You do know that's a fifteen-hour flight?"

"Do you think I give a shit?"

"We've decided to go our separate ways?" I blurt out as soon as Rose opens her front door.

Her mouth falls open, and it takes her a few seconds to grasp that I'm actually standing in front of her. I was on a fifteen-hour flight, and I probably look like I've been dragged through hell.

I have mentally, to be honest. My mind has been frantic with uncertainty since I saw the video, and I wasn't sure what I'd be walking into when I showed up here.

"Knox." My name sounds so sweet, coming from her lips. I've missed that.

"We've decided to go our separate ways?" It kills me more, each time I say it. Those seven words have been haunting me.

Her blonde hair is braided down the side, and she's only wearing a sports bra and sweatpants.

She holds up her hand, struggling to come up with the right words to explain how she blindsided me with this. "Let ... let me explain."

"Let you explain? You explained plenty to the entire world! What happened to you wanting to keep our relationship private and between us and *us only*?"

She looks behind her shoulder before stepping outside and shutting the door behind her. "We talked about this." Her voice lowers to almost a whisper. "We agreed that trying to keep a relationship while you're away on tour … or in the spotlight, period, isn't realistic." Her eyes focus on the ground. Just like at the airport, she can't even look at me.

"That's bullshit. I'm perfectly capable of holding a relationship and being committed to you while I'm on tour *and* in the spotlight. It's you—*you and you only*—who is so afraid, so goddamn scared of what people will say. You're so worried about the possibility of your heart getting broken that you won't even listen to it when it's happy!"

She finally looks up at me, and when she does, I can see the shame on her face. I can see her fighting with herself to pull away. *She loves me, so why is she doing this to us?*

"This is what I was afraid of," she finally says. "The destruction of our friendship because we crossed that line."

I run my hands over my face and shake my head to hold back my hurt. "What we have is more than friendship, and you know it. Don't try to minimize it for your convenience."

"I'm not! You want me to be honest, to be real, and that's what I'm doing right now! You have this silly fantasy that everything will work out between us. It's unrealistic. Why can't you see that?"

Silly fantasy?

I take a step back from her. "I'm awake, baby. Trust me, my eyes are completely open now."

Tears start to fall down her cheeks, and I'm trying my hardest to stop my own. I've never felt this shattered, like someone ripped me open with promises and then infected me with lies. *Why should I allow her to see me suffer if she doesn't give a damn that she's the one causing the pain?*

"I don't want to hurt you, Knox."

"You already have! Why did you open up and give me what I wanted if you didn't plan on letting me keep you? Why did you get my hopes up if you weren't going to give me a fair chance? I can hold a relationship. I've done it before, and I did it for years. Maybe it's you with the relationship issues."

"You're probably right," she says softly. Her response shocks the shit out of me. "I have commitment and trust issues that will tear us apart. I'll never be able to trust you, and a relationship without trust is a relationship that's never going to last. If you don't answer your phone one night, I'll think you're cheating. There's no changing that. I don't know why I'm like this, but I am."

I close the space between us to grab her hands in mine. "Let me show you that it doesn't have to be that way. Let me prove your fears wrong."

She pulls away. "I'm sorry … I can't," she whispers before clearing her throat and straightening her back. "I know you have a show soon that's halfway across the world. You need to get going. Don't ruin your career over me."

I throw my hands up in defeat and start to back away from her. "You're going to regret this one day, and when you find someone you love as much as I do you, you're going to die when you feel the same rejection and heartbreak that I'm feeling right now. I promise you, it's not pretty, and it'll tear you apart."

43

Rose

"Are you fucking kidding me?" Claire screams as soon as I get back inside. She's standing in front of me, arms crossed, face fuming. She points to the door. "That man was out there, begging you to give him a chance. He loves you. Don't shut him out because of your insecurities."

"Stay out of my business," I answer, walking around her.

I knew she'd be eavesdropping on our conversation. The girl has ears like a hawk.

"No, I won't. You're my best friend, and I love you. It's my job to be in your business and tell you when you're acting like a fucking coward, and quite frankly, you're acting like a fucking coward!"

Her words of honesty shove through my chest like a knife. *Do I regret ending things with Knox?* Yes. But I'd rather live with regret than go through a Knox heartbreak that would tear me apart worse than what it already is.

"I don't want that life!" I scream.

"You're not choosing that life. You're choosing *him*. He comes with baggage, yes, and if you're not thinking clearly, so do you."

"Whatever." I run up the stairs and slam my bedroom door shut.

"Fucking coward!" Claire yells again.

Tears are still slipping down my cheeks when I fall down face-first onto my bed.

I almost made a run for it when Claire looked through the peephole and said Knox was standing at the front door. I even considered not answering and acting like I wasn't home, but there was no way she would have let that slide. She threatened to let him in and record our entire conversation if I didn't go out there and hear what he had to say.

"Fucking coward!" Claire yells *again.*

And I know I'm going to be hearing those words all night.

I grab my remote, turn on my TV, and crank the volume up.

I have to drown her out before she convinces me to change my mind.

Three days have passed since Knox walked away from me.

Three days of fucking hell.

I've lost track of how many times I've picked up the phone to call him. It's killing me, knowing I led him on and then pulled away when I felt like the time was right. I knew I'd eventually have to leave him on tour and go back to school, so I never should've let it go that far, but I couldn't help myself.

People always fall in love at the wrong time and in the wrong place. Love is never convenient. It's the most difficult yet satisfying journey you'll go through in life.

Damn it, why can't our hearts just beat for us and that's it? Why do we have to feel emotions through them?

I miss our little conversations. I miss his dirty, annoying texts. I miss eating breakfast with him every morning. You don't realize how much you miss something until it's gone and you know you'll never get it back.

"Have you come to your senses and called him yet?" Claire asks when I walk into the kitchen.

She asks me this same question every morning, making me feel even more like shit.

I grab a mug from the cabinet and pour myself a cup of coffee. "I told you to stay out of my business." I start adding creamer while waiting for her to continue her preaching.

"And I told you, that isn't happening. If I was making a mistake like this with Dixon, you'd call me out on my bullshit, and you know it. I'm your best friend. I want you to be happy, and Knox Rivers makes you happy." She pauses and then grins wide. "Wow, I never thought I'd say something like that."

"Trust me, neither did I," I grumble, taking a sip of my coffee.

"Why are you so afraid of love?"

I set my cup down on the table before plopping down in a chair. "I'm not afraid of love."

She snorts, and I give her a dirty look.

"I'm scared of that kind of relationship. The one where every girl wants the guy I'm dating, where creeps are following me around, and where magazines print pictures of me and talk about Knox cheating on me. I don't want that shit. Never have. Never will."

"You won't even deal with it to be happy and be with the man you love?"

"I thought I was in love before, but it was immaturity and delusion. I honestly don't trust my heart anymore."

"Quit comparing him to Adam's bitch ass. Knox turned down every girl while you were together. He could've pulled a move like the douchebag and snuck around with some skank in a dirty-ass bathroom, but he didn't."

"That's not what I'm doing. I'm comparing him to every

single guy out there who has girls throwing themselves at him. So, drop it. I'm sick of hearing you lecture me about it."

"Fine. I tried, and as your best friend, I'll be here, waiting for you to cry on my shoulder when Knox starts dating someone else."

I cough on my drink, and coffee splatters from my lips onto the table. Claire grins. The girl is smart.

"See? How did it feel when I talked about him being with another woman? It hurt, right? It's something that will happen though. So, be prepared."

"I hate it when you make sense."

"Text him. Call him. Do *something* before it's too late."

"I'll think about it."

I get up, pour myself another cup, and go back to my bedroom.

"Before it's too late!" Claire yells to my back.

I pick up my phone from my nightstand.

I set it back down.

Then pick it up again.

Why did Claire have to implant the thought in my mind of seeing Knox with another woman? It pains me to even think about him putting his hands on someone else, his lips kissing hers like he did mine, and him doing the kind, romantic gestures he did with me.

Whoever that lucky bitch will be, I already hate her.

I pick up my phone again and start typing before I change my mind.

> Me: I don't want you to hate me.

There. I started the conversation.

But what if he doesn't answer?

What if he ignores me?

My chest tightens, and I start to grow dizzy while I wait to see if I'm going to get a response. I'm mad at myself because I'll be waiting all day with my phone in my hand until I get one now.

My phone beeps, and I'm almost afraid to look at it. I slowly bring it up and read the text.

Knox: I could never hate you.

His answer makes me feel even more like shit.

Me: I'm sorry.

I jump when the phone starts to ring in my hand.
It's Knox.
Should I answer it?
It might kill me more to hear his voice.
I have to answer it, considering I just texted him.
"Hello?"
"I thought it might be easier to talk. Emotions can get mixed up in texts."
His sweet voice soothes me, and all of that built-up tension and anxiety in my body vanish at the sound of it.
"Maybe we should talk when you get home. I texted you because I've felt like complete and utter shit since you left my house. I should've handled things differently."
I should've invited him in, so we could have a real conversation, and I definitely shouldn't have sucker punched him with what I said to the paparazzi.
"That's *months away.* I can't be unsure about us for that long. I thought every shot I had with you was gone until I got that text. You sending me that proves you don't want us to be over."
"You're right. I can't pull away from you, but you're in an entirely different country and time zone than I am. That's a problem."
"And? We have phones. We have the internet. I can book a

private plane for either one of us in minutes. We don't have to send a raven to talk to each other."

"I know."

"I miss you, and it's killing me, not talking to you. Your first day of school is tomorrow, and I haven't even been able to see how you're feeling about it."

"Let's take it slow. We'll consider ourselves friends right now, okay? But I promise we'll try when you get back."

"Friends who have phone sex and send naked pics?"

I laugh. "Possibly."

44

Knox

"So, Rose finally reached out?" Mason asks on the phone.

"Yeah."

I've been keeping him updated on the whole situation with Rose, and he's trying to help me stay in a positive mood and keep my hopes up. She's been texting me back and forth regularly for the past week since our conversation on the phone, but we still haven't gotten back to where we were before.

We're both holding back in fear of it not working out now. I don't want to dive in too fast and have her leave me underwater if she changes her mind again.

"And she's come to her senses?"

"I still haven't figured that out yet. The woman is confusing as hell. She said she wants to wait until I finish the tour before jumping into a relationship."

"What does that mean? I like the girl, and I want to see you happy, but that's kind of fucked up."

"I don't know. The back-and-forth shit, I can't handle it. She's playing the same games Stella did. She wanted me, then she wanted space, and then when she saw I was hanging out with other women, she wanted me again. I swear, it's like whenever I fall for a woman and develop real feelings for her, it's one who wants to fuck with my head and doesn't know what she wants."

"I'm sorry, brother. Do you want me to talk to her?"

"No. Nothing will make her more uncomfortable than my brother calling and trying to be all Dr. Phil or some shit."

"I understand. I thought it might help."

"I know, and that's why I love you, but I think, this one, I have to figure out on my own."

"I'll talk to Gretchen and see if she has any tips for you. Women think a lot differently than we do, bro. I'm not even kidding. When she goes into her psychoanalyzing bullshit and tries to do studies on me, I run for the hills."

I laugh. "You love her psychoanalyzing bullshit."

Gretchen is in medical school to be a psychiatrist.

"You're right, but just don't tell her that. I have class in thirty minutes. Good luck on your show tonight and everything else."

"Thanks, brother. Have fun in class."

He stops me before I hang up. "And you know what this is the best time for?"

"I know."

"Get it done."

I hang up and pull my notebook from my luggage.

Then, I start to morph my feelings into my next song.

"I love Thailand, man," Spencer says, walking into the living room of my suite.

I finished my show an hour ago and just got out of the shower. Some of my friends flew into Thailand for my show, so I feel like I owe them an enjoyable time tonight.

"Every time I come here, I beg Yasmine to quit modeling, so we can sell everything and move here."

I pull my shirt on and run my hand through my wet hair. "I have a feeling that Yasmine isn't going for it."

"Nope. She's too much into her work to even think about settling down somewhere, which I don't understand. She doesn't have to work. I have plenty of money to provide for us for the rest of our lives."

Spencer created a social network app that blew up. He makes a killing in ads and has even had billion-dollar offers to purchase it, but he declines every one. He doesn't want to be a sellout. He has millions, and he's dating one of the biggest supermodels in the world, who is also cool as shit, so I don't blame him for wanting to settle down off the grid.

I sit down and watch him go to the minibar to make a drink. He drains it and then stares straight at me. I can tell he's about to say something I don't want to hear.

"What the hell is going on?" I ask.

"You're not going to like this, and I want to point out in advance that it's not my fault, but a few extra people decided to tag along on this trip to see your show. I tried to stop it, and so did Yasmine, but everyone accused us of being assholes, taking your side."

My shoulders curl forward in dread. "Spit it out and don't bullshit me."

"Stella is here."

"Motherfucker," I hiss.

We hang out in the same crowds, so I knew occasionally running into her would happen, but I wasn't counting on her flying thousands of miles to see me.

"She decided to come last minute with Jasmine." Jasmine is Yasmine's sister. "We couldn't exactly kick them off the jet, and they had already purchased tickets to your show, so we couldn't stop that either."

I groan, tipping my head down and shaking it. "This isn't going to look good, man."

He plops down in the chair next to me and drops the hand holding his drink in the middle of his legs. "Look, she wants to talk to you or some shit. I don't know if you're involved with anyone at the moment, but she kept blabbering about still having feelings for you." He grunts. "It sure put a damper on the whole plane ride."

Spencer is another one who texted me the video of Rose saying we were done. He hasn't brought it up since, most likely trying not to drag up bad memories if we broke up, so I haven't had a chance to tell him I've talked to her.

"It's cool. Thanks for having my back. I'm trying to work shit out with Rose, so Stella showing up here is the last damn thing I need. It's going to look bad. If you and the gang are here, they'll know we're going out, and paparazzi will be waiting to find something to take a picture of."

"Don't bail on us. I've been waiting to go out with my boy for months, and Thailand is our motherfucking city."

"I'm not bailing, but I need to make sure I keep my distance."

He pulls out his phone. "I'm texting Yasmine right now to let Stella know you're not interested in anything other than a simple hello."

I snort. "You must not know Stella."

I look up when I hear a knock on the door.

"Yeah … I told George to let them up."

"*Fuck.* Let the ex-girlfriend dodging begin."

I need to figure out a way to leave the club without looking ungrateful that Spencer and my friends chartered a private jet to come see me.

I love hanging out with my friends, especially when I'm in a different country where I don't know anyone, but Stella being here is putting a huge buzzkill on the occasion. I'm trying to stay as far away from her as I can, but she's inching closer and closer as the night gets later.

I'm nursing a beer and watching everyone have a great time around me when I notice her coming my way.

Shit.

I tense. Whatever is about to happen most likely isn't going to be a brief and friendly conversation. I see the determination in her eyes.

"Your show was amazing," she says, sitting down next to me on the couch in the back of the club. "It reminded me of how I used to go to every show of yours and watch you perform. The love you have for your art is beautiful. I forgot how much I enjoyed it."

"Thank you," I reply.

The music is blaring around us, and she leans in closer so we can hear each other better. "Remember last time we were in Thailand?"

I nod, and she lets out a light laugh.

"I told you it was my dream vacation, and then you took me for my twenty-first birthday. I'll never forget that. It's the best birthday I've ever had."

"I'm glad you had fun." I'm trying not to act like an asshole. Maybe her intentions aren't bad.

"Do you miss me?"

"I'm happy with where I am right now."

"You didn't answer the question."

"How do I answer your question without sounding like a dick? I loved you, and there will probably always be a special place in my heart for you, Stella, but that's it—a place in my heart for the first girl I loved, but not the only one. I don't miss you because what we had wasn't meant to last forever, and we both know that. We outgrew each other. I'll always consider you a friend. That's it."

"You don't mean that," she whispers, her lower lip trembling. She starts shaking her head over and over again. "Tell me you don't mean that."

"I do. I don't want to hurt your feelings, but if you came here with the hopes of us getting back together, it's not going to happen. I want to be up-front about that right now."

"Let's try again," she pleads, scooting in closer.

"I'm sorry, but that's not what I want."

"We have history that we can't throw away. We've dated other people, but we always end up back together. Let's stop wasting our time and try again. We're older now."

Stella is upset that I'm moving on with someone else. Sure, I've dated and fucked other women, but they were never anything serious like I have with Rose. I've never felt something as strong as I feel for her. And Stella knows it, which is why she's here. She knows when I love and care about someone because, at one time, she was who I loved.

"Thank you for coming to my show, but that's not what I want."

"*Please*." Tears are streaming down her face, causing her mascara to run with them. "I hate seeing you with someone else."

"I hope you find someone to make you happy."

I slide away from her and go on the hunt for Spencer to let him know I'm taking off. He and Yasmine are staying in my suite, and I want to make it clear that under no circumstances can Stella crash with them. I don't care if I have to pay to get her a separate room myself.

I'm almost to him when I notice a guy with a camera phone in his hand, tracking my every move.

Motherfucker.

This isn't going to look good.

I call Rose as soon as I get back to my room. It goes to voice mail.

It's one in the morning here and eleven in the morning there, so there's no way she's still sleeping. She's an early riser.

I hit her name again.

No answer.

I hit the text icon.

Me: Call me as soon as you can.

45

Rose

"He keeps calling me," I tell Claire. My phone starts ringing again. I hit the Ignore button. It beeps. "And texting."

This is why I wanted to keep my distance from a relationship with Knox. Even though we agreed to take things slow and not make anything serious, it still hurt when I saw the picture of him and Stella in the club. They are in Thailand together—a woman does not fly that far to see a man, uninvited. This is what I was afraid of, and it's killing me more than I expected.

"Answer your phone and quit acting childish," Claire demands. "Listen to what the man has to say."

"You mean, listen to his excuses? No, thank you. I don't want to interrupt him and his girlfriend."

"He's trying to call *you*, his girlfriend, so obviously, you wouldn't be interrupting shit."

I take one of my pillows next to me and throw it across the room in an attempt to deflate some of the anger rising through me. "Why would he do this? He knows I'm stressed out about classes and about him hanging out in clubs with women."

My phone starts ringing again. Claire reaches across the bed, snags it from me, and answers before I have the chance to stop her.

"Hey, Knox," she says. "Yes, she's right here. Hold, please."

I shoot her a dirty look when she hands the phone off to me.

Listen to what he has to say, she mouths before jumping off my bed and leaving the room.

At least she's giving me some privacy, which is surprising.

My chest tightens when I put the phone to my ear. "Hello?"

"You've seen them, haven't you?" Knox rushes out.

"Are you asking if I saw the pictures of you cuddled up with your ex-girlfriend in some club?"

"Hold up. I wasn't cuddled up with her."

"My bad. I'll correct myself. Are you asking me if I've seen the pictures of you *hanging out* in some club with your ex-girlfriend in a country I'm sure she doesn't frequent often, which means she came there for you?"

"It doesn't look good, I know, but let me explain."

"Fine, explain away."

"Some friends came to see the show, and Stella decided to tag along. I didn't know she was coming until they were already here. I made it clear to her that she and I are completely over. You know I'm in love with you and I don't want anyone else. If I was fucking around with her, would I be calling you right now?"

I stay quiet.

"Do you want to FaceTime, so you know I'm here alone, wishing you were next to me?"

"That's not necessary."

"Then, tell me you believe me. Tell me you trust me."

I want to believe him, but that still doesn't change the fact that there's some doubt lingering in my thoughts. I watched my dad pull this move time and time again when he had girlfriends. He'd talk to them on the phone, assuring them he was alone and going to bed when, instead, he'd have another girl over as soon as he hung up.

"You don't believe me," he says softly. "Why?"

I need to be honest with him. "You have these gorgeous and rich women there, wanting to be with you. I'm this broke girl with pink stripes in my hair, who's crashing at her friend's house while attending college. That's pretty self-explanatory. It was a summer fling, Knox, but we're too opposite. It'll never work. Maybe temporarily, but not permanently."

"Sunshine, that doesn't mean I don't like pink streaks and snarky attitudes. I'll take the pink hair over everything and everyone. It's much more authentic, fun, and satisfying. I can promise you, you're not some fling. You're my forever."

"I don't want to be that jealous girl," I whisper.

"Then, don't be. You have no reason to be jealous of anyone. You're the only one getting my attention. *You.* Do you hear me? *Trust me, Rose.*"

"The problem is that I can't."

I'm still trying to erase the images I saw of him and Stella from my mind, but it's impossible. I'm trying to fight off ideas of them messing around, but I'm losing the battle. No matter what, my heart will always remember what's happened in the past.

"Don't … don't do this," he begs. "You promised. You swore to me that you'd try."

"I did try!"

I pull my phone away when he tries to FaceTime me and hit the Reject button. I can't do that right now. It'll kill me.

"You won't even look at me?" he yells.

I stay silent, and he lets out a sharp laugh.

"You're going to throw everything that we've built away because of some ridiculous fear of another woman getting my attention? If I'm interested in fucking other women, why do I call you every single damn night? Why am I always checking in, so you know you're the only one on my mind?"

"But she's there! Last time I checked, Thailand is more than a hop and a skip away. She came there to see you!"

"And? I didn't ask her to. You're going to be around men daily in your classes. Do I wonder about you connecting with any of them? Yes, the idea has crossed my mind, but I trust you. I wish you could do the same with me."

I'm crumbling inside, but I keep my voice straight. "You focus on your tour right now, and I'll focus on school. We'll talk when you get back, okay?"

"You're making a mistake."

"Space is good for relationships sometimes."

"No, space is a bullshit excuse for someone being weak and scared."

"Then, maybe I'm weak," I croak out.

"You promised! You promised you'd fight for us."

"Some promises can't be kept."

He scoffs, and his voice turns cold. "Fine, you win, Rose. All promises are out the door. It's over. We're over.."

The line goes dead.

I stare down at my phone, debating with myself on whether I should call him back as I wipe away the tears running down my face.

I feel like a heartless bitch right now, but it's for the best. I can't be blamed for protecting my heart.

"Fucking coward!"

I look up at the sound of Claire's voice to see her standing in the doorway with a look of annoyance on her face.

I hold my hand up, not wanting to hear her make me feel even worse. "I told you to stay out of my business."

"You keep pushing him away like this, and one day, he won't come back."

"Good."

Her eyes narrow in on me at my response.

"I have too much shit to focus on right now than some silly relationship that'll never last."

"Coward," she spits out again. "It's not a silly relationship if you love each other."

I throw my hands up. "How do you think I feel, Claire? I'm about to go to classes, and all I can think about is him hanging out with her. A girl doesn't fly across the country to see an ex who doesn't want anything to do with her."

"Did he know she was coming?"

"He said no."

"Then, there's your answer, genius. He didn't invite her."

"She posted a throwback picture of them kissing on Instagram *the same night*. How do you explain that?"

"She's obviously trying to get in your head. Shit, I'd do the same thing if Dixon started dating someone else. It's what you do when you're desperate. She knew she could get to you that way."

"It doesn't matter. He pretty much said he was done and hung up on me."

"Whatever. You're going to be the one who regrets it in the long run."

46

Rose

Ten Weeks Later

The sound of my phone ringing wakes me up.

I blindly slide my hand around on the nightstand in the dark until I find it.

It's three in the morning, and Knox's name is blinking across the screen, surprising the hell out of me. We haven't talked since the Stella situation in Thailand.

I quickly hit the Answer button. "Hello? Is everything okay?"

Phone calls this late are never good. They're either drunk dials or tragedies.

I'm praying for a drunk dial.

"No," he murmurs, blowing out a deep breath.

"What's going on?"

"I had a break in my schedule for a few days and decided to come home. I wanted to sleep in my own bed, shower in my bathroom, and all that good shit. I get here after an exhausting ten-hour flight and walk into a complete nightmare. I wasn't sure who else to call but you. You're the only person I know that's on my team and gives a shit about *my* side of the story."

I gulp in air. "What happened?"

"Nate decided to turn my house into the fucking Playboy mansion. It's completely trashed. The police are here now, and I can't even begin to list all of the shit that's missing." He pauses. "My guitar is gone, Rose."

My chest caves in, and my eyes start to well up at the sound of hurt in his voice. I'm positive he's holding back his own tears. His most prized possession—his guitar—has been taken from him. Sadness shatters through me. I want to kick Nate's ass myself.

I flip on my lamp, hop out of bed, and start searching for something to throw on. "Do you want me to come there?"

"Don't worry about it. It's late. I feel bad for even waking you up."

"I'm on my way."

He can't go through this alone. I won't let him.

"Rose …"

"I'm on my way."

"Okay."

The relief in his answer tells me I'm doing the right thing.

Cop cars are blocking access in front of his gate when I pull up. I'm shuffling through the glove compartment in search of the gate opener when an officer knocks on my window.

"Sorry, miss," he says when I roll it down. "This is a private drive."

"I'm here to see Knox," I tell him.

He chuckles, giving me a condescending look. "You and every other pap and fan around here."

"I'm not a pap or a fan. I'm his assistant."

He's still giving me that look, like it's not the first time he's heard someone say that.

I grab my phone from the cupholder. "Hold on. I'll call him right now."

He crosses his arms and nods while I hit Knox's name. I tell him the situation when he answers, and he says he'll handle it.

"The girl in the Jeep is his assistant," are the words that come through the officer's radio. "Please have everyone make a note that Rose Graves is always allowed on the premises."

"Sorry, only trying to do my job," he says. "Especially given the situation why we're here. I want to give you a heads-up—it's not pretty."

"I understand. Better safe than sorry."

He tips his head down and gestures for me to go forward when the gate opens.

Knox is waiting for me in the driveway and meets me when I get out of the Jeep. I can see the pain on his face. The loss. The hurt. The fight with himself on how he's going to deal with Nate. He was only trying to help someone and ended up getting screwed over.

He moves in closer, trapping me between him and the car, and his eyes meet mine. "I kicked him out," he whispers. "Am I wrong for that? I threw all of his shit out of my house and told him he's never welcome here again."

I reach down and grab his hand. "I would've done the same thing. He needs to give you space. He took advantage of you."

We stand there, silently staring at each other for a few minutes until we hear the click of a camera.

"Fuck," he hisses, scrubbing his hand over his face. "They're like cockroaches. They always figure out a way to slither in somewhere and take a picture."

I keep my head down when he snags my hand in his and leads me through the front door and into the house. My stomach sinks when I take a look around.

The place looks like it's been dragged through hell. There are marks, holes, and graffiti all over the walls, and I swear I see splatters of blood. The floors look like they've had almost every drink imaginable spilled on them, and half of the furniture is either ruined or missing.

He throws his arms out. "Welcome to the home I've worked my ass off for."

"We'll get it fixed," I say, trying my hardest to sound reassuring.

He picks up a vase and throws it across the room. It hits a wall and shatters to pieces. "That'll take months! I don't want to look at this. The sight of it makes me fucking sick. This doesn't feel like my home anymore. I feel violated in here."

"Then, come stay with me, and I'll talk with Thomas about getting this cleaned up." The words leave my mouth before I even think about what I'm saying.

I can tell he's just as surprised as I am when he turns around to look at me.

"You don't have to do that. I can stay at a hotel."

"You're right. I don't have to, but I want to. You've been staying in hotels and the bus for months. You came here to sleep in your own bed …"

"That's not happening again. Who knows what venereal diseases it's infested with? I had the door locked, but that doesn't stop thieves. I'm half-tempted to burn this thing to the ground."

"It might not be as comfortable as yours, but let me tell you, my bed is pretty damn comfy. Claire's parents are big on expensive furniture."

He raises a brow. "You sure about this?"

"Absolutely. You'd do the same for me, if not more. Grab whatever you need."

My head is spinning when he loads his bag into the backseat. I've asked Thomas to return the Jeep numerous times, but he always says Knox will contact me when he gets back. I feel like a fraud, driving it around, but I have no other means of transportation and had no idea where to take it.

The ride is quiet on the way back to the condo. I hit the

brakes, waiting for the gate to open, and notice Knox powering down his phone.

"Not in the mood for calls tonight?" I ask.

"I probably won't be in the mood for calls for the rest of the week," he says, letting out an exhausted breath. "I don't even remember the last time I left this thing off for more than five minutes. I always seem to be connected, and for once, I want to get a break from it all."

"I get it."

When everything with my dad went down, reporters were blowing me up for stories, and everyone I went to school with wanted to get the scoop. I had to make the decision to either turn my phone off completely, which was difficult because I wanted to keep in touch with my dad and his attorneys, or change my number. So, I changed my number, which was a big lifesaver when the pictures of Knox and me went viral.

I turn off the ignition. "Claire is asleep," I tell him. "If we wake her up, you'll never get to bed because she'll be asking you twenty-one questions."

"So, don't say a word or trip into shit?"

"Exactly."

I switch on a light when we make it inside and turn around to look at him. *Follow me*, I mouth, walking upstairs.

He takes a look around when I shut my bedroom door behind us. "You know, I've never been inside here. I feel like you've seen every room in my home, but yours has been a big mystery to me. It's nice, seeing this side of your life."

I sweep my arms out in a circle. "Take a look around. Textbooks and my laptop are pretty much my life right now."

He rubs his forehead, laughing. "Oh, sunshine, there's more to you than textbooks."

I start to respond when something hits me. "Shit," I hiss. "We forgot your bag in the car."

"We did. Is it okay if I borrow something of yours to sleep in?"

"Sure," I answer around a laugh. "I have some of the best lingerie that will fit you perfectly. What are you, a B cup?"

He thrusts his chest out. "How did you know?"

I'm glad I'm taking his mind away from the house.

"Although anything in those drawers probably looks much better on you, I'll work with what I have."

I can't stop myself from licking my lips with excitement when he grabs the bottom of his T-shirt and drags it over his head. He's more in shape than he was before, the muscles in his chest more prominent, and my hands are itching to see if his skin feels the same.

"You cool with me taking my jeans off?" he asks, breaking me away from my thoughts.

I shrug. "It's nothing I haven't seen before."

"I'm sure you've missed the view."

"That's definitely one thing I've missed."

He raises a brow. "I'll have to keep that in mind."

I pull off the sweatshirt I had on over my pajama top and climb into bed. I look over at Knox while he steps out of his jeans. Exhaustion fills his face as he joins me and pulls the blankets over us.

He flips over to look at me. "Is it cool if we snuggle?"

I rest my head against the pillow. "You're pushing the limits tonight, aren't you?"

"It'll make a man feel better when he's down."

I fake an annoyed laugh and turn around. "*Fine.*"

He moves in closer and throws his arm over me, making me feel more comfortable in my bed than I ever have, and the heat of his body relaxes me.

"Thank you, sunshine," he whispers into my ear, tightening his hold like he never wants to let me go.

47

Knox

I wake up to an empty bed, and I'd think last night was a dream if the sheets didn't smell exactly like heaven. She still uses the same body lotion that reminds me of pineapples and lavender.

I crawl out of bed to head to the bathroom but stop myself and start getting dressed. I know she said Claire would be in freak-out mode if she saw me, so I'm hoping she's already left because I have to piss like a racehorse.

I duck down the hallway—thankful it's clear—and go into the bathroom. I walk down the stairs when I'm finished and find Rose in the kitchen.

"Morning, sunshine," I greet, moving into the room.

She has a pan on the stove and is cracking an egg into it.

She gives me the world's most gorgeous smile. "Good morning. How did you sleep?"

"Perfect actually. The best sleep I've had in weeks, but I was disappointed when I woke up in an empty bed."

"All of my classes are at the butt crack of dawn, so I can't sleep in anymore, even on the weekends. My body won't let me. It sucks, but I'm more productive now, so that's a plus."

"It's the opposite for me. My days are short, my nights long." I point to the stove. "Do you need any help?"

"Nope." She nods toward the stool at the island. "You sit down right there."

"You sure?"

"Positive."

I do as I was told.

"The tour seems to be doing well," she goes on. "Thomas said it's been nominated for numerous awards and you've even added more shows."

She's trying to steer away from talking about Nate destroying my house. I appreciate it because I'm not sure if I'm ready for that yet. I'm still trying to wrap my mind around the fact that my own family deceived me.

"Revenue- and review-wise, it's great, but it's been one of the most emotional journeys I've ever been on," I reply.

She scrunches her face up. "Why do you say that?"

I lean in, resting my elbows on the counter, and lock eyes with her. "You came into my life because of the tour, yet I lost you for the same reason. I came home to a destroyed house, and I've lost respect for the majority of the people in my family. I honestly feel like there's nothing for me to look forward to when it ends."

Her eyes dart down to the pan, and she moves back and forth on her feet, looking uncomfortable. "Some of those are an easy fix."

"The house, yes. The broken relationships and my guitar, not so much."

"We can have your team keep an eye out if someone tries selling your guitar or pawning it. I'll search for it every day, checking eBay, Craigslist, everywhere I can. We'll find it."

She uses a spatula to swipe up the egg, drops it onto a plate, and then hands it to me.

"How do I deserve you?" I ask, sighing. "Even if we're not together, how did I get so lucky to have you in my life?"

She pauses in the middle of cracking another egg and opens her mouth to respond … and then shuts it. Heat radiates in my chest as I keep my eyes on her face. It's still there—her love for me—and I want to drag it all out of her, so she can see it too.

"I think we're lucky to have each other," she whispers.

"Well, isn't this a surprise?!"

I turn around to find Claire strolling our way with a shit-eating grin on her face. An anguished groan comes from Rose.

"I see someone snuck in sometime during the night."

"It's a long story that no one wants to talk about right now," Rose immediately says, giving her friend a serious look.

The girl always has my back.

I look back at Claire. "My cousin trashed my house and pretty much let everyone rob me. So, I called Rose, and she offered to let me crash here. That okay with you?"

"Absolutely," Claire answers, the grin still on her face. "Stay as long as you'd like. Make yourself at home."

I shake my head. "I appreciate it, but I don't want to be a burden. I'll book a hotel for a few days until I can find something to rent temporarily. I'm selling that house. I don't even want to set foot in it again."

"You only have a few weeks left on tour, right?" Rose asks.

I nod. "Which means I need to buckle down and get my shit together."

"I can help out, look for places, and email them to you, so you can focus on your shows."

"You would do that?"

She smiles. "Of course. It's the least I can do for you paying my tuition."

"My mom has this bomb real estate agent," Claire says. "I'll ask her if she has anything on the market you might like. I can also get her to list your house?"

I nod. "That sounds great."

Claire walks over to the fridge and pulls out a bottle of water. "I'm headed to the beach to meet Dixon. He has a tournament today. You guys want to tag along?"

"Probably not," Rose answers. "I have a feeling all eyes will be on Knox, and Dixon might not appreciate that."

I nod in agreement. "Yeah, I think we're good. I need to relax for a bit. Tell Dixon we said good luck."

"I will," Claire says and then looks over at me. "Hopefully, you're still here when I get back. If not, fingers crossed I'll see you again soon."

We're relaxing on the couch post-breakfast, and Rose is spread across the length of it, resting her feet on my lap, watching TV.

I love this. It feels like we're back on the bus, having our Netflix binges, completely comfortable and happy around each other.

I grabbed my phone and powered it back on about ten minutes ago, and I'm replying to all the text messages from last night and this morning. I start to feel the frustration rising through me as I text back and then decide to quit, so I don't ruin my time with her.

I release a heavy sigh, toss my phone on the coffee table, and rub the back of my neck, shaking my head. Rose raises a questioning brow when I look over at her. I can tell now she wasn't watching TV—she was staring at me.

"Texts from my mom," I explain. "She thinks I overreacted with the whole Nate situation."

She grimaces. "Are you shitting me?"

"I wish I were, but according to her, family shouldn't turn their back on family."

She straightens up against the pillow behind her. "That seriously pisses me off. If anything, she's the one turning her back on you for not supporting your decision and for letting people take advantage of you, her son. Did you tell her about the guitar?"

"Sure did. Her response was that it's not like I can't buy another one."

"No disrespect, but fuck her."

I crack a smile. "You're incredible, you know that?"

"I'm incredible because I said fuck your family? I doubt those words have been described as amazing that often."

"You're amazing because you care about me and only me. You don't give two shits about my money, my fame, or opportunities. Shit, you could've quit school and had me take care of you, but you wanted to do it on your own. You want to be independent, and that's incredible. It makes me happy. It lets me know I can trust you."

She slips me a shy smile. "I'm glad to make you happy. You can always trust me. Don't ever forget that." She grabs her coffee mug, brings it to her lips, and lightly blows on it.

I shift around, feeling my cock get excited underneath my jeans as I remember how she used to wrap those pouty lips around it. "You keep doing that, sunshine, and I might have to make you happy and bend you over this couch."

Her nose wrinkles in confusion. She's so damn adorable. "If I keep doing what?"

"Blowing that coffee cup."

She rolls her eyes. "I'm not *blowing* this coffee cup. I'm blowing into it. What's up with you and being turned on by my reactions with food? Moaning when I take a bite of cake. Blowing on my coffee. I told you to see a doctor about it."

"Your *blowing* is what's turning me on. Stop doing it or do something about it."

She ignores my comment, takes a slow sip, and swallows it down. "Will you be honest with me?"

"Always."

"Have you ..." She hesitates. "Have you hooked up with anyone since me?"

"I haven't even touched anyone since you." I level my eyes on her. "Have you been with anyone else?"

Please say no. If the word yes *comes out of her lips, it'll crush me.* I know she's not mine anymore, but I feel like there are parts of her she's still letting me have.

I reach down to wrap my hand around her ankle and start massaging her foot.

She stays quiet, her curious eyes meeting mine. "If you haven't been with anyone … and I haven't been with anyone …"

I start to knead my knuckle into her heel.

"It sounds like it's been a while for the both of us."

My hand freezes, a smile dancing on my lips. "Sounds like a predicament with an easy fix."

I lean in closer, but her hand smacking into my chest stops me.

"Promise me one thing before we do this."

I raise a brow.

"We keep this casual, okay?"

I nod. "We keep this casual."

She moves, straddling my lap before I even finish my sentence, and circles her arms around my shoulders.

"I've missed you," she whispers. "I've missed this." She leans in and captures my lips with hers.

"You have no idea how much I've missed you," I say into her mouth before slipping my tongue inside.

She tastes just as sweet as I remember.

My hands trail down her sides, settling on the curves of her hips, while she slowly starts to grind against my hard-on. I push her dress up, dragging it over her head, and run my hands over the lace of her bra before removing it.

She sucks in a breath when I unravel her hair from the tie, watching the waves of color cascade across her chest, hitting right above her hard nipples. Her head drops back when I latch my lips around a pink bud and suck hard at the same time I start rubbing her over her panties.

The room grows hot as she tears my shirt off, throwing it to the ground, and I shiver when she runs her warm palms over my chest.

"Rise up for me," I say.

She whines in argument when I guide her toward the end of the couch.

"Don't worry. You won't be whining long."

"Good. Now, fuck me, Knox Rivers," she rasps out. "I need you."

"Not as much as I need you."

I settle on my knees behind her, bend her over the arm of the couch, slap her ass, and rip off her panties. Goose bumps traveling up her skin when I slip my hand between her thighs and spread them apart. She's drenched for me, dripping down my fingers.

Her back arches, and she starts to buck against my hand when I slide two fingers in, curling them into her heat and hitting all of her favorite spots.

"Have you touched yourself, thinking about me, since you left?" I ask, my voice rough.

"Knox," she moans out.

I pull my fingers out of her and play with her clit, waiting for an answer. "Answer me or no more."

"Yes!" she gasps out. "I have—so many times. It's always you."

"Fuck yeah." I shove my fingers back in, working her harder until her orgasm shatters through her.

Her panting and the noise of me unbuckling my pants are the only sounds in the room. My cock springs forth, and I stroke it a few times after pulling down my jeans and boxers. I nudge it between her legs, moving it back and forth along her folds, teasing her until she's writhing underneath me in need.

"You're all I think about. I jack off to the memory of you every day," I say.

She gasps when I fill her up.

"Only you, sunshine."

I push my chest into her back, moving my hand around to play with her tit, and pump in and out of her.

She intoxicates me—the most powerful drug I can take, the strongest drink I can consume.

There's nothing casual about this.

And I'm going to prove that to her.

"You're going to stay the weekend, right?" Rose asks when I wrap a towel around her after stepping out of the shower.

We decided to clean up after our *casual sex* with some shower sex.

"Why?" I ask. "Would you like me to?"

She focuses on getting dressed, not looking over at me. "I mean … I don't have any plans this weekend, just some homework, so it would be completely fine."

I grab her around the waist and pull her into my side. "You missed me, didn't you?"

She squirms, trying to fight me off as I tickle her side. "No! Stop!"

"You did."

She pushes away from me, laughing. "Fine. *Yes*, I did miss you."

I drop my towel and grab my pants. "Thanks for the invite, sunshine, but I think I'll be leaving now."

Her jaw drops. "What?"

"Can I borrow the Jeep, or do I need to call a car?"

She stares at me, unblinking, and stutters for words.

I bend down and kiss her forehead. "Of course I'm staying. I'll stay as long as you let me."

Rose slams the fridge shut and leans back against it. "If we go out in public, there's no doubt we'll be noticed, and they'll be drilling you on details about your house."

"Then, what are we going to do? Starve to death?" I question. "I'm going to die over here. We can order in or have George bring us something."

We've been hanging out all day, and my stomach is grumbling as it starts to get dark outside. Rose was planning on going grocery shopping today, so we're running low on food. Good thing California has delivery places out the ass.

"We can do the whole snowed-in kind of thing without the actual snow?"

She chuckles. "Sounds good to me."

"Just don't get sick of me and throw my ass out in the fake cold."

"We were together every day for almost three months. I don't think I could ever get tired of you."

"I like hearing you say that. I thought you'd given up on me."

Her eyes soften. "I didn't give up on you."

"Sure seemed like it. I mean, you said you couldn't do a relationship with me anymore. If that's not giving up, I don't know what is."

I'm giving this conversation a one-eighty—taking it from a small *what's for dinner* talk to a *what's going on in our relationship* one.

Her shoulders slouch. "You have to see where I'm coming from. I saw the things my father did on tour. I saw the women who threw themselves at him. At Adam. I even saw it when I was on tour with you. If we were together, I'd spend all my time worrying about you caving in to their advances. I can't stress about that and try to get my degree."

I raise my voice, shoving my finger into my chest. "I'm not your father. I'm not Adam. I'm *me*, and you know me. I'm not that man. You saw me on tour. I can do commitment. How long were we together before we had sex? Was I fucking other women while I waited? No. I can go without sex. It might be unfortunate, but it's not the end of the world. Have you heard of masturbation?" I stop and chuckle. "Of course you have. You have your fair amount of vibrators."

"So hysterical." She rolls her eyes and pushes off the fridge. "I understand where you're coming from. Feed me, and we can talk about this more, but you know I'm cranky on an empty stomach."

"Is there hope?" I have to ask, or it'll kill me.

"There's most definitely hope."

I stay the entire weekend with Rose. George did a grocery store run, so we cooked dinner together, found a new Netflix show to binge-watch, and made love every night and morning. Claire stayed at Dixon's to give us privacy.

I don't want to leave when it's time to go.

I want to stay in this imaginary world, where we're both normal people, living a normal life.

I grab her hands in mine. "Tell me this good-bye is going to be better than the last one. Promise me I'll see you again."

She tightens her hands around mine. "I promise."

48

Rose

"Do you want to hear a super-awesome story?" Claire asks, strolling into my room and flopping down on my bed.

"Nope," I answer.

Whatever it is, I doubt it's going to be *super awesome* and more along the lines of some lecture about Knox.

George picked him up early this morning to catch their jet. Knox said he'd text me when he landed, but I haven't heard from him yet. The flight is around fourteen hours, so I'm not too worried.

Him staying this weekend pulled at my emotional strings, showing me how much I truly missed and cared about him.

"So, I walked out of my bedroom the other morning, and this gorgeous man was sitting in the kitchen. Who was this good-looking man, you ask?" Claire goes on in excitement.

"Nope, sure didn't," I grumble.

"It's Knox Rivers, and he stayed with my roomie *the entire weekend.*"

I've been dreading having this conversation with her. She's dialed down on the whole *you made a mistake, breaking up with Knox* speech, but now, I'm sure it's going to be a daily thing again.

"He needed somewhere to stay. I wanted to help a friend out."

She snorts. "You are so generous. You weren't only helping him with a place to stay either. You were fucking him as a friendly gesture too?"

"Exactly." I start to focus on my notes. Well, I act like I'm focusing on my notes.

"One minute, you want him to stay away from you, and the next, you want him inside of you. Make up your mind before he starts making out with someone else."

I shrug and keep my eyes down. "If he does, he does. I can't stop that."

I look up when she pushes my shoulder.

"Uh, yeah, you can, dumbass. You can date him."

"I have to get to class." I get up, grab my laptop to slide it into its case and then into my book bag, and throw it over my shoulder. "Like always, it was a pleasure, chatting with you about Knox."

"I'm sure it wasn't as great as the pleasure he was giving you last night," she yells to my back as I'm walking out. She laughs when I throw my hand up and flip her off.

I have to get my mind off Knox and back to my real life now.

Knox: The real estate agent Claire hooked me up with sent me some listings. I'll be home next week. Want to check them out with me?

It's been two and a half weeks since Knox left my condo, and it's been hard, staying in touch with our crazy schedules. He's been busy with his shows, and I've been swamped with schoolwork and finals approaching.

Me: I'd love to.

"Who are you texting?" Claire asks. She arches a brow and pops a fry in her mouth while waiting for my answer.

I set my phone down on the table at our favorite lunch spot and sigh. "None of your business, *Mom*."

She scrapes her hands together and gives me a serious look. "Stop fucking with his head, Rose."

"You don't even know who I'm talking to. It could be my dad."

"Unless your dad illegally had a cell phone smuggled through someone's asshole into his prison cell, I know that's a lie."

"He needs a friend to look at houses with. He and his mom still aren't on speaking terms, and his brother is in Texas. I figure it's the least I can do for everything he's done for me."

"No, what that man needs is for you to get your head out of your ass and be his girlfriend."

"My head isn't in my ass. It's in my finals and how I have to pass them."

"I wasn't aware you couldn't have a boyfriend *and* pass a test. You can multitask. I've seen you straighten your hair and paint your fingernails at the same time. *And* did you know that happy people perform better on tests?"

"Drop the whole Knox thing, okay? I'll talk to him when he gets in town. I promise."

"Holy mother of all hotness and romance," Claire screams, barging into my room. She jumps up and down in excitement, squealing like a child.

"What in the world are you yelling about over there, psycho?" I ask.

"You have to see this … or listen to this, to be more precise."

"Okay," I drawl out.

She grabs her phone, hits a button on her screen, and turns up the volume.

Knox's voice flows from the speaker, and Claire starts dancing in place.

She's afraid to open up,
Hiding behind a broken mask, afraid to be up-front,
But I can see through her.
I can see the sunshine through the rain.
With one touch, she lets me have my way,
Giving me only a sliver of her until it turns dawn.
I call this our secret of the day.
Every piece of her I uncover takes my breath away.
Open up, sunshine. Come my way,
As we uncover our secret of the day …

She's a rose.
I'm her thorn.
One a symbol of love and the other of sin.
But without one, the other wouldn't exist.
She blushes pink when I whisper in her ear.
I tell her what she needs to hear.
That my secret of the day is that I can't live without her.
And never forget that just like a thorn does the rose, I'll always
protect her.

Thorns and roses.
We're bound and tied.
Please don't run and hide.

You are my forever, sunshine.

A buzz shoots through me, kind of like when I drink too many energy drinks, but it's a Knox high. I'm drunk on him, transfixed with his every word as I keep listening to the song that I know is about me.

"Sunshine?" Claire says. "This song is *so* about you."

I wave off her comment. "You don't know that."

"He's smart. I'll give him that. He's winning you back little by little, easing himself back into your life."

"We'll see."

She replays the song and starts moving her hips to the beat. A few seconds later, we're both singing along to the words.

She holds her arms out. "Come on! Let's dance to the song you were the muse for!"

We dance until the song ends, and Claire insists I text Knox.

Me: New song?

She replays the song, and my phone beeps with a reply.

Knox: You listen to it yet?

Me: Yep! Claire has it on repeat and is
throwing a dance party in my bedroom.

Knox: Tell me you joined her?

Me: Sure did. It's beautiful.

Knox: I had the best inspiration.

"You're blushing. Blushing is a good sign," Claire says, pulling me out of my conversation.

"I'm overheated from dancing."
"Whatever."
We break out in dance again.

49

Knox

"The tour is over. How do you feel?" Thomas asks.

I arrived back in the city last night after my final stop of the tour in Latin America. Thomas picked me up and is letting me stay in his guesthouse until I find a new place here. I haven't been back to the house that Nate trashed, but according to my new assistant, Anna, all of my belongings have been cleared out, and someone has already put an offer in on it.

"Exhausted. Eighty performances in six months in I don't know how many countries drain you."

"People might give you shit, but you're a hard worker. The tour is getting fantastic reviews. Now, we need to get you working on a new album. 'Thorns and Roses' is blowing up the charts. Women are loving the romantic side of you, and Anna says you've been writing a lot on the road."

"I already have studio time scheduled. But first things first. I have to find a place to live."

"You can stay here for as long as you'd like."

"I appreciate it. I'm meeting with my realtor in about an hour, so hopefully, she has some good shit lined up for me."

"You want me to come along?"

"I'm picking up Rose, and she's coming with me."

His brows bump together. "Rose?"

I nod.

"Interesting."

"Why is that interesting?"

"According to her father, she's seeing a new man, and he's about to propose."

My back straightens, and I feel all the color draining from my face. "What?"

Thomas laughs and pats me on the back. "I'm fucking with you. I like you two together. She keeps you grounded, so make things right with her now that you're home for a while."

"Trust me, I'm trying."

Me: I'm five minutes out. You ready?

Rose: Yep! I'll be waiting outside.

She walks to my car and opens the passenger door as soon as I pull up.

"Hey, stranger," I greet, giving her a smile.

"Hey," she says. She's acting shy … like the last time I saw her, I wasn't eating her pussy. She folds her hands in her lap. "So, what are we going to be looking at today?"

"The realtor sent me pictures of a few homes, but there's one I think might be the winner. I'm having her show us it first, and then we'll go from there."

"Sounds good to me."

I put the car in reverse, back out of the drive, and head through the gate. "How did your finals go?" I ask, turning out of her neighborhood. "You didn't fail, did you?"

She laughs. "No, thank God. I did pretty well and took

some extra credits this semester, so I won't have to take on such a heavy course load this coming semester."

"Good. You'll have more time to hang out with me."

She grins. "I guess so."

The house we're looking at is only a ten-minute drive, and the realtor, Debbie, is already there. She jumps out of her red Mercedes when I pull up and struts over to us in her black heels.

"Knox," she says, hand shooting out my way. "It's nice to finally meet you."

I shake her hand, giving her a smile, and her attention then moves to Rose.

"And you must be Rose. Knox says he can't buy a house until you see it first."

"That's right," I say as Rose gives me a strange look.

"You're both going to love this place," Debbie says.

We follow her up the walk and into the home.

"Your assistant said your style was modern. This is twelve thousand square feet. Price is a little over eight million, so we're in budget, and it also has a guesthouse."

"Let's see if the pictures did it justice," I say.

If the place looks anything like I saw online, this will be my next home. It's nothing like my last one, which was a total bachelor pad. This one is homier and more settled down. I won't be throwing any wild-ass parties here. I've learned my lesson of trusting people around my shit.

Debbie gives us the tour, and I can tell Rose loves it.

"What do you think?" I ask her when Debbie leaves the room to take a phone call, but I'm pretty sure it's to give us time to talk.

Rose takes a look around. "I think it's absolutely breathtaking."

I smirk. "Beautiful enough that you'd want to live here?"

Her blue eyes narrow in on me. "If you're seriously trying to hint that you're giving me this house or something ridiculous along those lines, I'm telling you no right now, and there's no changing my mind."

"That's not what I'm hinting at. What do you think about staying in the guesthouse? It'd be perfect for you."

"Why? I already have a place with Claire."

"You'll have more privacy here and a place of your own. The guesthouse is just as beautiful as this home with a living room, a full kitchen, and a kick-ass master suite with an awesome bathroom."

Her hesitation is evident, so I move on to reason number two on the list I had lined up for this moment.

"It would also help me—give me peace of mind. If you're here when I'm gone, I know it'll be taken care of. You won't pull a Nate on me, and my mom won't try to get another one of my family members to move in, so I can take care of them."

She's still giving me that nervous look.

"You don't have to give me an answer right now. Think about it and then let me know, okay?"

She bites into the edge of her pink lip and nods. "Okay."

"Final thoughts?" Debbie asks, interrupting us as she comes back into the room with her hands thrown out and a bright smile on her face.

I glance over at Rose, and she nods.

"I think we'll take it," I answer.

Both Rose and Debbie pick up on my choice of words. *We'll take it.*

Debbie claps her hands in excitement that she's about to get a nice little commission check. "Perfect. I'll make an offer on it today."

I shake Debbie's hand when we make it back outside, and we tell her good-bye. Rose slides back into my car after I open up the door for her.

"You hungry?" I ask when I get into the driver's seat.

"Starving actually. I planned on making lunch before you picked me up but decided against it when I realized Claire was waiting for me to come out of my bedroom, so she could give me instructions on what to say to you today."

"She's on Team Knox, isn't she?"

"She's definitely on Team Knox."

"I knew I liked her."

I grab my phone and text Anna to set up lunch plans somewhere we can go without having cameras in our faces. I've had enough radio and TV interviews to last me for the next few months, and I don't want them bringing up Nate trashing my house.

I pull into the back entrance to the Italian restaurant and park the car. I get out, open her door, and then lead her into the building. The chef is waiting and takes us to a table in a vacant room.

"I haven't been to this place in forever," Rose says, sitting down. "It's one of my favorites. My dad and I used to come here all the time, but it's a little too overpriced for my budget now."

I smile and make a mental note to thank Anna for making a good decision. "So, how's the new job going?"

Thomas mentioned that Rose has been doing some light work for him when she's not busy with classes.

"It's fine. Thomas works around my schedule, which is nice. I'm also doing my community service at the city's social work office, and they told me I have a job lined up as soon as I get my degree."

I love the way her face lights up at the mention of her new career starting.

"That's awesome. I'm excited for you."

Would I rather her get her degree and work for me? Absolutely. But I can't ask her to give up her passion because I know what it feels like to love what you do.

"And it's all thanks to you. Thank you for helping with my tuition."

"If you thank me again, I'm going to bend you over this

table and spank you. It's not all thanks to me. It's all thanks to you and your hard work."

We keep the rest of the conversation light and catch up on what's going on in our lives until we finish our lunch and get back in the car. When I pull in front of the condo, I stop her before she gets out.

"I'm having a Christmas party for the kids at the hospital on Saturday. Come with?" I ask.

She smiles, nodding. "Text me the details, and I'll be there."

50

Rose

I collapse onto my bed and let out a long sigh. I couldn't have had a better day with Knox at the children's hospital. We handed out gifts and ate too much candy and cookies, and Knox sang every Christmas song known to man. I didn't want to leave.

There's something about making other people feel better that lightens your mood and brightens your day. My problems seem so insignificant. Being there today told me I'm doing the right thing with my life.

Knox sits on the edge of my bed with his intense eyes pinned on me.

"What are your intentions with me?" I ask.

What Claire said has been on my mind.

Does Knox have ulterior motives?

He situates himself so that we're facing each other. "I'm not sure if you want me to be honest with you."

"I certainly don't want you to lie to me."

He clears his throat. "You cage yourself up and lock me out whenever I'm honest with you. You put a restraint against your heart in fear. I don't want you to pull away."

I flinch at his response. "I don't cage myself up. I'm a *realist.* You can't blame me for not wanting to live in some fairy tale."

"If you're such a realist, then be real and follow your heart. *Realists* don't run from shit. They face the truth. They face *reality*. So, until you decide to do that, you're a pessimist."

I cross my legs and straighten up my back. "Then, let's face the truth. *Secret of the day.* Tell me what's on your mind."

"My intentions are to win you back," he confesses, no bull-shit. "I'm fighting to prove to you that you want it as much as I do. You know I'm in love with you—deeply, madly, and passion-ately in love with you—and I know you love me. Sometimes, it takes longer for your mind to open up and listen to your heart. I understand you want space, but my intentions are to let you have your space, but share it with me at the same time. You saw … *you felt* … how happy we were on tour. We can do that again. We can have a great and happy life together."

I open my mouth, ready to keep building up those walls, but he stops me.

"I'm still telling you my secret," he goes on. "I'm off tour. You're close to graduating. Nothing is holding us back, except for you making up your mind on whether you want to live life happy or scared."

Damn, that was some secret.

There's no way telling him I'm afraid of the dark will top that.

I rake a hand through my hair. "You're still going to be trav-eling," I start to ramble. "I'll be focusing on work here. The sun might not come out tomorrow. It'll never work."

His hand disappears into his pocket, and he pulls out his phone.

"What are you doing?"

His lips tilt into a smile. "I'm searching for the exact defini-tion of pessimist."

I snatch his phone from him. "Funny."

He blows out a long breath, the smile fading, and something else appears. Determination. "You're never going to be happy if you're always thinking about the what-ifs. *What if* the world ends tomorrow? *What if* I get tricked into selling my voice to Ursula and can never sing again?"

I roll my eyes and slap his shoulder. "Oh my God."

"I'm serious! Do you think it's smart to quit right now because there's a *chance* something could go wrong? If something bad happens, we deal with it *together*. Adversities are much easier to go through when you have someone at your side."

"You know it's hard for me to put myself out there. You know why!"

He places his hand on his chest. "It's hard for me just as much! But I did it for you." He scoots in closer and moves his hand to my chest, right over my heart. "I gave you a part of me that you can easily break, but I know I'm in good hands. Do the same for me."

I've been so fearful of him playing games with my heart and hurting me that I never thought that I was the one causing pain for the both of us.

My fear is hurting him.

It's now or never, Rose.

I can't continue to live my life, afraid of love. I can't retire my heart when I haven't even given it a chance to work properly.

I look down at his hand on my chest, my heart pounding against my rib cage right underneath it, and I'm finally connecting with the love I have for him. Love should come first before everything.

"I love you, Rose, more than words can describe. I could write a million songs, and it still wouldn't say enough. I want us to be together. I will do everything in my power to make it work."

I place my hand over his as tears start to fall from my eyes. "I love you, Knox. You own me—mind, body, and soul—and I will give you my all. Be patient with me, but know that I'll be here. There's no more leaving, no more turning my back."

"That's all I'm asking for—for you to give me *you*." He pulls my hand from his and brings it to his lips. "Now, let's go furniture shopping for our new house."

"What?" I stutter out.

"You heard me. I put in an offer on the house, and they accepted it. You're moving in, and, babe, you'd better listen when I say, it will not be in the guesthouse."

I giggle as he helps me up and drags me into his arms.

My heart feels full.

He pulls away when his phone beeps and reads the text on the screen. I notice his hands start to shake.

"What is it?" I ask.

He swallows a few times before answering, "They found my guitar."

I suck in a breath and cover my mouth. I've been looking everywhere for it, and I'm so glad he's going to get it back. "Thank God. I'm so happy. You have no idea."

"Two things I love have been brought back to me today. This is the best day of my life."

51

Knox

It sucks that I can't be sitting in the crowd, watching her like everyone else, but this is her day, and there's no way I'm letting myself take that away from her. I won't let this celebration be about me.

Which is why I'm sitting in a back office, watching the ceremony about to start from a TV screen as they record it.

"Would you like a drink or something?" the woman who escorted me in asks as she stands in the doorway.

I hold up my bottle of water. "I'm good, and thank you for doing this."

She grins. "It's no problem. We appreciate it. A celebrity in the crowd would take away from what these students have worked hard for."

I relax in the chair and watch the introduction, the valedictorian speech, and all of that good stuff. My back straightens, my legs spreading wide, when they hit Rose's row.

I throw my hands up, and pride fuels through me when they call her name and she walks across the stage. Her smile spreads from ear to ear when she's given her diploma, and she looks into the camera and blows me a kiss before going down the stairs.

She did it.

My girl is now a college graduate. She's already secured a job with Los Angeles County Department of Children and Family Services, and she's set to start next week. She's going to change the lives of children, and I can't wait to ride along with her on that journey.

She's already taken one with me. It's time I do the same for her.

"Happy graduation!"

I untie the blindfold covering Rose's eyes, allowing it to fall to the ground, and wait in excitement for her reaction.

She jerks back to look at me, her eyes searching mine. "Wait … what?" she stutters out. "What is this? Are we moving?"

I take her hand and lead her up the walkway to the white house with blue shutters. It's a large home, equipped with ten bedrooms, eight bathrooms, and two large family rooms, so there will be plenty of space for everyone.

There's a *Sold* sticker slapped across the *For Sale* sign in the front lawn, and I'm planning on replacing the sign with something else when she decides on a name.

Rose's dad got out of prison a few weeks ago and has been helping me get everything ready for this day. It's been a pain in the ass, trying to keep it a secret, but Claire did a great job of distracting her. The reaction on her face tells me she had no idea.

"This is a home where you can start a foundation that gives children somewhere safe to go until they can get a foster family or adopted."

A white Honda pulls up, and I wait for the woman to get out of her car and reach us before I keep going.

"This is Trish. She, along with two others, will be the house moms here. There will be an adult here twenty-four/seven, so the children will be well taken care of."

Her eyes widen. "Are you being serious right now?"

I nod. "You said you wanted to give kids more hope. We have to start somewhere. I think this can be our somewhere."

Her hand falls to her chest, and her gorgeous blue eyes start to water. A gush of breath leaves me when she wraps her arms around me and starts to jump up and down.

"Thank you," she chokes out when she pulls away. She swipes the tears from her face. "This is the best present anyone has ever given me."

"We don't have a name for it yet," I tell her, circling my arm around her waist and bringing her into my side. "I wanted it to be your choice."

She covers her mouth. "I don't know …"

"What about Thorn & Roses Foundation?" her dad suggests, coming up behind us.

"The Thorn & Roses Foundation," she repeats. "I love it."

Epilogue

Rose

Ten Years Later

I step out of the car and into the suffocating Houston heat and smile when I notice the bicycles scattered along the circular driveway.

Just a typical day at the Rivers' home.

I keep telling them, one of these days, someone isn't going to be paying attention and run the bikes over. But kids will be kids, and mine seem to have selective hearing.

I carefully shut the door behind me and peek into the back-seat window.

Nola is nervously biting her fingernails and looking down at her lap. She was quiet the entire ride here, giving brief one-worded answers, and I hope she starts to open up more.

She did when I found her, telling me everything that had happened in her six years of life, and it still pains me when I think about it.

She's out of her comfort zone, and it'll probably take her a few months to adjust to living here, but I want her to love it.

I wave my hand toward me, asking her to come out, and she

does. She straightens out her new pink dress and starts to play with the bottom of her dark braid.

"Welcome to your new home," I tell her.

She looks up at me with wide brown eyes. "This … this is where I'm going to be living?" she whispers, and I nod. "It's like a castle."

"A castle fit for a princess."

A lopsided grin spreads on her face.

I was given Nola's case two months ago when police were called to a home after someone complained about a rancid smell coming from their neighbor's house. Fury raged through me when I walked in. She was living in absolute filth, and she was severely underweight, only thirty pounds at six years old. Her parents were addicts who only cared about their next high instead of their child's dinner or nightly bath. Needles and syringes littered the home along with animal feces and cock-roaches.

I had to get her out of there.

It took me a month to go through the court system and legally adopt her.

She's our fourth child. Knox and I had our first baby girl eight years ago and then decided to go the adoption route. We have two homes—one in LA and this one here in Houston, where we tend to spend most of our time. Knox had a custom studio built in the house, so he does most of his work from here. Estelle lives next door, so the kids always have a fresh supply of cookies.

I look back at the sound of a door shutting when Knox gets out of the car. "I hope she loves it," he whispers to me, stopping at my side.

I take his hand in mine. "So do I."

He leans back against the hood. "This is the life, sunshine."

I laugh. "Is this the life you imagined you'd have ten years ago?"

"Did I imagine I'd be married to the most beautiful, magnificent woman in the world while still selling records and having a house in Houston with rug rats running around? No. I never imagined I would be this happy."

"Secret of the day: I love you," I whisper.

"Secret of the day: I love you more."

Books by Charity Ferrell

BLUE BEECH SERIES

(each book can be read as a standalone)

Just A Fling

Just One Night

Just Exes

Just Neighbors

Just Roommates

Just Friends

TWISTED FOX SERIES

(each book can be read as a standalone)

Stirred

Shaken

Straight Up

Chaser

Last Round

MARCHETTI MAFIA SERIES

Gorgeous Monster

Gorgeous Prince

ONLY YOU SERIES: A BLUE BEECH SECOND GENERATION

(each book can be read as a standalone)

Only Rivals

STANDALONES

Bad For You

Beneath Our Faults

Beneath Our Loss

Pretty and Reckless

Thorns and Roses

Wild Thoughts

RISKY DUET

Risky

Worth The Risk

About the Author

Charity Ferrell is a Wall Street Journal, USA Today, #1 Amazon, and #1 Apple bestselling author. She resides in Indianapolis, Indiana. Angst is her happy place, and she loves writing about flawed people finding love.

FIND HER ON:

www.ingramcontent.com/pod-product-compliance
Lightning Source LLC
Chambersburg PA
CBHW050756190726
48285CB00005B/1685